"You're always we__ Martine. I made th__ ago."

"What are you committed to, Jimmy?" Martine's voice was barely a whisper, and the sound was shaky, like her legs that didn't want to support her, like her fingers that trembled when they cupped his hand where it rested on her cheek.

Jimmy moved closer, kissed a trail to her ear, then glided down to the corner of her lips. He toyed with her, teasing her lips apart, briefly tasting her, giving her a taste of him, before he lifted his head and met her gaze. His was fiercely protective and possessive and hot.

"You, Tine," he answered gruffly. "I'm committed to you..."

* * *

Dear Reader,

The heroine in this book, Martine Broussard, first appeared in my 1999 release, *Murphy's Law*. Best friend of that book's heroine and owner of a voodoo shop that catered to both tourists and serious practitioners, Martine captured a few hearts besides my own. Dedicated readers periodically asked for her story over the years, and I wanted to give it to them. I just didn't have a hero for her.

Then, after more than fifteen years of waiting, in walked Jimmy DiBiase. Martine knew Jimmy from a very short-lived and unhappily ended relationship years ago, and she didn't remember him the least bit fondly. But underneath all that hostility—okay, yes, there was more hostility, along with aggravation and annoyance and irritation. But underneath *that*, Martine's little heart squeed just about every time Jimmy came around.

That was when I knew Martine and I both had our guy. Add a few murders, a little voodoo, secrets and threats from the past—and, of course, some of New Orleans's incredible food—and, as they say down there, *Laissez les bons temps rouler!* Let the good times roll.

Marilyn

DETECTIVE
DEFENDER

Marilyn Pappano

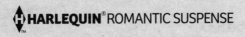
HARLEQUIN® ROMANTIC SUSPENSE

Recycling programs
for this product may
not exist in your area.

ISBN-13: 978-1-335-21893-3

Detective Defender

Copyright © 2017 by Marilyn Pappano

Printed in U.S.A.

www.Harlequin.com

Oklahoma, dogs, beaches, books, family and friends: these are a few of **Marilyn Pappano**'s favorite things. She lives in imaginary worlds where she reigns supreme (at least, she does when the characters cooperate) and no matter how wrong things go, she can always set them right. It's her husband's job to keep her grounded in the real world, which makes him her very favorite thing.

Books by Marilyn Pappano

Harlequin Romantic Suspense

Copper Lake Secrets
In the Enemy's Arms
Christmas Confidential
"Holiday Protector"
Copper Lake Confidential
Copper Lake Encounter
Undercover in Copper Lake
Bayou Hero
Nights with a Thief
Detective Defender

Silhouette Romantic Suspense

Scandal in Copper Lake
Passion to Die For
Criminal Deception
Protector's Temptation
Covert Christmas
"Open Season"

Visit the Author Profile page at Harlequin.com for more titles.

For the people who have loved New Orleans with me:
Dale
Meg
Susan

And for the special cops in my life:
Brandon and Robert

I love you all!

Chapter 1

It was a strange winter. The sky hung heavy and gray, the clouds so dense that the sun hadn't managed to break through in days. Damp cold drifted through the French Quarter streets, spreading its chill with each bit of ground it covered. Martine Broussard had lived her entire life in southern Louisiana, and she couldn't recall any winter that been so relentlessly bleak for so shamelessly long.

Tugging her jacket tighter, she regretted not taking a few moments to run up the stairs from her shop to get a heavier coat before striking out for the river, but Paulina had been so insistent on the phone. *You have to come* now. *I really have to talk to you, Tine.*

When a ghost from your past broke twenty-four years of silence with both fear and anger in her voice, what could you do besides go *now*?

No one sat on the benches in Jackson Square or lounged on the grass, a rare emptiness that was as strange as the chill. The walkways along the four sides saw a bit more traffic, but people seemed eager to go from one place to another. Like them, Martine didn't linger but lengthened her stride instead. It was only a handful of blocks from her shop on Royal Street, and the walk to the river normally took ten minutes or so as she strolled and dawdled and exchanged hellos with fellow Quarter residents. This afternoon she cut the travel time in half, jogging across Decatur, crossing the trolley tracks, reaching the Moonwalk in record time. It was even colder here by the river, but that wasn't what caused the prickling of her nerves.

It was the sudden absolute sense of…*wrong*. This weather was wrong. The phone call from Paulina was wrong. The panic in her voice was wrong. The queasiness in Martine's gut was wrong. It was a normal Tuesday in a normal week in a normal January in a normal French Quarter, and the uneasiness, the nervousness, the weirdness, were all wrong.

But it *wasn't* a normal day, a normal week, a normal month.

The broad path stretching in both directions atop the riverside levee was empty. There were trees, benches and trash cans, all shrouded in swirling fog, but not a sign of life in either direction. Martine reached inside her jacket, touched her fingers lightly to the charm that lay beneath her shirt, then gripped it as a figure materialized a dozen feet ahead of her. A gasp escaped her before she recognized Paulina, but even recognition didn't slow the pounding of her heart.

"Never thought I could hide behind a little tree,

did you?" her old friend commented. Though she still looked very much like the girl Martine had grown up with, she was significantly different, too. Teenage Paulina had always carried an extra ten pounds that gave a soft roundedness to her beauty; she'd rarely been without a smile; her blond hair had gleamed and her blue eyes had glistened with life, love, anticipation and promise.

This woman needed an extra ten pounds to fill out the hollows in her face. Her hair hung dull and limp, and her eyes were hollow, too. She wore black pants that bagged on her skinny frame, a dingy white shirt and a gray fleece jacket that helped her blend into the steely day.

She would have been voted "the girl most likely to..." if their generation had done such things. Most likely to sleep with the boys. To talk back to the teachers. To flirt with the handsome football coach. To get suspended for being a wild child and named homecoming queen in the same year. To go to college, to live life loud, to run wild and travel far, to have the perfect career, marry the perfect man, birth perfect children.

Like the day, the weather and everything else, that title would have turned out to be wrong.

Realizing she was still clenching her charm, Martine let it drop and slowly closed the distance between them. "It's been a long time, Paulina."

"Not long enough. I'd hoped I'd never see you again."

Though the baldly spoken sentiment stung, Martine couldn't take offense because subconsciously she'd reached the same conclusion long ago. For fifteen years they'd been best friends—the two of them plus Callie and Tallie, the Winchester twins, and Robin Railey—but one June night had ended that. Robin had refused anything to do with them starting the next day. The twins had moved their summer visit to relatives in England ahead by a month and left without a good-bye, and Paulina had escaped to college two months early. As far as she knew, none of them had ever returned home.

"Why don't we get out of the cold? Get some coffee?" Martine gestured vaguely to her left, her wave taking in Jax Brewery and Café du Monde.

Paulina shook her head and went straight to the point. "Someone knows."

Without thought, Martine reached for the charm again, caught herself and forced her hand away. A chill swept through her, unsettling and eerie and totally irrational. She knew that last part in her brain—had tried to convince her friends of it twenty-four years ago but never could. She gave herself a mental shake and Paulina a faint smile. "Knows what, Paulina? That five girls who'd had too much weed played some silly games in the woods one night?"

Paulina's features looked as if they would crack if she tried to return the smile. They were masklike, the coloring off, the contours exaggerated, the eyes shallow and empty of any emotion that might come down on the lighter side. A not-real mask of how a real Paulina might look if she were scared to death.

Scared to death? Because of something they'd done when they were kids?

"They know what we did, Tine. I don't know how—maybe they saw us, maybe Callie or Tallie or Robin told someone—but they know, and they're…they're…"

Her gaze swept the area, her eyes wide. She hunched her shoulders and lowered her voice. "They're coming after us."

Martine shuddered, reminded of too many late girls' nights watching horror movies on TV or wandering the entire town after everyone else was in bed, snitching tomatoes from Mrs. Bush's plants, peaches from Mr. Everard's trees, sharing plans and jokes and stories to scare the pants off each other. Paulina had always been best at those, holding a flashlight so her face was mostly shadows, creating voices for every character, including low, growly, vicious ones for the villains. She'd never failed to make Martine shriek with good-natured fear, followed by laughter.

But a look at Paulina showed the great release of laughter wasn't on the agenda today.

Again, Martine gestured toward the more populated area a few dozen yards away. "Come with me, Paulina. I'll buy you a cup of coffee and some beignets. You always said they were God's dessert, and they're as good today as they were then." She even took a few steps before realizing that Paulina hadn't moved.

"Have you talked to Callie or Tallie or Robin?" the woman asked. "Heard anything about them from your family or on Facebook?"

Retracing her steps, Martine returned to her original spot. "No." The end of their friendships had come too fast, had been too hard. She'd moped around alone and lonely after they'd abandoned her, until finally she fled, too, though not far: only the fifty miles to New Orleans. She'd put them out of her head and eventually out of her heart, and she'd made new friends and built a new life with no room for them. The day she'd realized she could think of them dispassionately—*Oh, that blonde looks like Paulina* or *She reminds me of Robin with the way she walks*—had been a very long time coming.

"Well, you can't talk to Callie. She's dead. They tried to kill Tallie, but she got away. No one knows where she is. I haven't been able to find Robin, so I don't know if she's still alive. And that leaves you and me, Tine. Me, I don't stay in one place very long. You, though...you're living over there on Royal Street. Hell, you're even listed in the phone book. You need to leave. Run. Find a dark little hole and pull it in on top of you, because they're coming after us, and they're not going to stop until we're—we're..."

She said the last word in one of those scary-story voices, little more than a whisper but still loud enough to echo inside Martine's head: "Dead."

A passing ship chose that moment to blast its horn, both muffled and amplified by the heavy air. Martine gazed at it a moment, headed downriver. Once it reached the Gulf of Mexico, its crew could go anyplace they wanted in the world. A tiny part of her wished herself on the deck, where soon the sun would shine and all of life's possibilities would open up before her again.

But she couldn't run away, wouldn't, especially from a problem that wasn't even really a problem. Those foolish kids from twenty-four years ago hadn't done anything deserving of punishment. Besides, she had a business here, a home and the best friends a woman could be blessed with. Who gave up perfect to run from unfounded fears?

Apparently Paulina. When Martine turned away

from the ship and back to her friend, Paulina was quickly disappearing into the mist ahead. "Paulina, wait!" Boots with three-inch heels weren't made for running, especially when the ground was damp, but she got close enough to snag the trailing hood of Paulina's jacket. "Paulina, please, let's talk about this. I'll get you a place to stay. You can get a good night's rest, tonight I'll cook your grandmother's gumbo, and in the morning we'll have beignets and coffee and straighten all this out."

Paulina's gaze took on a scornful cast as she spun around to face Martine. "You don't believe me, do you? You, with all your voodoo and charms and black-magic curses—you think I'm crazy. I knew Tallie would doubt me. She and Callie never had half a brain between them. And Robin...she always thought I didn't have half a brain, either. But you—you make your living off this stuff, you're surrounded by it all the time, and you think I'm crazy."

"I don't, Paulina, I don't think you're crazy at all. I just want—I want to understand it. I want to know what's happened. I want to wrap my head around it. We can do that together and maybe even find Robin. Just come back to the shop with me. Come on, we'll talk it all out and—and find some way to make things right, okay? We always made things right, didn't we?"

Stiffening, Paulina gave her a haughty stare. "You think I don't remember your lying-your-ass-off voice? So innocent and sincere that every adult you used it on believed every word you said?"

Heat flushed Martine's face. She hadn't realized when she slipped into the voice, but she'd recognized it by the end of her little speech. Her best friend Evie called it her dealing-with-psychos voice. A popular French Quarter psychic, Evie had her own version, the tourists-wanting-their-money's-worth voice.

"I'm sorry, I'm sorry. I didn't mean—" A screech rushed up from the fog that hid their feet, making them both jump. An instant later, an angry little dove flew up into view, hovered for a moment to chitter at them— they must have interrupted his dining on whatever scraps he'd found below—then darted off.

At the same moment, Paulina darted off, too. She moved fast and silent, either sure of her footing or not caring if she took a wrong step. Martine watched her go, tugged her coat even tighter and headed back to the shop.

Jimmy DiBiase didn't have the typical wanderlust. He had no desire to travel to every state in the union. He didn't like flying enough to want to spend hours in the air to tour Britain, France, Italy or Greece. He didn't care about China or India or Vietnam or any of hundreds of foreign places he'd never been. He'd been born and raised within spitting distance of the Mississippi River, and he was happy to stay within that same narrow range.

But he did like moving.

When he woke up, he knew automatically that it was Wednesday, and without looking at a clock, he knew it was too early for him to be awake, for which he could thank the person calling his cell. He knew it looked like another grim, dreary day, and he needed to take a leak, but he didn't know where the bathroom was because, not for the first time in his life—or even this year—he didn't know where he was.

First things first. He picked up the cell, setting it on the table next to the mattress. The mattress and the box spring were the only other furniture in the room, and the tile seemed to radiate out from them in dark shiny waves. Shoving his hair from his face, he answered the call as he sank back under the covers. "What time is it?"

"Five fifteen." The voice belonged to Jack Murphy, the homicide detective he worked with most often, and he sounded as unready to roll out of bed as Jimmy. Understandable when he had a beautiful wife curled up next to him. "Spare me the complaints, James. We got a case."

"How'd we get a case when our shift doesn't start for nearly two hours?" Jimmy sat up and swung his feet to the floor, then saw the wall of windows on the other side of the room. This was his new apartment. He'd seen it only once before and never in the dark, but there was no mistaking all that glass eight stories above the ground.

"Personal connection," Murphy said. "I'll pick you up in five."

"I'm at the new place."

"I'll be out front."

The call ended, and Jimmy thought for about ten seconds about stretching out again, but there was nothing in the world he loved as much as his job—not even sleep when his head was thick and his ass was dragging. Add in Murphy's personal connection to a homicide case, and he moved fast enough that he was standing on the sidewalk when Murphy pulled to the curb.

Jimmy slid into the passenger seat, angling the computer away to give himself some space. He fastened his seat belt and reached for the travel mug of steaming coffee in the holder nearest his seat. A carefully wrapped muffin sat on top of the cup—carrot and walnut, by the smell of it. Evie Murphy was a princess among wives. Murphy was damned lucky to have her.

Jimmy's behavior in his one and only marriage had proved he didn't deserve any kind of wife. The way he'd treated Alia must have seriously pissed off the gods; judging by the sorry state of his relationships since then, it seemed they were done with him.

With his dark hair standing on end and his tie looped around his neck instead of tied, Murphy was stoic and silent, not yet awake. He drove through the freaky, patchy fog, following empty streets past houses where outdoor lights cast dim halos. It wasn't raining, but everything was wet, and the dampness helped the cold penetrate deeper into a person's bones. Jimmy hadn't even begun to warm up until his muffin was gone, he'd downed half his coffee, and a swirl of ghostly blue and red emergency lights ahead announced their destination.

"A cemetery?" He glanced at Murphy. "You volunteered me for a case in the middle of the night at a cemetery that looks like a set for *Halloween 47: Everyone Dies*?" Then he realized he hadn't shown the courtesy of asking about the connection. "Do you know the victim? Does Evie?"

"No."

"Favor to family?"

"No."

"A former employee? A neighbor? Parents of one of your kids' friends?"

Murphy parked near the other vehicles and shut off the engine. He pulled on gloves before picking up his own coffee. "The only thing the victim had on her was a prepaid cell phone that had made only one call—to Charms, Notions and Potions."

Jimmy blinked. He was familiar with the business name. He'd worked half his life in the French Quarter and spent the other half partying, celebrating, crashing or living there. The cutesy name belonged to a shop owned by Martine Broussard, Evie's best friend, where up front she sold tourist stuff: good luck charms, candles, voodoo ritual kits, how-to books and worry dolls, along with the usual New Orleans T-shirts, coffee mugs and mass-produced voodoo dolls. In the back room she offered the serious practitioner stuff. Her market for that was mostly local. Tourists rarely ventured through the door separating the two rooms.

Family friendship aside, Jimmy wasn't sure he would have dragged himself out before dawn to *Halloween 47* just because the murder victim had called Martine's voodoo shop. Maybe she'd wanted directions. Maybe she'd been looking for a love potion or an Obatala candle for self-purification, or maybe she'd wanted to know if the bar across the street whose name she couldn't remember was open yet.

Not that it mattered. Murphy had wanted the case, and they had it. Now it was time to get out of the car, wander into the cemetery and start working it.

The cars belonging to the officers assigned the initial call and those of the crime scene technicians were parked along the street. Bright lights had been set up some fifty yards away among the graves, and a canopy had been erected to protect the body from the elements.

As Jimmy buttoned his overcoat, he noticed it was starting to rain, just small half-hearted drops, as if the fog had worn itself out and was liquefying in the sky.

He'd spent a lot of time in cemeteries—investigated a few murders that took place there, attended plenty of victims' funerals to see who else showed up and even gone to a few funerals for friends or distant relatives. Cemeteries didn't normally creep him out, but there was something about this scene…the weird weather, the unusual hush of the voices, the edginess that kept everyone focused on their duties. He wasn't the only one who'd rather be home in bed.

Yellow-and-black crime scene tape draped limply from crypt to crypt, cordoning off the area where the body lay. Uniformed cops stood outside the perimeter, detectives and crime scene investigators inside. Between them, he caught a glimpse of legs, ankles showing between sodden pants hiked to the calves and canvas sneakers, the skin unusually colorless under the bright lights.

"Detectives." A grim-faced patrolman lifted the tape so they could duck under, keeping his back to the scene. He looked so young that this was likely his first body, and he was doing his best to avoid it.

It was far from Jimmy's first, and probably just as far from his last.

"What do we know?" he asked, shoving his hands into his coat pockets.

It was a uniform who answered. "Neighbor out with his dog saw suspicious activity by the angel." He gestured behind him with one hand. "Myself and my partner didn't see anything from the street, but when we walked over here, we found…" He gave the body a quick nod that prevented any details from registering.

Everyone under the canopy mimicked his look at the victim, then turned to the angel. It adorned a spire atop the crypt twenty feet away, its gray marble turned dingy by time and weather. Her face was tilted to the sky, her wings stretched out. In prayer? Pleading? The promise of protection?

Had the victim seen the angel? Had she had a chance to pray? Or had she already been dead when she was brought here?

"She has no ID," Leland, the senior of the crime scene guys, said. He and Jimmy had started with the department at the same time, Jimmy an ambitious patrol officer, looking for arrests, wanting to make a meteoric rise through the ranks, and Leland a lab rat, perfectly content with handling corpses. The dead were so much less annoying than the living, he'd insisted. He'd risen through the ranks, too, to the point that he often had to deal with the living, as well. "No driver's license, no credit card, no jewelry, nothing. Just two hundred bucks cash in her jacket pocket and the cell phone with its one call."

"So it wasn't a robbery."

Jimmy didn't notice who'd stated the obvious—not him, not Murphy. He studied the woman instead: wet hair of dirty blond or light brown. Thin face, sunken cheeks, deep shadows under her eyes. Lines at the corners of her mouth and eyes, signs of worry or general unhappiness. Her T-shirt clung to her in wet folds, once white but now a vague shade of gray. She'd lost weight recently, judging from the long loop of drawstring that held her pants around her skinny hips and from the way her skin sat uncomfortably on her frame. Her clothes were cheap, maybe secondhand, but something about her didn't strike him as a secondhand-clothes person. There was a line on her left index finger where she'd long worn a ring, not a tan but a bit of shiny skin where the ring had rubbed back and forth, and all ten of her nails were bitten to the quick.

What there wasn't was an obvious cause of death. She didn't look like she was just sleeping, though Jimmy had seen his share of dead people who did. No, it was apparent with the quickest of glances that this woman was dead. The lights were out; the soul wasn't home.

Which meant the cause was on her back side. "Can you roll her over?" he asked, and the crime scene guys moved to comply. Something dark stained the back of her head. Blood, possibly from a blunt object, possibly the entry wound of a small-caliber bullet.

"There's something under her shirt," Leland said, and they returned her to her original position. He pulled up her T-shirt to reveal a large bandage, sticky clear film protecting some type of dressing. It was centered over her chest, crossing her breasts, extending above and below several inches.

"So she has surgery, someone kills her and dumps her in the cemetery?" It was the same voice that had stated the obvious earlier. This time Jimmy looked and identified its owner as one of the crime scene guys who'd so far managed to stay on the perimeter, not doing much of anything. Maybe one of their lab rats who'd thought working out in the field would be fun, or maybe a new guy who was destined to get on Jimmy's last nerve pretty quickly.

Ignoring his coworker, Leland began peeling back the edge of the dressing. He worked it loose carefully, teasing the adhesive from the skin, as gentle as if his patient were alive and watching, then abruptly he stopped. He looked a moment, then folded back the flap of bandage as his distraught gaze met Jimmy's. "I think we've found the cause of death."

Jimmy and Murphy both leaned forward, concentrating on the small area of chest that had been revealed—not pale smooth skin but a wickedly ugly wound and, inside, emptiness. Not real emptiness, of course, but the essence of something missing. Something important.

"Damn." Jimmy breathed the word the same time Murphy did, then looked to Leland for confirmation. Leland nodded.

"The killer removed her heart."

After a restless night, Martine gave up any hope for peaceful sleep, pulled her robe on and shuffled to the kitchen to make a cup of coffee. She'd had dreams all night—ugly, unsettling ones involving deep shadows, woods, birds screeching that had raised the hairs on her arms. If she were fanciful, she'd say the fog was keeping the happy dreams at bay. It didn't want her nights to be any more cheerful than her days had become since it moved in.

"It's just fog," she groused, pouring cream and sugar into her coffee. "A cloud of tiny water droplets hovering above the earth. It doesn't think or care or even know you exist, Tine."

The old, almost forgotten nickname made her pause before taking the first sip of coffee. Where was Paulina this morning? Had she checked into a motel or crawled into a hole and pulled it in after her? Had she stayed safe last night? Had she gotten anything hot to eat?

Was she crazy?

Martine had tried to put all the memories behind her when she got back to the shop yesterday, a task made easier by an influx of tourists. They'd worn a variety of N'Awlins T-shirts, a few had sported Mardi Gras beads or feather boas around their necks, and they'd done their best to project the carefree, good-time-in-the-Big-Easy air that most tourists came by naturally, but it had been a struggle for this group. Even inside the brightly lit shop, they'd huddled together in small numbers, their voices muted, lamenting the lack of sunshine and the mild weather they'd expected. They'd been worried without knowing why, and they had cleaned the shelves of every single good luck charm and candle in sight before leaving the way they'd come.

After the shop was closed, after Martine had finished off a po'boy from down the street and locked herself inside her cozy apartment, the memories had come knocking again. A search of the internet had proved true one of Paulina's claims: Callie Winchester had died three months ago in Seattle. The details reported by the news outlets were scarce, but the obituary confirmed it was their Callie. Her parents, who'd once lived two blocks from Martine's family, were now in Florida, and her twin, Tallie, made her home in London.

Callie…dead. Though Martine hadn't seen her in twenty-four years, though she hadn't thought about her much in twenty of those years, it hurt her heart to know she was dead. Callie had always been so vibrant, full of humor and wild ideas that usually ended in trouble for all of them. She'd been beautiful, with sleek black hair that reached down her back, olive skin and gray eyes, and she'd done a perfect imitation of her posh mother's British accent, but there had been nothing refined or elegant about her huge booming laugh. Tallie, identical in every way except the laugh, had compared it to a braying jackass, which merely made Callie laugh even harder.

And now she was gone. Someone had stolen her very life and discarded her for someone else to deal with, as if she were no more important than an empty burger wrapper.

That thought raised goose bumps on Martine's arms and stirred an ache in her gut. She was browsing through the pantry, looking for something to settle it, when the doorbell rang, echoing through the floorboards.

The clock on the microwave showed the time was 7:23. No one came to visit her before nine, and rarely without a phone call to alert her. Maybe it was just some punk, walking along the sidewalk and pressing doorbells. But no sooner had that thought cleared her brain, the bell rang again, seeming more impatient. Her nerves tightened, and apprehension throbbed behind her eyes. Whoever was downstairs on this ugly dreary morning after her ugly restless night couldn't possibly be good news for her.

Unless it was Paulina, come to take her up on her offer of coffee and beignets.

Hope rising over the dread, Martine hurried down the stairs as the bell rang a third time. Reaching the bottom, she jerked the security chain loose, undid the dead bolt lock and yanked the door open, prepared to meet her friend with a smile and a comforting hug—

But it wasn't Paulina. Jack Murphy stood on the stoop, dressed in the white shirt and dark suit that were his usual work clothes. He looked as if he'd slept in them, hadn't had time to shave and had forgotten to comb his hair, and his eyes were dark and somber with shadows.

Panic clutched Martine's chest, cutting off her breath. "Oh, God, please tell me nothing's happened to Evie or the kids."

His eyes widened, an instant of alarm followed by sudden regret. "No. No, God, no, they're fine."

Her knees going weak, she sagged against the door-jamb, one hand pressed to her chest. "Aw, jeez, you about gave me a heart attack! Don't do that again!" For emphasis, she poked him with one finger. "Not ever!"

"Is she always this ditzy?" a voice drawled from the curb, and Martine realized Jack wasn't alone. He'd brought along her least favorite police officer in the world—her least favorite *person*. It was too damn early in the morning—too damn early in the year—to face Jimmy DiBiase.

Especially when she was wearing what passed for pajamas and a robe: tank top, shorts, an old boyfriend's flannel shirt. She was exposed from the top of her thighs to her bare toes, to a letch like DiBiase with a freakishly cold fog silently creeping everywhere. No wonder her skin was crawling.

She was torn between slamming the door and flee-ing upstairs to wrap up in her favorite quilt and inviting Jack inside while pointedly leaving DiBiase in the cold.

Neither action would surprise Jack; he knew DiBiase was an acquired taste for most women besides strippers, hookers and cop groupies.

Then the realization clicked in her brain: Evie and the kids were okay, but Jack was still here, still in work mode. That meant someone else... "Who is it? Anna Maria? Reece? Jones? Alia? Landry?" Her brain was spewing forth names faster than her mouth could get them out.

Paulina's voice sounded faintly through the mist, sending a bone-deep shiver through Martine: *They're coming after us, and they're not going to stop until we're dead.*

Dear God, could it be her?

"I'm sorry, Martine," Jack said. "I'm handling this badly. We've got a...victim." The grimness returned to his expression. "No ID, nothing but a call to your shop yesterday afternoon."

Martine thought longingly of the quilt, and of the coffee she'd left on the kitchen counter. She needed warmth. She needed a lot of it to melt the ice that suddenly coated everything inside her, slowing her heartbeat, making it difficult to breathe. Paulina had warned her, had told her they were in danger, and Martine had done nothing. Had let her walk away. Had let her die.

Because she knew in her heart Paulina was gone.

"Oh, God." She swayed forward, and a hand caught her arm, holding her steady. It was a big hand, strong, the skin olive-hued, the fingers bare, and the overcoat sleeve above it was gray. Jack's overcoat was black. She knew, because she'd helped Evie shop for it. Which meant this coat belonged to DiBiase.

The hand holding her up was DiBiase's hand. For

one brief moment, she let herself accept the warmth and comfort and strength that seeped from him, just one moment when she was too weak to do otherwise. Then, with the stubbornness she'd been legendary for back home, she tugged free, folded her arms over her chest and hid her fisted hands against the soft flannel.

"I guess you should come in." Her voice was flat and numb, a pretty good match for the dismay and sorrow building inside her. She'd been a fool for letting Paulina walk away. Paulina had obviously not been herself; she'd needed taking care of. Needed someone to pretend to believe her, to take her home and help her until she was better able to help herself.

Twenty-four years ago, Martine had been the person Paulina turned to first, before anyone else. *Oh, Tine, he broke up with me for good. Tine, I'm failing algebra, and my dad will take my car away for sure. Tine, my mom and dad are fighting again. Tine, I think I'm pregnant, but I'm too young to have a baby!*

They had been best friends—had had a bond that should have been unbreakable. But now, after all those years, when Paulina came to her again, Martine had let her down. She hadn't even tried. She'd just wanted to get out of the cold and go back to her shop and take care of business. She'd wanted to stuff the past back into its cramped little corner of her brain and never take it out again.

At the top of the stairs, she turned left into the kitchen. "I'll make coffee," she suggested with the same numbness.

"We'll do it." Jack touched her arm. "Go get some clothes on."

She glanced down. Her legs and feet were an unflattering shade of blue, thanks to the cold, and goose bumps covered every bit of skin. When she lifted her gaze again, it automatically went to DiBiase, who was also just lifting his gaze. *Jerk. Self-centered, unfaithful, two-timing, arrogant—*

Giving him a look of loathing, she went down the hall to her room, where she dressed in comfort clothes: fleece pants, a long-sleeved shirt, thick wool socks and cozy slippers. By the time she returned to the kitchen, the two men had their coffee, and Jack had reheated hers in the microwave until it steamed.

"You want to go into the living room?"

Martine paused, then shook her head. "In here."

Jimmy was the last to walk through the doorway she'd indicated. She went first, turning on lights, opening curtains, and Murphy followed. Jimmy stood at the threshold, taking in everything before invading it.

He would admit, he didn't know Martine well. That time he'd tried to get her to go home from Murphy's party with him had been only their second meeting, and since then she'd looked at him like he was some kind of bottom-feeder. He did know that he wished things had happened differently back then, that she and Evie Murphy were like sisters, that his ex-wife, Alia, had been welcomed into their group last year and that Martine ran the voodoo shop below: part good fun, part legitimate business. He knew she was serious and mysterious and superstitious and sometimes wild and worrisome.

This room didn't seem to go with any of that.

It had once been a dining room, he suspected, from the general size and shape, the proximity to the kitchen and the arched doorway into the living room. Now it looked like it belonged in a suburban house, reigned over by a crafter who indulged creativity in the lulls between being World's Best Soccer Mom and World's Best Cheer Mom. The woman belonging to this room drove an SUV, had a closet filled with conservative trendy clothes, was organized enough to keep complex schedules for four kids in her head, never missed a PTA meeting and terrorized any mother who did.

It looked nothing like the Martine he'd offended a few years ago.

It held a large rectangular table, the top etched with a one-inch grid, and four perfectly matched chairs. Every available inch of wall space was covered with white bookcases, and the shelves were filled with books, craft supplies, an array of tools, fabric and a lot of things he didn't recognize, all of it in color-coordinated hampers or boxes. The lamps in the room gave off bright white light; for the first time in a week or more, he could see clearly again. The fog had lifted, at least inside this small space.

Martine settled on one side of the table. Jimmy sat on the opposite side next to Murphy. She opened a white bin, neatly labeled with the years, and pulled out a photograph, laying it on the table in front of him and Murphy.

Jimmy leaned forward to study the shot of the smiling blonde in an off-the-shoulder gown. Gaudy decorations behind her suggested a high school prom, an innocent time. It was funny the things twenty-plus years could change and the things they couldn't. This pretty, smiling, well-nourished, blue-eyed blonde shouldn't have a thing in common with the underweight, hard-worn, weary woman they'd seen in the cemetery this morning, but he had no doubt they were one and the same.

Murphy knew, too, but he still offered his cell phone to Martine. She glanced at the picture—quickly the first time, as if afraid there might be damage she didn't want to have in her mind, then for a still quiet moment. Shivering, she held her hands to her coffee mug before lifting it for a drink.

"Her name is Paulina Adams. We grew up together in Marquitta. She called yesterday afternoon and asked to meet me by the river." Her voice sounded hollow and distant, making its way through a thick haze of shock and emotion and guilt and sorrow. Jimmy had heard that voice a hundred times from a hundred different people, when he broke the news that someone they loved had died. God, he hated that part of the job. Today, because it was Martine, he hated it even more.

"Did you meet her?" Murphy asked. Of course she did. Jimmy wouldn't even have asked.

"She, um…she looked like she'd been having a tough time. She was frightened. She said…" Her breath sounded loud in the room. "She thought someone was trying to kill her. I thought she was being paranoid. But I guess it's not paranoia if someone really is out to get you, right?" Her smile was faint and sickly and slid away faster than it had formed.

With prompting from Murphy—a lot of it; the hesitations and pauses started long and got longer—she related the conversation with Paulina. Paulie, she'd called her, and in return Paulina had called her Tine. After a time, she fell silent, locking gazes with Murphy. "How did she die?"

Death notifications were Jimmy's least favorite part of the job, and definitely the least favorite part of *that* job was answering questions like that. No one wanted to hear that their sixteen-year-old daughter was raped before she was murdered, or that their elderly father had been beaten with a baseball bat by the thugs who broke into his house. Certainly Martine did not want to know that her friend's heart had been cut from her chest.

"We're waiting for the autopsy report," Murphy said gently. All cops, no matter how tough or gruff or abrupt, had a gentle side—even Jimmy himself. Granted, the only people who ever saw his were the victims and the officers he worked with. Martine couldn't see anything when she pretty much pretended he didn't exist.

"Why would someone want to kill Paulina?" he asked, part curiosity, part to remind her that he did exist.

Martine breathed deeply, her fingers running along the edge of the storage bin in a slow back and forth pattern. Her nails were painted dark red, and heavy silver rings gave an elegant look to her hand. Those hands could perform magic. He'd felt it for himself that last night, when everything had been full of promise. He didn't know even now what he had expected at the time—a few hours, a few dates, maybe even something serious—but what he'd gotten was rejection and her never-ending scorn. Most of the time, he was okay with that. Most of the time, he provoked her just because he could. But sometimes he caught himself wondering *what if…*

Realizing he was watching her, she stopped the rubbing and clasped her hands. "I don't know. Before yesterday, I hadn't seen her in twenty-four years."

"But you were best friends."

"Were," she repeated for emphasis. "In school."

"What happened?"

Again she drew a deep breath. He wasn't sure if it was meant to imply her annoyance at being questioned by him or if she was using the time to figure out the right answer. Right answers never needed figuring. The truth came easier to most people than evasions or lies.

"We were kids. We went to the same school, the same church, had the same interests. Then we graduated and…things changed. We changed. The ones who went to college went elsewhere. The ones who didn't moved elsewhere, too. We wanted to see what the world had to offer, and we lost touch after a while." A narrow line creased her forehead. "Are you still in touch with your best bud from high school?"

"I am. I introduced him to his wife. His kids call me Uncle Jimmy."

The crease deepened into a scowl. "Of course they do." Snideness sharpened her tone. "Most of us move on after high school. We all found new lives and new friends."

"And yet when Paulina was having a tough time, when she thought someone was going to kill her, she came to you, someone she hadn't seen in twenty-four years. Doesn't that seem odd? That she wouldn't go to one of those new friends you all replaced each other with?"

Martine's face flushed, giving her the first real color he'd seen since she'd found them at her door.

Anger? Embarrassment that she didn't have an answer for a perfectly reasonable question? Guilt that if she wasn't outright lying, she was at least not being entirely truthful?

He had to give her credit: she didn't shove back from the table, pace around the room or throw him out of her house. He'd watched plenty of people do all three. He'd even been on the receiving end of a few punches in the process of being thrown out. No, Martine might have surpassed the limits of her tolerance for him, but she retained control.

"I don't know where Pauline's new life and new friends are," she said, a clenched sound to her words. "I don't know where she went after school, what she did, how she lived, whether she married or had children, if she kept in touch with her family or anyone else. No one could have been more surprised than I was when I heard her voice on the phone, or when I saw her, or when she ran off into the fog. We were friends a lifetime ago, but after twenty-four years, she's as much a stranger to me as she is to you. I'd have better luck coming up with suspects who want *you* dead than Paulina."

If the conversation hadn't been so serious, he might have laughed at that. He'd been a cop for eighteen years. Everyone could come up with a list of people who wanted him dead.

She slid her chair back and stood, replaced the picture in the bin and closed the lid. "I have to get ready to open the shop, and I need time to…"

Jimmy silently completed the sentence for her: grieve over a stranger who'd once meant the world to her. He needed time to figure out whether he believed everything—or even anything—she'd told them. His first two questions for himself after an interview were *Did she lie?* and *Why?* He wasn't looking forward to telling Murphy he believed his wife's best friend had lied.

Murphy made the small talk to get them out the door—*thanks, sorry, take care*—then they took the stairs in silence. The street was just as empty of life as it had been when they came.

Murphy started the engine and turned the heat to high before thoughtfully tapping his fingers on the steering wheel. "Notice how she just happened to have that box on the table? The yearbooks were inside there, too. A lot of pictures, souvenirs, old cards. Seeing Paulina yesterday upset her more than she wanted to show."

"Maybe she was wondering how Paulina went from that kid at the prom to that woman on your phone. Or maybe seeing her made her nostalgic for the good old days."

Murphy snorted. "I know you didn't miss the fact that she wasn't telling us everything, so don't make excuses. I love Martine, but I'm not here because she's my kids' godmother. My job is to find who killed Paulina and why."

"But you can't forget that she's your kids' godmother, can you, and that makes the job harder. Evie and the kids would never forgive you if you treated her like a suspect or an uncooperative witness."

"Hey, I can be tough," Murphy said in self-defense. "I once handcuffed Evie and took her to jail."

"Yeah, and you'll never do that again, will you?" That arrest had been the end of their relationship the first time around. Once Murphy realized he'd been duped, he'd had to solve a few murders, arrest a few corrupt feds and grovel like hell to get back into Evie's life. In Jimmy's opinion, that was a hell of a lot of work for one woman.

Which probably explained why he hadn't stuck with just one woman in a long, long time.

Chapter 2

Oh, God, she'd lied to the police—and not just to the police, but to Jack.

Groaning, Martine dragged her hair into a pony-tail. Instead of being bouncy and perky like it should be, it just dangled limp and heavy—the way she felt, coincidentally. She'd put on makeup as soon as the detectives had left, but she'd had a hard time finding the balance between enough and too much. Even now, she couldn't tell whether she looked like someone who'd had a shock or someone trying to pass for a clown.

She hadn't actually lied to the police. She just hadn't volunteered a few things, like the fact that Paulina believed their voodoo curse was the reason for the threat against her. Or that one of their other best friends had been killed just a few months ago, allegedly because of the curse. Or that Tallie, Robin and Martine herself were on the supposed hit list, too.

Martine couldn't get past the cold hard fact that the others ignored: their voodoo curse wasn't real. It had been far more Dr. Seuss than Marie Laveau. They hadn't raised any spirits; they hadn't disturbed the peace between this world and the other; they hadn't done anything a million stupid kids before and after them hadn't done.

What had happened to William Fletcher had been a coincidence—not even a surprising one, according to gossip. He'd been warped in his tastes and careless in his pursuit of them, and Callie and Tallie's mom had often said that one day the consequences of his actions would catch up with him.

That Saturday night they had.

But it wasn't her fault, or Paulina's or the others'.

Heaving a sigh that echoed with restlessness and sadness, she pulled on a bright yellow-and-pink madras plaid rain slicker and a pair of boots and headed out. Back in the day when the shop was new and finding its way, she'd made time to bake goodies for her employees' breakfast and breaks, but business had luckily picked up about the time her baking interest waned. Now she visited Wild Berries, a small shop on Jackson Square, and bought treats far better than she could make.

The strange dampness made her pull the slicker hood over her head as she walked. It wasn't raining exactly. It was more as if the drops of water were suspended in air and broke only when a person bumped into them. The few that trickled down her face were ridiculously cold and sent shivers all the way to her feet.

And all the weather people could say was *Unusual weather patterns* or *Maybe a break this weekend.*

Anise, one of her employees, kept insisting the sun was never going to shine again, but then, Anise was a gloom-and-doom sort of person. With her distinctive Goth appearance, Martine hadn't decided whether she added to the ambiance of the shop or scared the customers instead.

When Martine stepped inside Wild Berries, a bell dinged overhead, and a small high voice sang out, "The sun will come out tomorrow…"

She slid her hood back to revel in the brilliant smile the shop owner, Shelley, gave her. Even on her worst day she summoned more optimism than Martine could even imagine at the moment. Shelley was happy, she'd once told Martine—truly, seriously, contented all the way down to her soul. Martine knew days of deep satisfaction, but she envied Shelley her pure unwavering light.

"How's business?" Martine asked as she strolled the length of display cases, her mouth watering with each new discovery. Lemon and brown sugar and chocolate perfumed the air, along with buttery pastry and cinnamon and coffee. If it was possible to absorb calories by osmosis, Wild Berries was the place to do it.

"My early birds are reliable. It's slow right now, but it'll pick up by lunch. How about your place?"

"People come, buy and go. Let me have twelve of your most decadent creations, would you? Make one lemon with a sign that says 'Hands off. For Martine's pleasure only.'"

With a laugh, Shelley folded a brightly decorated cardboard box and began filling it. "I thought I saw you pass by yesterday afternoon, but you were moving so fast, I wasn't sure."

Martine kept her smile in place by sheer will. "Yeah, I—I had a—a meeting." With a woman who'd been murdered twelve hours later. God, that sent a chill through her soul. She wondered about Paulina's parents: Where did they live now? When would they be notified? How thoroughly would the loss of their only daughter devastate them?

And more questions. Had she been married? Was there a husband out there worrying where the hell his wife had gone? God have mercy, what if there were kids feeling the same?

And what about Tallie and Robin? They should know, too, because they'd been Paulina's friends, too. The five of them had shared a lot of history.

And they deserved a warning because, even if Martine didn't believe in the paying-for-their-curse business, it seemed someone else might.

Paulina had believed it, and she was dead. Callie had believed it, and she was dead, too. Martine couldn't have helped Callie, and she hadn't helped Paulina, but if she at least contacted Tallie and Robin…at least gave them a heads-up…

A flash of color wavered in front of her, and she blinked hard, bringing the plastic bag holding the pastry box into focus. Shelley wore her usual smile, but it was tinged with a bit of concern. "You okay, Martine?" she asked, and Martine was pretty sure it wasn't the first time.

"Yeah, sure. Nothing a few days on a tropical beach wouldn't cure."

"You and me both. Sun, sand, cabana boys…my dearest dream. Maybe the lemon tart will take you away for a few moments, at least."

Martine traded her debit card for the bag, then looked inside and located the tart underneath the box's cellophane lid. In fine print across the pastry, Shelley had written with frosting, *Reserved for Martine*. With a laugh, she pocketed the debit card again. "My employees are most grateful, and so am I."

"Have a good day. And don't let the weather get you down. No matter how dreary, it's still New Orleans, and that beats a sunny LA or New York or Chicago any day."

Martine waved as the bell dinged above her again. Shelley was right. A bad day in New Orleans was better than a good day anywhere else. She'd had a lot of dreams growing up, but in terms of distance, they'd ended fifty miles from her hometown. She enjoyed traveling, but at the end of every trip, she was happy to be home where she belonged.

Would always belong.

And no one—no old friend, no murderer, not even Detective Jimmy DiBiase—could take that from her.

She was halfway past Saint Louis Cathedral when the nerves between her shoulder blades prickled. The power of a look never failed to amaze her: this one was as physical as an actual touch, and it made shivers dash down her spine. She tried to casually glance over her shoulder to see who was watching her, but when she moved her head, the hood of the slicker stayed where it was, instead giving her a good look at the pink lining. Stopping and actually turning around was a bit obvious, but when she reached the intersection, that was exactly what she did.

It was truly raining now, so much more normal than the earlier damp that some pressure deep inside her eased. The few people around were intent on getting to their destination, except for a crowd of tourists huddled beneath a lime-green golf umbrella and conferring over a map. No one showed any interest in her. No one seemed to notice she existed, despite her yellow-and-pink slicker.

Nerves. She wasn't a person usually bothered by them, and they were making her jumpy. Bad weather, slow business, Paulina, DiBiase... It was all enough to give anyone a case of the creeps.

Satisfied that was it, she headed down the street again. Her path took her past the house where Evie and Jack lived, with its smaller entrance leading to her psychic shop. Guilt curling inside, Martine ducked her head and lengthened her stride. She would talk to Evie soon, but not yet.

Only half a block separated her from the dry warmth of her shop when footsteps sounded behind her and, too quickly for her to take evasive action, Detective DiBiase caught up with her and flashed that grin most women found so charming. She had once found it charming. If he ever caught her in a wildly weak moment, she feared she might find it so again. "Wild Berries. I like their stuff."

One of the lessons Callie and Tallie had taught her early on was that ignoring people who didn't want to be ignored was a waste of time. They had pestered her relentlessly until she gave in and dealt with them. She fell back on that now. "Think of more questions, Detective?"

"A few. You have one of those caramel bread puddings in there?"

Crossing the street between parked cars, she dug

in her pocket for her keys, unlocked the shop's old wooden door, jiggled it a bit and pushed it open. Rain made the wood swell and stick, but the door with its wavy glass was decades old. She hated to replace it with something new and inferior.

The lights that were always left on—one above the display window, others over the checkout counter in the middle of the room—banished some of the gloom but not enough for Martine. She flipped switches as she walked through the shop, pushed aside a curtain of beads and went into the storeroom/lounge, where she set down the pastries, then stripped off her slicker. She didn't need the slight squelching sounds behind her to know that DiBiase had followed. Just as she'd been aware of someone's attention at the square, she felt it now.

Damn, had he followed her all that way without her realizing it?

"What do you want?"

His gaze slid to the pastry box inside the wet bag, reminding her of a hopeful puppy. Grimacing, she shoved it across the table toward him, then started the coffee. The clock ticking loudly on the wall showed ten thirty, but it was still set to last summer's time so she had thirty minutes before opening the store, probably twenty minutes before Anise arrived. Wonderful. DiBiase could annoy her that long without even trying.

"You like lemon tarts, huh?" His deep Southern drawl scraped along her skin, an irritation she couldn't banish, like the cold, the fog and now the rain. "Appropriate."

Her gaze was narrowed when she faced him. "What does that mean?"

"Well, you are a bit sour."

He helped himself to a generous serving of cheese Danish, the ruffled white liner contrasting vividly against his dark skin. On a general scale of attractiveness, he ranked high. Even Martine couldn't deny that. With dark hair, devilish eyes, the grin and muscles that still impressed though his college football years were long behind, every woman she knew thought he was gorgeous. The problem was, he knew it and took advantage of it. Everywhere he went, he was waylaid by women wanting great sex, and he was happy to comply.

Even six years later, it still embarrassed Martine that she had almost been one of them.

It angered her that, on rare occasions, she even kind of regretted that she hadn't been.

"Consider the company," she said in response to his calling her sour. Then she turned her back on him and her thoughts, lifted a couple of boxes from the storage shelves and carried them to the front of the store.

Of course Jimmy followed her—not to the counter where she was ripping open the boxes with too much enthusiasm, but through the beaded curtains. He turned down the first aisle he came to and followed it around the perimeter of the shop. Despite living in Louisiana his whole life, he had little personal experience with voodoo. His parents had seen to it that the family was in church every Sunday—in their small town, it had been more a social event than a sacred one—and they had never encouraged questions about other beliefs. When he'd thought as a kid that he was so much smarter than them, he'd assumed it was because they were so tenuous about their own beliefs that they didn't feel qualified to debate them. Later he'd realized that their unwillingness to debate had also been more a social thing than religious. In a small town, it was easier to go with the flow.

Most of the merchandise on the shelves could be bought in a dozen places in the quarter. Some was strictly fun, some for tourists, some for posers. But in the room behind a door marked Private, that was where the real stuff was, according to Jack—the stuff that couldn't be picked up just anywhere. The stuff for the practitioners, the true believers.

Jimmy watched Martine over a display of crudely made dolls and wondered if she was either, or merely a supplier of goods. Her mouth was set in a thin line, and her brows were knitted together. She didn't want him here, and that was okay. In his job, he was used to people distrusting him. The prejudice against police officers that had surged in the past few years made a tough job a hell of a lot tougher. When it got bad, he wondered why he spent his days wearing a gun, walking into dangerous situations, doing his damnedest to protect communities that didn't appreciate it, but the answer was simple. He was a cop. He'd saved a lot of lives. He'd helped out a lot of people. He'd found justice for a lot of victims.

It was what he did best.

That, and piss off pretty shop owners who had a thing about fidelity.

As he finally circled to the counter, Martine began sliding small plastic bags onto rods extending from a display case. "Don't you have better things to do this morning than aggravate me? Like, I don't know, telling Paulina's parents what happened or, here's an idea, maybe even finding the person who did it?"

"Her parents live in Alabama. The police over there are making the notification. By the way, her name is Bradley now. Was Bradley."

Her fingers slowed, the tips tightening briefly around the plastic package that held an astrological charm. "Did she have children?"

"No." That always seemed a good thing to him with murder victims. Not having kids meant less damage, less grief. *But without children, what do they leave behind?* his father sometimes asked. Jimmy figured the old man didn't want the family name dying out. He was the only son his dad had, and neither of his sisters had been willing to hyphenate their married names. Poor Pops was stuck.

Jimmy picked up a worry stone from a dish filled with them, his thumb automatically rubbing the depression in the middle. "When Paulina called you yesterday, what did she say?"

"She wanted to meet me."

"No chitchat? Hey, long time, how are you?"

She glanced out the window, and Jimmy followed her gaze. The fog had risen high enough to cover a few inches of the glass. It was like being in a dream: the street disappeared from sight; a man walking his dog, both of them legless; a delivery truck driving by, its wheels invisible. There were going to be a lot of trips and falls and battered shins as long as this lasted.

"She said, 'Tine, it's Paulina. I need to see you. Meet at the river as quick as you can get there.' I told her I was busy. I had customers. She said, 'You have to come now. I really have to talk to you.' So I went."

Still rubbing the stone, he walked around to stand near her. "First contact in more than twenty years, and she demands you meet her on a day like yesterday, then tells you that someone's after her."

Martine paused a moment before nodding. After hanging the last of the charms, she stuffed one empty box inside the other, moved a few feet to a tall display of candles, guaranteed to bring a person health, riches, love or whatever else his heart desired, and started rearranging them.

"Did she ask you for money?"

"No."

"For help?"

"No."

"For advice? Sympathy? Directions? Did she want to say goodbye? Did she leave a message for her parents or her husband?" He watched each tiny shake of her head, then impatiently asked, "Then why the hell did she bother calling you, Martine? Just to say, 'I think someone wants me dead. Hey, I like your hair that way, and I hear your shop's doing pretty good. I'll probably die in the next twenty-four hours, so I won't be seeing you again. Have a good life'?"

"Stop it!" she demanded. "She's *dead*! Show a little respect."

"I'm not disrespecting *her*." It was part of the problem today: everyone wanted respect, even when they were lying, cheating, stealing, killing and telling the rest of the world to screw themselves. Martine didn't want to be questioned again, she didn't want any pressure even though she'd been less than forthcoming the first time around. Whatever she was hiding could be nothing. It could be personal, between her and Paulina.

Or it could be integral to solving the case. It wasn't up to her to decide.

Her face was pink, her breathing unsteady, when the rattle at the door announced a newcomer. A woman—early twenties, shiny black hair, pale face, dark makeup, black clothes—stepped inside, gave a shake like a great big dog, scattering rain everywhere, then looked up at them through water-splattered glasses. "The sun's never gonna shine again," she said in a doleful voice. She shuffled over, a huge black tote bag hanging from one shoulder, and stopped a few feet away. "I'm Anise."

Though he could feel hostility radiating from Martine—or maybe because of it—he grinned at the girl. "I'm Jimmy."

"Don't talk to him, Anise," Martine snapped before the girl could open her mouth again. "He's not welcome around here. In fact, if you could do a few wards to banish him from the premises, I would be most grateful."

Jimmy shifted his full attention to Anise. "You can banish me? Where, like, I wouldn't be able to walk in the door?"

"Maybe. I'm just a novice, but I'm pretty sure I can at least make it very uncomfortable for you to be here." She pushed her glasses higher on her nose.

He made a dismissive noise. "Your boss can do that with nothing more than a look." Once upon a time, she'd made him very uncomfortable with no more than a look…but in a most desirable way.

The color in Martine's face deepened. She murmured something—he saw her lips move but heard no words and figured it was a prayer of some kind—then with a deep breath faced him. "You should go now."

He good-naturedly shook his head. "You should tell me the truth now. All of it."

"I—"

"Have kept all the good parts to yourself, like why someone wanted Paulina dead, what happened to your friendship, why she came to you. You're a bad liar, Martine. I know it, and Jack knows it."

The look she gave him was defiant, with her jaw jutted out and her eyes darker than usual. A muscle quivered in her jaw, and her lips were thinned. He moved a few steps closer and lowered his voice for his last volley. "I intend to find out what you're holding back and why. So I'll be back, Martine, no matter how many wards Anise casts. I'll find out the truth, and God help you if anyone else gets hurt in the meantime."

For a long moment, their gazes locked. There was the usual annoyance and dislike in her eyes that sparked the usual regret in him, but along with them was fear. He hadn't thought she was even capable of the emotion.

It made him that much more determined to find out what the hell she was hiding.

Without enough customers to keep two employees busy, much less four, after a few hours, Martine gave up, said goodbye and went out the front door. The stoop to her apartment door was only a few feet away, just one big step when she could actually see it, but with the fog lingering, she went down the shop steps, up the other steps and let herself inside. The staircase was narrow and dimly lit, and she reminded herself for the tenth time to buy a couple of higher-wattage light bulbs for the top and the bottom.

As soon as she got to the top, though, the airy colors and tall windows that usually let in the sun made her forget about the stairs. They were just the gauntlet she had to run to reach the cozy comfort of her home.

Grabbing her laptop, she went into her workroom, curled in a chair next to the window and logged on to a search engine. There she paused. Paulina and Callie were dead. Tallie was in hiding, and Robin had long been lost, according to Paulina. Martine had zero idea how to find them, so she did what she used to do when she was stumped: she called her mother.

Bette Broussard still lived in the house where Martine had grown up, not that she spent a lot of time there. A few years after divorcing Martine's father, Bette had made herself over into a travel writer, taking advantage of everything the internet had to offer, and had become successful enough that these days, "vacation" meant staying at home for longer than a weekend. She'd finagled her travel-tip columns onto some very prestigious websites, had her own YouTube channel and boasted social media followers in the mid–six figures.

It had taken Martine five years just to get her shop's very simple website online.

After a couple of rings, her mother's husky voice greeted her. "Ha! When I got up this morning, I crossed my fingers and turned in a circle three times, chanting your name, and here you are!"

"You know, you could have picked up your phone and called me without risking getting dizzy and falling."

"I can't fall. I'm sixty-five years old. It could be dangerous."

"Just because you say you can't doesn't mean it can't happen anyway." Would that it were true. Martine would be spinning in circles and chanting her heart's desires until she passed out. *Paulina can't be dead. Callie can't be dead. Tallie and Robin and I can't be in danger. I can't have to see Detective DiBiase one more time.*

"In my world, it does." Bette said something in an aside, and Martine heard a British-sounding, *Yes, ma'am, of course, ma'am.* "Where are you?" she asked.

"Home. Where are you?"

"London. That was Chelsea. She's my translator on this trip."

"They speak English in London, Mom."

"Yes, but apparently they don't think *I* do. It was impossible to get anything done with them constantly asking me to repeat myself."

"Because they love your accent." Her mother sounded as if she'd stepped straight out of Southern belle charm school, her words all rounded and sweet and enchanting, gliding slowly one into the next and putting a person in mind of sultry afternoons on a veranda, sipping mint juleps and saying *y'all* a lot.

DiBiase's accent was pretty much the male version of Bette's.

Martine scowled hard until the thought disappeared from her mind.

"What's going on with you, Tine? You rarely call me in the middle of your workday."

Too late, of course, Martine rethought the call. Did she really want to deliver sad news to her mother while she was on a business trip? Bette had adored her daughter's friends, and they'd felt the same about her.

But her mom was always on a trip. She could handle news, and she would want to know.

"You remember Paulina? And Callie?"

Bette snickered. "That's like asking if I remember your father. Those girls practically lived in our house. I never really knew what happened between you all, but you know, it was like losing part of the family. One day I had all five of you underfoot, and the next you were all gone. Moved on. I knew it was inevitable, of course, but I wasn't prepared for it. Then your father left, and I…"

Martine remembered her mother's shock as well as her own when Mark Broussard had packed his bags and moved into his fishing cabin ten miles outside town. He hadn't had an affair. He hadn't wanted a divorce. He'd sworn he was happy and loved Bette and Martine as much as ever. He'd just needed some time alone.

Bette had given him time—six months, a year, two, her life effectively put on hold—and then she'd given him an ultimatum: life together or divorce. He'd refused to choose, so she had.

Twenty-plus years he'd lived in that cabin, working when he had to, fishing when he could, communing with nature and his own spirit and still insisting that he loved Bette and Martine as much as ever. It was strange, but Martine believed he was genuinely happy.

Bette's sigh was long and blue, then her voice brightened. "Have you heard from the girls? Is that why they're on your mind after all this time?"

"Sort of. I saw Paulina for a few minutes yesterday. She was, uh…" Martine had to stop, had to close her eyes to push back the tears that threatened. When she thought it safe to continue, her words wobbled with emotion. "She was murdered last night, Mom."

For an instant, the silence on the line was thick, then her mother's own voice wobbled. "Oh, honey... Good Lord, how awful. Her poor parents... Was it a mugging or a robbery or what?"

Her fingers aching, Martine switched her phone to the other hand. "I don't know. Just...her body was found this morning, and Jack is assigned to the case."

"Well, it's good to know New Orleans has their finest on the case. Still...so sad. Heavens, I can't imagine what Paulina's parents are feeling right now."

"Not just Paulina's parents. It's weird, Mom, but she told me Callie had been murdered a few months ago."

That bombshell rendered Bette speechless. Martine worked her boots off, then drew her feet onto the chair and gazed forlornly out the window. The tiny courtyard below that never failed to make her smile failed now. The fountain was turned off, the bright-colored cushions for the chairs stored downstairs. The plants drooped as if they might collapse under one more drop of rain, and everything looked sallow and depressed, in need of a dose of brilliant sunshine.

"Poor Callie," her mother said at last. "And poor Paulina. What a sad, sad coincidence."

A lot of people didn't believe in coincidence. They insisted there was a great plan, that everything happened as it must. Her mom wasn't among them. She thought coincidence was a lovely wrinkle that delighted her more often than not.

Could it be coincidence? Martine really wanted to believe it. Life was dangerous. Some people were willing to kill for a pair of shoes, a handful of change or because they felt slighted. It could be just really bad luck that first Callie, then her old friend Paulina had become victims. Just because their lives had been connected didn't mean that their deaths were.

But she couldn't quite convince herself of that.

"Mom, I wanted to get in touch with Tallie and Robin to let them know about Paulina, but I don't have any idea where they are. Do you have phone numbers or addresses for their parents?"

"I'm not sure, but I do know their mothers follow me on Facebook. I'll look them up and email their info to you right away, okay?" There was a brief pause with the faint sound of typing in the background. "And Tine? Be careful, honey. It would rip my heart right out of my chest if anything happened to you. I love you more than my life."

Martine swallowed hard. "I love you, too, Mama."

After disconnecting the call, she gazed down at the courtyard again. The barren branches of the crape myrtles faded into the brick wall behind them. The fog lifted here, swirled there, but thanks to the protection of four walls, it mostly just hovered.

It made Martine feel cold and damp and heavy.

Her gaze went distant as her mind shifted back to the conversation. She'd never imagined she would be contacting Paulina's or Callie's parents. Never imagined she would be offering condolences on their daughters' deaths. Never imagined two of her four former best friends would be murdered. Never imagined for even an instant that Tallie's or Robin's or her own life might be in danger.

Movement in the courtyard caught her attention, drawing her to her feet and closer to the window. Nothing was there, just the fog bumping into the walls that constricted it, then slowly settling back into its lazy ramble. Still, a shiver passed through her, leaving her ice cold as she sank back into the chair.

Danger or coincidence: Did it matter? Either way, it didn't change what she had to do.

Resolutely she typed a message on her phone, drew a deep breath and hit Send.

Now all she could do was wait.

Jimmy had a hundred favorite hangouts in New Orleans. Today it was a bar on Bourbon Street, relatively small, with wood floors, tables closely spaced and tall French doors usually open to the sounds, sights and smells of the Quarter. Today the cold kept all but the main entry closed, but he didn't mind. There was blues on the sound system, he had takeout from his favorite Cajun restaurant and his ex-wife was seated across from him.

Alia had provided the takeout, easily enough for four people and most of it for herself. She had a passion for food that few people he'd ever met could match. Luckily, she was also blessed with a passion for working out and a metabolism that favored her.

She buttered a piece of corn bread but paused before taking a bite. "So this new case of yours…the victim was a friend of Martine's."

"Yeah, best friend from high school." He didn't ask how she knew. She was a special agent with the Naval Criminal Investigative Service. She was also friends with Evie and Jack, and her husband, Landry, was co-owner of the place and tending bar at the moment. She had a lot of sources.

"I bet she's thrilled with you," Alia said with a smirk.

"She likes to pretend I don't exist."

"A lot of people like to pretend you don't exist, Jimmy." There was no bitterness in Alia's voice or her smile. She liked him a lot better now that she wasn't married to him, which was only fair. He'd been a crappy husband. He just hadn't…cared.

Oh, he'd loved her. He still did, in different ways. But he'd been younger, stupider, more reckless, less understanding. Marriage had been more about taking a chance than making a commitment. Practically everyone in his circle of friends had been married and divorced at least once; it was no big deal. You tried it; if it didn't work out, you moved on.

Now he knew—years too late—how idiotic that attitude had been. He'd hurt Alia, hadn't done himself any favors and had convinced a lot of people that he was a complete jackass.

Alia had gotten over him and was much happier with Landry than she ever would have been with him. Jimmy had gotten over himself, too. But a lot of people still thought he was a jackass.

He didn't often admit it, but on occasion he found himself wishing Martine wasn't among them. After the way things had ended between them before they'd even really started, he should have forgotten her—written her off as one of the few women he couldn't seduce. But she was a damn hard woman to forget.

"I also heard the killer removed her heart," Alia went on. "Is that true?"

This time Jimmy scowled at her. "Did Evie tell you that?"

"Ew, Jack would never tell Evie anything that gross. Isn't that a voodoo thing? The heart of your enemy makes you strong?"

"I think around here it's more of a movie thing. I'd have to ask someone who knows more about voodoo than me."

"Ooh, and Martine is just such a person."

He scowled again. "Yeah, we'll let Jack handle that. I'll stick to digging through the victim's life and finding out all her secrets." That part of the job was both interesting and off-putting. Cops were curious; it was part of the job. But wasn't Paulina Bradley entitled to a bit of privacy after her death? Wasn't it bad enough that she'd died violently, alone and afraid? Did it have to come to light now that she was a lousy housekeeper, that she read porn, that she daydreamed about things she would never accomplish? Did it matter now that she kept chocolate stuffed in her underwear drawer, that she had a crush on her neighbor or that she drank too much when her husband was gone?

"It's kind of like a car wreck," Alia said sympathetically. "You know you should look away, but you have to see what happens. There's so little dignity after a violent death."

"I do my best." His phone buzzed with an incoming text message, and he finished his last bite of gumbo before picking it up. "Crap. Jack's out of town—"

"Since when?"

"Don't know. He got me out of bed two hours early this morning to take this case, then he headed to the coroner's while I interviewed the guy who called 911. Let's see… Lincoln, Nebraska, PD picked up his double-homicide suspect that jumped bail last month, and he's on his way to get him. And Martine's decided to share some information with him that she didn't give earlier."

Alia grinned. "She's going to be disappointed when you show up instead of Jack. Maybe you should politely remind her that the sooner she tells you everything, the sooner she'll be rid of you."

"Yeah. Though I don't think she's gonna fall for anything polite after I called her a liar a couple hours ago." He stood and shrugged into his overcoat. He hated the coat; it was constrictive and awkward when he was running or needed to draw his pistol or Taser. He could dress down, like most of his fellow detectives, but he shared one quirk with Jack: work clothes meant shirt, coat and tie. Old-fashioned but respectful of the job and the victims and the families they dealt with.

"Aw, Jimmy." Alia stood and straightened his collar for him. "I'd chastise you, but you've seen me do worse with an uncooperative witness. Just remember, she's also our friend."

Not *his* friend, he thought as he waved to Landry, then walked out onto the street. At the time they'd met and almost made it to bed together, he hadn't cared about having female friends. But, like he said, he'd gotten over himself since then. He had more than a few female friends now. It said an awful lot for Alia that she was one of them.

When he reached Martine's store, he wiggled and jiggled the swollen door to open it, stepped inside and reached back to close it. When his fingers wrapped around the knob, electricity jolted through them, minor, little more than static but enough to make him jerk his hand away and swear softly.

"What happened?"

He glanced from his hand to Anise, still looking as gloomy as the weather, even though a spark of interest lit her black-rimmed eyes. "I got shocked."

"Hmm. That wasn't the effect I was going for. I'll have to try again." Turning without a sound, she disappeared into the depths of the store as if he was no longer there. A lesson she'd learned from her boss, probably.

His nose wrinkling against the particularly strong odors of the incense on the shelf beside him, he headed for the central counter. The kid slumped over a textbook there straightened to his full height of six foot four, maybe five. He was thin, long-necked, long-armed, long-legged, long-haired and apparently short on words. No *Can I help you?* or *How are you today?* He just stood there, giving Jimmy a long steady owl-like gaze, and waited.

Jimmy showed the kid his badge. "Martine?"

The kid lifted his gaze to the ceiling, then accompanied it with one long thin finger pointing straight up.

"Niles, we're not supposed to talk to that guy," Anise called from the back. "Don't tell him where Martine is."

Niles, poor guy, turned red and very slowly folded that finger back down, then hid his hands behind his back for good measure.

Jimmy grinned at him and went back out the front door. Once again, when he touched the knob to close the door, a shock fired through his fingers. It might not be painful, but it was going to become annoying pretty damn quickly.

He stepped across from one stoop to the other and

was about to ring the doorbell when the door opened with a haunted-house-worthy creak. The hair on his neck stood on end, and his hand was already sliding beneath his coat to the .40 holstered on his belt before the thought even crossed his mind. He stilled when a woman with wild hair and pink glasses popped out from behind the door.

"Did I startle you? I'm Ramona." She squeezed by, then patted his arm. "Go on up, Detective Murphy. She's waiting."

She was definitely expecting Jack. Jimmy was going to piss her off this time just by walking into the room. But that was okay, because this time he wasn't leaving without some answers.

Chapter 3

Customers sometimes thought that because Martine knew something about voodoo, she must know all the other woowoo stuff. They asked if she was a witch, a psychic, a medicine woman, if she could talk to the dead or read auras or throw the bones. She patiently explained that she had knowledge but no powers. She never knew who was calling before looking at caller ID. If she met a premonition, she wouldn't recognize it, and all she ever knew about a person was what anyone else with eyes could see.

But as the footsteps reached the top of the stairs and turned automatically to the right, a shiver ran through her. She didn't need supernatural powers to know that Jack had stood her up, the rat, and sent DiBiase in his place. Anyone who shared her dislike for the detective could have told the same thing just based on instinct, pheromones or the hairs dancing on their nape. There was nothing special about it.

Nothing special about instincts or hairs dancing on her nape. But pheromones, those man/woman chemicals that signaled interest and attraction and desire ... those were pretty damn special.

But not in play here. Not between her and DiBiase.

He stopped in the workroom doorway, slid off his damp coat, looked around, then hung it on the corner of the door. His hair was damp, too, the bright overhead lights glinting off it. He raised both hands as if to stall whatever criticism she might offer. "Jack had to go out of town to pick up a prisoner."

"A fact he failed to mention when he texted that he would be over soon." But as she said the words, she acknowledged that wasn't exactly what he'd said. She'd said she wanted to give him information about Paulina, and he'd sent back three words: Be there soon. He couldn't be held responsible, he would argue, if she wrongly assumed he meant *he* would be there soon, could he?

Blowing out her breath, she gestured to the chair across from her. The plastic bin was out again, this time sitting on the seat beside her. She wished she'd thrown out this stuff years ago, that she'd run farther than New Orleans and changed her name and never, ever heard from her one-time friends again, because then maybe Callie and Paulina would be alive, and even if they weren't, she wouldn't know about it.

But maybe something in this bin or some bit of information in her memories would help lead the police to their killers...or killer. Maybe it would save Tallie and Robin from the same fate.

Maybe it would save Martine, and then she truly could bury the past.

DiBiase sat across from her and pulled a notebook, small and scruffy, from his jacket pocket. Silently she slid a paper across to him. "Those are the names of Paulina's and my best friends when we were kids. I don't know anything current about them, except that Tallie lives in London. The names underneath—that's their mothers' Facebook accounts. They follow my mother. Paulina had been looking for Robin and Tallie for a while, and she couldn't find them, and Callie…"

"Callie?" DiBiase's gaze was razor-sharp. She wasn't the only one in the room with instincts, and she would wager his were far better developed than her own. He'd known from the start that she was holding something back. He hadn't been happy then, and he would be even less so when she told him.

Sighing, she slid another piece of paper to him. It was a printout of Callie's bare-bones obituary. "She was murdered three months ago in Seattle. Paulina told me about it."

Hands trembling, she folded them together and waited for the explosion of anger that was sure to come. DiBiase read the obituary, his mouth thinning, his eyes going dark and hard. Taking out his cell phone, he placed a call, withdrew an ink pen from his pocket and began making notes in tiny neat lines on the paper. "Hey, this is Jimmy. I need the short version on a homicide in Seattle three months ago… Yeah, the eighteenth. Victim's name was Callista Jane Winchester. Can I hold while you get it for me?"

His stern gaze cut back to Martine. "She went by Callie?"

She nodded, and he made a note on the obituary page. "And her sister. Tali…whatever?"

"Taliesin. It was the name of Frank Lloyd Wright's house. Their father was an architect." She caught herself before rambling further afield and mumbled, "We called her Tallie."

He noted that, then a distant voice came from his phone. He started writing again, murmuring *Okay* at appropriate times. If Martine had to compare his writing with the fonts on her computer, she would guess his font size was slightly less than eight points, which was as small as her fonts went. From her vantage point, across the table and upside down, it looked like an incredibly detailed pattern rather than words.

Abruptly his pen stopped, and everything about him went cold. Martine shuddered, reached to pull a quilted throw from one of the shelves and wrapped it around herself. Obviously, he'd learned something that surprised or sickened or angered him. *Please don't let it be proof that Paulina and Callie were killed by the same guy.*

His conversation lasted a few more minutes, and when he laid the phone aside, he sat back and looked at her. She couldn't recall ever seeing him so serious. Despite his job, or maybe because of it, he was usually looking at the bright side of life, quick with a grin, a joke or, if there was an available woman, a pickup line. He didn't take much seriously, she sometimes thought, beyond annoying her.

He was taking whatever information he'd just gotten very seriously. "What do you know about Callie's death?" His accent was less noticeable when he was this intense. He sounded businesslike, no-nonsense. Life might be a joking matter to him, but death wasn't.

"Just what's there. I—I don't even know if I believed Paulina when she told me. She was…melodramatic."

He stared at her a long time, making her shift positions awkwardly, sending a rush of heat through her. She felt like the bug pinned underneath the microscope, and he was the scientist unsympathetic to her plight.

After a moment, he broke the eye contact. "Okay, let's pick up where you started withholding information this morning. You met Paulina at the river. She'd been having a tough time, she was frightened, she thought someone was trying to kill her."

A childhood memory flashed through her brain: her mom and dad sitting her down after some minor infraction at school. *Always tell the truth*, her father had said, and when she'd asked why, he'd explained: *It's easier than remembering a lie.* Her mom had swatted him on the shoulder and corrected him: *It's the right thing to do.*

She'd pretty much lived by that rule, for both reasons, but this afternoon, nothing was easy, and she wasn't sure which actions were right. But she'd committed herself to telling everything, and although it irritated her that DiBiase thought her a liar, and embarrassed her that he had reason to think so, she was going to take the route that was neither easier nor guaranteed to be right.

"What was the first thing she said to you?"

"That she'd hoped she would never see me again."

A slow blink was the only emotion he showed. Not

quite what he'd expected, she guessed, given how close she and Paulina had once been. "And you said?"

"I offered to buy her some coffee, to get out of the cold. I thought she looked underfed."

"And?"

Ducking her head, Martine pressed the bridge of her nose to ease the tension gathered behind her eyes. She was tired and blue and melancholy and sickened by the recent events. She wasn't sure she could bear one more day of the nerves that had been stretched taut ever since hearing Paulina's voice on the phone or the creepy bleak weather or the sensation that something terribly wrong was connected to it. She didn't want to know what had happened to her former friends, wanted to erase them from her memory, wanted to jump on to the first plane heading to London and ask her mom to cuddle and pamper and coddle her into a brighter, sunnier, safer place.

As if London didn't have fog and rain.

"Martine." DiBiase's voice came from nearby, and she looked up. He'd moved around the room, transferred the plastic bin to the table and seated himself beside her, all without her hearing a thing. The intensity was still etched in the lines of his face, but it wasn't so harsh now. She couldn't have blamed him if it was. She'd been less than helpful so far with his investigation.

"Did you go for coffee?"

She shook her head. "Paulina—Paulina said, 'Someone knows.' She didn't know who or how, but they knew, and they were coming after us. She said Callie was already dead, that Tallie and Robin had disappeared and might be dead, and that they—this someone—wouldn't stop until they had also killed us."

It took every bit of air in her lungs to get the words out, and for one awful moment she couldn't replace it. Her chest was tight, her brain too dazed to give the command to breathe, so that when her body couldn't wait one instant more, her lungs dragged in oxygen with a terrible, broken wheezing sound.

DiBiase laid his hand on hers where it curled tightly around the quilt. His skin was warm against the ice of her own, his palm large enough to cover her fisted hand, his fingers closing tightly around hers in a way that made her feel safe. It allowed her to breathe evenly, regularly, and chased away the panic.

It took a few heartbeats for her to realize that for the first time in years, hostility wasn't foremost among her emotions toward him. She was grateful for his steadiness and solidness and for the sense of security he gave her.

Many deep breaths later, the moment passed. She wiggled her fingers free of his, found a tissue to wipe at her eyes, then searched wildly to find even the slightest sarcasm. "Do they teach you that in detective school? Calming Hysterical Females 101?"

He didn't move back to his original seat, but he did lean back, putting some precious space between them. "I have two younger sisters. I had advanced training in how to make females hysterical by the time I was ten. Calming them is sort of the same stuff in reverse."

"Huh. I never thought of you as having sisters to torment."

"Or be tormented by."

"Then you probably also have a mother and a father."

His look was wry. "And grandparents, three nieces and two nephews. No, I didn't magically come to life as the perfect guy. I had to work to get where I am."

She smiled very faintly, then looked past him at the stark-white pieces of paper on the table. Grimness settled over her like a cloak, icy and awful, and it echoed in her sigh.

"You ready to go on?" DiBiase asked.

If she said no, would he give her more time? Or would he try to wheedle, cajole or charm her into continuing? Ten minutes ago, she would have said he couldn't have done it, but he'd just proved her wrong.

She nodded.

"What was Paulina talking about? What did this someone know?"

She opened her mouth, then closed it again. Her dad had been wrong. Telling the truth wasn't always easiest. She could think of at least a hundred lies that she could tell with far more polish than the truth would get. Her mom had probably been correct that it was the right thing, but Martine would give anything to keep their foolishness from that long-ago night to herself.

Anything except someone else's life.

Jimmy listened to the creaks of the old building, the occasional vehicle sounds from outside and not much of anything else. Any pedestrians out there weren't lingering; the residents weren't walking their dogs; no one's windows or doors were open to share their music. It was quiet in a city that was rarely quiet, a strange-enough occurrence to set a vague unease niggling between his shoulder blades. New Orleans was a city of magic and myth—the unexplained often happened in this town—but this weird combination of cold and fog and murder carried a sense of menace he couldn't recall experiencing.

It was just coincidence. The logical part of his brain knew that, but it felt like...more.

"Martine." He liked the sound of her name. Liked the feel of her. The smell and the taste of her. It had been a long time since their night-gone-bust, but a man didn't just forget the feel of a woman like her in his arms.

This time when she opened her mouth, words came out, determination dragging them one by one. "Our last year in high school, we had a new teacher, Mr. Fletcher. We called him Fletcher the Letcher. He was about our fathers' ages, and he was creepy. It wasn't anything hugely overt. He looked at girls when he thought no one noticed him. If we got caught in a crowded hallway with him, he was always accidentally bumping into us, brushing against our boobs, fondling us but, of course, never on purpose. He was just a jerk. As far as we knew, he never took it any further, never did anything that he couldn't *claim* was an accident, but it was gross. We really hated him."

Jimmy reached for the printouts she'd given him and wrote a couple of lines. Maybe Fletcher the Letcher *had* gone further, with his victim too embarrassed to confide even in her best friends. That kind of betrayal of authority could certainly cause a teenage girl who otherwise had everything she needed to succeed to wind up terrified, paranoid, on the run and then murdered.

"The Saturday night after graduation," Martine went on, "the five of us went out in the woods near our houses. Someone brought some weed, and someone sneaked a bottle of booze from their house. We decided it would be fun to put a curse on Mr. Fletcher, to—to stop him from being such a perv. We put together a crude voodoo doll out of a bandanna and twigs and Spanish moss, and I made up a chant, something really juvenile about making him stop bothering the girls. At the end, we stuck a stick through its chest, and Paulina skewered its crotch with a metal nail file. It was just… silly. A game. None of us knew anything about voodoo. We were high and tipsy and stupid. That's all it was."

Using the lid from the storage box as a table, Jimmy used his own shorthand to document the story while waiting for her to go on. In his experience, there was always more, and he had the patience of Job when it came to waiting.

Martine pushed back the quilt and stood, pacing to the nearest window, then to the next one, then flipping the switch on a space heater tucked into the corner. She'd changed the loose pants she'd worn this morning for faded jeans that clung to her hips and every inch of her long legs, and added a chambray shirt over the long-sleeved T-shirt. With all that, she was still pale, her skin still bearing the faintest tinge of blue. She'd always been so confident, so capable, that he wouldn't have thought her afraid of anything.

But, of course, she was. She feared the one thing everyone did, even him: something happening to the people she loved. Hadn't her initial response to seeing Jack this morning been fear that trouble had befallen Evie and the kids?

Arms folded across her chest, she paced the length of the room on the opposite side of the table, making a neat little turn at each end. "We did our moronic ritual, stayed until the weed was gone and the booze was gone and it was late and we were sure we could get into our houses and into our rooms without our parents catching us, and then we went home. The next morning…" Her voice faltered, and so did her steps. She stood at the window, staring out, but Jimmy knew for damn sure it wasn't the courtyard or the building next door she was seeing.

"The next morning we heard Mr. Fletcher had been found dead. He'd been shot in the chest and in the groin. A day or two later, his wife was arrested. She confessed, said she didn't want a trial and went to prison."

"But you were convinced—" He considered it a moment, then changed tacks. "Your friends were convinced that somehow your ritual had caused his death. Had made her kill him."

Still staring out, she nodded. "It ended everything. Our entire lives' worth of friendship. I tried to tell them it was ridiculous. We had no power, no experience, no knowledge. We'd been playing a dumb game, and it was just a coincidence that he'd died, but they felt so guilty. They left town, put as much distance between all of us as quickly as they could. As far as I know, other than the twins, none of us had any contact until Paulina showed up yesterday."

Like Jimmy had told Alia, he didn't know much about voodoo, despite a lifetime in Louisiana. He respected it for the religion it was, but as for the curses, the gris-gris, the powerful magic… Maybe he was skeptical, but he didn't believe the most skilled voodoo priestess could kill a man using nothing more than a doll and words. And Martine and her friends had been, by her own admission, far more stupid kids than skilled medicine women. Young, easily influenced and gullible enough to believe they had unleashed forces that cost a man his life.

"He wouldn't be the first philandering husband whose wife took her revenge on the family jewels," he remarked.

She glanced over her shoulder at him, a faint movement that might have been a smile tugging at her mouth, then sat down again.

"I take it you never told anyone about this."

She shook her head.

"And they probably never did, either."

"I don't believe so. They were too scared and ashamed."

"So who did Paulina think had discovered the secret?"

"She didn't say."

He tapped his ink pen but didn't quite let it touch the pad. The noise when it did tended to annoy the hell out of Jack, Alia or anyone else he was working with. They preferred not trying to think with the relentless *tap-tap-tap* for accompaniment, so he'd learned to be satisfied with just the movement.

"She obviously thought it was tied to Fletcher's death. Maybe because of Callie's death? Do you know how she found out about that?"

"No."

"Other than thinking someone was out to kill her, how did she seem to you? Like someone going through a bad time that would pass or maybe someone with real long-term problems?"

"Someone *was* out to kill her."

"Yeah. I'm just trying to figure out what her mental status was before you saw her, before she took off from home in the middle of the day and disappeared for the next three months. Her husband's driving over from Alabama, so I'm meeting him tomorrow, find out what he knows."

Martine shrugged, her features sad. "She was troubled. She looked like she wasn't sleeping at all, like she'd lost a lot of weight. Her clothes didn't fit. Her skin didn't fit. I remember thinking she looked…scared to death. And she accused me of thinking she was crazy."

"Did it cross your mind?"

She was reluctant to answer. It always surprised him how many people took to heart the bit about not talking badly of the dead, when it was usually the bad parts he needed to solve a crime. Once a person was dead, there were no more consequences. Secrets didn't help anyone.

Finally she nodded. "It did. You can't imagine the difference from that night in the woods and yesterday. She used to be so bright and happy and full of life, and then she looked like an escapee from a horror movie set."

A pretty good comparison, Jimmy thought, remembering his first impression of the graveyard where the body had been found. *Halloween 47: Everyone Dies.*

If it turned out that Paulina hadn't been unnecessarily paranoid, *everyone* could—would—logically include Martine.

Every muscle in his body knotted. He would be damned if he would let that happen. Even with the grudge she nursed against him, life wouldn't be the same without her in it.

"So…can I ask a question?"

His gaze flicked up to her face, and she seemed taken aback by the ferocity of it. He blinked, swallowed hard and worked to substitute something bland and far less intimidating. "I can't promise I'll answer."

"How was Paulina killed?"

Damn, he'd been expecting that. People who cooperated usually felt entitled to a little information in return, and they usually asked one of two questions: *Why?* Or *How?* There was never a satisfactory answer to the first; even if the victim was a lying, thieving, murdering thug, there was always someone in his world who'd loved him and didn't believe he'd deserved to die.

As for the *how*, Jimmy didn't believe it brought comfort, except along the lines of died-too-quickly-to-feel-any-pain. Shot, stabbed, beaten, run down in the street, drug overdose, bomb, burned alive, torture, ritual, poison…dead was dead. But families felt compelled to ask.

He carefully lined the edges of the papers she'd given him and folded them in half. "She had blunt-force trauma to the back of her head." Enough to render her unconscious, according to the preliminary autopsy reports, but not the cause of death. That appeared to be, as Leland had suggested at the scene, the removal of her heart.

The same manner of death as Callista Jane Winchester.

"There's something else."

"Yeah, but I can't…"

"Was it… Is it connected to Callie's death?"

Suddenly Jimmy felt tired. He couldn't count the number of times he'd talked to families about the horrible things done to their loved ones. No one outside of a coroner should know as much about the ends of strangers' lives as he did. It just wasn't natural.

But it was the career he'd chosen—or maybe it had chosen him. He was always too late to save the victim, but he usually managed to get justice for them and, often enough, saved another life or two along the way.

He fully intended to save Martine's life.

"Yes. I'm pretty sure it was. The…other details of the cases match." Exhaling heavily, he stood. "I've got a lot of files to read, a lot of people to talk to, but finding Tallie and Robin are at the top of my list. If they're alive, we'll keep them that way. You, too. Don't go out alone. Don't meet any other old friends who happen to call. Don't forget there's a killer out there."

For a long time, still pale, still looking as fragile as spun glass, she held his gaze. When she finally looked away to open the storage bin, her hands trembled. "I picked out some pictures of the girls in case…" She brought out an envelope and offered it, but when he took hold of one end, she had trouble letting go of the other.

"Thanks. It helps to put faces to names."

"I also have…" This time she pulled out the yearbook from her senior year. The girls, their friends and any possible rivals and Fletcher the Letcher, all in one book. He'd meant to ask for it but got distracted. She'd saved him a trip.

He accepted it, along with the plastic shopping bag she plucked from a box meant for the store, and slid everything inside to keep it dry. He needed only one more thing before he went back to the office: a source to talk to about the possible voodoo aspects of the case. He'd intended to ask Martine a few questions but not now. She was freaked out enough already. Asking *Who can tell me about the ritual taking of human body parts?* would send her over the edge. He would find his source another way. That was what he got paid the big bucks for.

"Look, Martine—"

"Please don't tell me not to worry."

"Oh, hell, no. Two of your friends have been murdered half a country apart. You'd damn well better worry." He shoved his fingers through his hair. "I just wanted to say… I'm sorry."

She didn't ask what he was sorry for—Paulina's and Callie's deaths, being a jackass, leading her on, pissing her off. Any of it. All of it. She just nodded grimly.

"If anything out of the ordinary happens, call me." He offered his business card. "Anything—a hangup, a customer who seems vaguely familiar or overly friendly, anything at all. Okay?"

Her face was as colorless as before. "Okay," she said in little more than a whisper. "Thank you."

"Now come downstairs and lock the door behind me."

She obeyed, moving so lightly on the stairs that he felt her presence rather than heard it. When they reached the dimly lit foyer, he hesitated, his hand on the doorknob, then faced her. "It'll be okay." They were meaningless words—*okay* might come in a few weeks, a few months, a few years or not at all, because no matter what happened in the end, Paulina Bradley and Callie Winchester were still dead—but people seemed to appreciate hearing them, and it filled some need in him to say them.

She drew a deep breath, squared her shoulders and straightened her spine. Her chin lifted a notch, and a smile touched her mouth. "My mama says everything will always be okay, because even though we can't change what's happened, we can change the way we deal with it. If the human race wasn't adaptable, it would have ceased to exist before it ever got started."

"Your mama's a smart woman." He opened the door, and the air in the small space turned cold and damp. After stepping outside, he gave her his usual grin. "You'll be hearing from me."

He closed the door and waited until he heard the lock engage before going down the steps. In the instant before the *snick* of metal sinking into metal, he heard her murmured response.

"Lucky me."

After rattling around her apartment for half an hour, Martine realized that DiBiase's instruction not to go out alone wasn't as simple as it sounded. She had excess energy to burn, and the best way to do that was to bundle up and head out for a rapid-paced tour of the Quarter. But she'd learned this morning how easily someone could follow her when her senses were hampered by her rain slicker, she didn't own an umbrella and she didn't find that physical misery made anything better.

Instead, she fell back on her number two energy-eater: she went back to the shop. Ramona had left for the day, Niles was out for lunch—literally this time, as well as figuratively—and Anise was ringing up a customer's selection of candles, oils and charms. Martine gave her own charm a gentle touch as she greeted both women with a nod, then went into the storeroom.

She was checking inventory when the clerk came into the room. "Is he gone?"

He... "Detective DiBiase? Yes." Martine didn't point out that he obviously wasn't in the shop, and she wouldn't have left him alone in her apartment. She loved her employees and counted on them quite a lot, but all of them were a little oblivious. Evie said the customers liked it, that it was part of the shop's mysterious, illusive air that some tourists expected.

"He got shocked both times he closed the front door." Anise's tone was distant, dreamy. "When he came in and when he left. Like static electricity, only not. That wasn't what I expected from the spell, but it's a start."

"Spell? What—" Oh, yeah, the comment Martine had made earlier about banishing him from the premises. Now who was being oblivious? Then she suppressed a shudder. The thought that Anise might actually have some power rather than mere interest in the paranormal was a little bit scary.

The clerk perched on the edge of the counter. "Why is he coming around anyway? Are you in trouble?"

Martine wished she could truthfully answer no to the question, but wishes were nothing more than hopes sent up into the ether. Some came true, but the rest evaporated into the mist, breaking into a thousand wistful pieces that never fit back together again.

"An old friend of mine from back home was murdered last night," she finally said. "I was apparently the last person to see her." She failed at suppressing this shudder. How sad for Paulina that her last conversation in life with a friend was the unsatisfying, borderline hostile exchange they'd shared.

"Wow. I've never known anyone who was murdered."

Martine had known Paulina. And Callie. And Fletcher the Letcher. What kind of normal law-abiding citizen knew three murder victims? Dear God, she hoped the list ended there. She wasn't afraid of death for herself. It was part of the cycle of life. But she wanted to go peacefully, naturally, not in a fit of someone else's rage.

"Evie's here," Anise announced, hopping to the floor a moment before the usual wiggle-rattle started at the front door. Again Martine wondered if her assistant truly might have power, but then she realized Anise could actually see the front door from where she'd sat.

Giving herself a figurative eye roll, Martine made a note to call a carpenter to repair the door. Some of the old building's quirks were charming. Her customers and friends having to wrestle the door to get inside wasn't one of them.

"I'll finish the inventory," Anise offered. "Or at least work on it until Niles gets back."

Thanking her, Martine walked through the bead curtain and met her best friend at the checkout. As was normal on Evie's visits, she laid a bag of baked goodies on the counter. Outside of normal was the big embrace she gave Martine. They were besties, but not usually the touchy-feely kind. Even so, the only thing that could have possibly felt better at that moment would have been a hug from her mom.

"I'm so sorry about Paulina," Evie murmured, squeezing extra tightly before releasing her. "And I'm sorry Jack sent Jimmy over in his place."

"It's okay." Martine sat on a stool next to the counter and watched Evie do the same. She'd been working today—she wore her fortune-teller look, with its long flowing skirt, snug shirt, lots of jewelry and mystique. Today it was part of her shtick, but truth was, she'd always loved long flowy clothes and scarves and wearing her weight in silver.

"Where are the kids?"

Evie replied cheerfully, "Nursery school, preschool and school. I know they're on their way home when I feel the shock waves disturbing the atmosphere."

"And Jack? Did he really go out of town?"

"Really. He called a few hours ago, asked me to pack a bag and picked it up on his way to the airport. How was Jimmy?"

Martine considered it. "Surprisingly not-Jimmy for the most part."

"You didn't think he had a mode that wasn't arrogant bastard? Come on, Martine, NOPD wouldn't keep him on nearly twenty years if he wasn't good at what he does."

"I knew. I just thought being charming and obnoxious and smarmy were the only things he was good at."

"Well, yeah, there's that, too. He's multitalented." Evie reached inside her bag and pulled out two bottles of water from an insulated bag, then set a small plastic dish between them, filling it with fresh raisin oatmeal cookies from the bag. "You haven't eaten lunch, have you?"

"I'm not hungry." That was a hard thing to say when Evie's cookies were sitting inches away. To appease the sudden gnawing in her stomach, Martine broke off a tiny piece, mostly raisin, and ate it. "I'm sorry I wasn't very cooperative with Jack."

"Ooh, he didn't tell me that." Evie smiled. "You know Jack. After our case, he doesn't tell me much about the job, and frankly I don't usually want to know much. The only way he would have brought me into this would have been so I could give you a smack or two and make you tell him everything."

Martine snorted. "Like you could make me do anything."

"Ha, I am so much more persuasive than you are. Remember my job—I talk money out of customers' hands every day."

She snorted again. Evie was an honest-to-God psychic who pretended to be a fraud. She gave the casual tourists value for their money, scattering tidbits of truth in the generic readings. Her serious talents, though, were saved for her serious customers.

Suddenly morose, Martine asked, "If I ask you a question, will you give me the truth?"

"You know I don't read you well, but yes. Of course I'll tell you if I know it."

"Don't you want to know the question first?"

"I know the question. You want to ask if you're going to die. And the answer is yes."

Martine's nerves tightened and her breath caught raggedly in her chest in the half instant it took Evie to go on.

"We're all going to die, sweetie. The only variables are when and how. But are you going to die now, the same way your friend did? No. And you know why? Because I don't even have to know Paulina to know that you're not like her. You won't run away. You won't try to deal with it on your own. You're wise enough to know when you need help and to accept it when it's offered."

"I'm not feeling very wise today," Martine murmured. Hadn't she just apologized for not cooperating with Jack? Hadn't she kept back important information during her interview with him and DiBiase this morning? Hadn't she wasted precious breaths wishing she could make this whole awful situation go away so she wouldn't have to deal with it?

"Eat another cookie," Evie said, pushing the plate closer. "I have it on good authority that cookies make everything better."

Realizing she'd consumed one cookie bits at a time, Martine picked up another. "Whose authority? Jackson or Jack?"

"Both, and Isabella and Evangelina." Evie's smile was a glorious thing to see. They made up the perfect happy family: handsome dad, beautiful mom, three gorgeous, smart, funny kids. No one would ever guess by looking at them the trouble she and Jack had gone through to get where they were. They deserved every bit of the light in their lives.

Martine rarely envied anyone anything. She loved her shop, her home, her family and her friends. She didn't earn a fortune, but she met all her needs and most of her wants and still had money in the bank.

While there was no great love in her life, there'd been more than one or two men who'd been great for those moments in time. As far as kids, she'd never known if she'd truly wanted to be a mother. For a long time, she'd expected it to just happen. It was how things worked in her experience: a woman fell in love, got married, had kids and lived out the rest of her life. She'd done the falling in love, the getting married, but kids/no kids had been an issue for them.

She loved Evie's kids. She loved their friend Reece's kids, too, but as for children in general, not so much. At some point, she'd accepted they weren't part of the plan for her, and she was all right with that.

She'd also mostly accepted that a good man wasn't part of her plan, either. But when she saw Evie's expression while talking about Jack, or Reece whenever she talked about Jones, she felt a little bit of jealousy. A whole lot of loneliness. Just not enough to settle for less than perfect.

How fitting that when she thought those last three words, it was Jimmy DiBiase's image that came to mind. If any man she'd ever met was so perfectly less than perfect, it was him.

"What are you thinking about?" Evie asked.

Because her friend really, truly liked DiBiase, Martine fudged her answer. "Just wondering how you got so lucky in the It's-a-Wonderful-Life jackpot."

Evie dithered over picking a cookie as if it were the most momentous decision of her day before sneaking a glance to Martine. "Do you still have dreams about Jake?"

The question startled her. She could honestly say

Jake Lassiter had popped into her mind only twice in the last four or five years, both times in the past minute. He was another blast from the past, even more unwelcome than Paulina had been. When she and Jake had married about a million years ago, she'd believed *she'd* won the jackpot, but her ambitious politician husband had been even less a believer of things that went bump in the night than Jack had started out, and he'd been entirely too convinced of his abilities to manage, maneuver and manipulate things—namely, Martine and the shop—to his advantage.

They'd had two good years together, then three stormy years followed by a divorce. So quick that by the time he'd informed Martine about it, it was all over but the signing of the papers. He'd agreed that she should keep everything she'd brought into the marriage, and she'd agreed that if she couldn't have him, she sure as hell didn't want anything of his, and *bang*, they were done. He'd remarried, this time a suitable up-and-coming politician's wife, before Martine had even caught her breath.

"I haven't thought of Jake in years," she said honestly. "It's funny. He was such a huge deal in my life for so long, and then suddenly he wasn't. Probably the last time his name crossed my mind was when he last ran for reelection. Wow." She sighed easily. "I tried so hard to forget him—"

"After you put a dozen curses on him."

"Two dozen, at least. And then I forgot him so completely that I forgot I was even trying."

"Hmm, if you can pinpoint exactly when you put him out of your head, and whatever else was going on in your life at the time, you could make a fortune in forgetting candles. They could be shaped like the groom half of the cake toppers people use at weddings, and they could melt down to nothing by the time the conscribed burning period is over."

"I like that. Just a goop of black wax, with the face the last part to melt, of course. In a grisly, eyes-wide-open scream." Behind Martine, the front door banged and rattled, then the bell announced a visitor.

"Just me," Tee, the mail carrier, called before she could rise from the stool. He wore the bulky slicker that covered the mailbags he carried, a knitted cap under the hood and navy blue shorts that reached his knees, with black socks and walking shoes. He joined them at the counter and counted out a half-dozen pieces for the shop: a utility bill, an invoice, three catalogs and a manila envelope.

"Have a cookie, Tee," Evie offered. "Take two or three."

The young man flashed her a grin. "Thanks, Miss Evie."

"And for heaven's sake, get some long pants," Martine added. "Your legs are turning blue."

"You know my motto. Neither snow nor rain nor heat nor gloom of night can make me give up my shorts." He kept one cookie to eat, wrapped the others in a paper towel Evie provided from beneath the counter and left again, as quickly and as noisily as he'd come.

Evie stood and stretched. "I guess I should head out, too. The kids will be home soon. The other day they locked Anna Maria in the reading room but forgot about the door leading into the house, so they were wildly disappointed when she got out that way and sneaked up behind them. I fully expect them to keep trying until they succeed, and then heaven knows what they'll try for an encore."

Yeah, loving her godchildren was best done from a safe distance. Though she wouldn't have to worry about a similar fate. Anna Maria's mistake was letting them know she was an instantly forgiving pushover. Martine kept them guessing about just how many lines they could cross before suffering the consequences.

"Thank you for the cookies and the conversation." Martine pushed the plate of cookies toward Evie, but Evie pushed them right back.

"Keep them. Give them to Jimmy next time you see him." Oh, she said it so casually, as if it happened all the time and was a choice on both their parts, but the look in her eyes was wickedly teasing.

A shudder ricocheted through Martine, one she greatly exaggerated to express her displeasure. "I should have just shot him at that party. I blame you, you know, for inviting me and Jack for inviting him and for not warning me in advance."

"Sweetie, you'd been married to a politician. I figured you'd recognize a good-for-nothing, sweet-talking charmer from a mile away with a blindfold on. Besides, Alia's forgiven him for all that. Why can't you?"

"She's a better woman than me. Besides, when Alia looks at Jimmy, then at Landry, she gets on her knees and thanks God for kicking Jimmy to the curb for her so she would be free for Landry."

Again, uncharacteristically, Evie hugged her. "No one's better than you. That's why I love you." Weaving around the counter, then the displays, she called back,

"If you don't have anything to cook tonight, order in. Don't go out by yourself. Better yet, don't go out at all. Don't answer your door without your baseball bat, and don't take any calls from numbers you don't know."

"What? Did DiBiase think I need reminding?"

"Oh, no. That's what Jack tells me every single time he has to work late. Love you."

"Love you, too." Martine watched Evie go, feeling a bit lost as she disappeared down the street. She delivered the bills to the desk where Anise was still working and left the rest of the mail in a basket on a shelf behind the front door to go through when she got home.

With even more on her mind than before Evie had come, she got cleaning supplies from beneath the counter and went to the front plate-glass windows. When she'd gone home for a visit one fall weekend during her parents' divorce, she'd found her mother cleaning with a vengeance. *You can never start spring cleaning too early*, Bette had said in what she'd obviously thought was a cheery manner that had struck Martine as far more manic than happy. Like a good daughter, she hadn't pointed it out, or mentioned that the only things she was cleaning belonged to Mark, or that her notion of cleaning was swiping with a cloth, then tossing the item into one box for trash, one for giveaway or one to return to him. Virtually everything had gone into the trash box.

Other than her small bin of high school memories, Martine didn't have anything to dispose of to clear her mind, but she could throw her energy into cleaning. Spring was the season of promise. When spring came, this week would be a distant memory and getting more so every day. The sun would be shining, the tourists would be happy, business would be booming and her life would be back to normal.

She would make it so.

Chapter 4

By the time Jimmy left his desk, the sun had already set, though it hadn't been visible to anyone within a hundred-mile radius of New Orleans. He thought about dinner, well aware that the refrigerator, cupboards and pantry in his new place were as empty as the day they'd arrived for installation. Some of his buddies had gone to a bar they favored that served damn good greasy hamburgers and crispy fries, but while the food sounded good, the company didn't. He'd left the station; he hadn't left work. There were things he wanted to read, notes to organize, thoughts to get down in some rational form.

He settled for picking up a pizza and going home. The apartment had a mostly open layout: living room, dining room, kitchen, office and gym sharing one large space, each area designated by its own carpet laid over black tiles and/or ceiling-to-floor drapes that opened and closed soundlessly at a push of a button. The bedroom and bathrooms actually had four walls and doors, so he didn't care much about the rest of it.

He changed into a pair of jeans and a sweatshirt from his long-ago college days, set his paperwork on one end of the island, the pizza on the other, and picked a stool in the middle. For the worst part of the eating, he would thumb through Martine's yearbook, which he could do with one-handed ease. With a small memo pad and a handful of paper clips, he opened the book.

He'd gathered recent photos of four of the five women. Robin Railey had been living in Illinois, a suburb of Chicago, the last time she'd renewed her driver's license. That had been the middle of last summer, but in early November, she'd moved from her condo, quit her job and apparently fled. No cell phone records, no credit card use, no social media activity, nothing going on with her social security number. She was like an illusion: here, then gone. The coworkers and friends he'd spoken to had worried about her for a while, but her absence from their lives meant she'd eventually faded from their thoughts.

Her parents should have been even easier to locate than Robin. They were in their sixties, an age when people tended to be more deeply rooted in their lives. A month after Robin left Illinois, Vince and Melissa Railey left their retirement community in Arizona. They'd told neighbors they were going where it "never got cold" and the cost of living was cheap. They told family they were taking a luxury round-the-world cruise and leaving their cell phones behind. They said they would be back in eight months, ten months, a year, or they might take up residence on the prettiest deserted island they passed. Their credit cards and social media, likewise, had gone unused.

In her senior picture, Robin had looked like your typical eighteen-year-old. Her hair was short, straight, her features were bland, and her occasional comments were those of a protected teenager. She didn't look like Martine's choice for a best friend, though to be truthful, that observation was based mostly on the fact that Robin wasn't Evie. Some people had been together too long and fit together too well to ever imagine anyone else in their places.

He finished his first piece of pizza, washed it down with bottled water, then sprinkled hot red pepper flakes over the next piece. After taking a large bite that left cheese stringing from his mouth to the slice, he turned a few pages to the Winchester girls' pictures. Beneath their photos were their proper names, Callista and Taliesin, both scratched out and replaced with their nicknames, one in hot pink ink, one in lime green, both in a very girlie style. The girls were mostly identical: Callie's lips a little thinner, the tip of Tallie's nose a little sharper. They wore their hair the same, the same makeup colors, but Callie wore a shirt left undone one button too low, while Tallie's denim jacket showed little of the modestly rounded neckline of her shirt.

He'd tried to contact Tallie and Callie's parents a half-dozen times and got nothing but voice mail. He'd requested a copy of Tallie's passport picture from the State Department and gotten that back, along with the information that the passport had last been scanned in London back in November—a few weeks after Callie's funeral, Jimmy guessed. His IT guy hadn't been able to find much of an internet presence for Tallie: no Facebook, Twitter, Instagram, Snapchat, LinkedIn or any of the other countless outlets. There were a few cached references to her on the website of the investment firm she'd worked for, but nothing whatsoever since her sister's obituary.

Wiping his hands, he rooted through his stuff for the email he'd gotten from the Seattle detective investigating Callie's murder, with all its attachments. Her cell phone hadn't been recovered, but her social media accounts boasted a lot of selfies, usually surrounded by a crowd, in clubs, restaurants, theaters, sometimes alone, often in lingerie or a bikini. Alone, she mostly wore a sly, secretive smile, staring straight at the camera as if she could see into the eyes of the person viewing the pictures. In a few, she looked pensive.

Then he came to the last picture in the file. Callista Jane Winchester, lying on her back in a cemetery, clothes damp, a wound to the back of her head, a large waterproof dressing hiding the brutal attack on her chest.

Related? the detective had echoed when Jimmy brought up the fact. *In what way?*

Mother of God, he said after Jimmy told him, and he could easily imagine the man making the sign of the cross. He was tempted himself, and he wasn't even Catholic. *I'll help however I can, but it's hardly even an active case here. No clues, no suspects, nothing.*

How could a person do that kind of damage to another human being and no one else know? It should be tattooed on their foreheads, the evil in their souls forcing its way out to warn anyone they met. To have the dead-cold ability to mutilate a person like that and the even deader, even colder ability to hide it from everyone who saw him… A person like that was too dangerous to walk free.

And their guy was not only free, he had likely set his sights on Martine. Of the remaining three, she was the easiest to find, the only one living right out there in public, not fifty miles from where they'd grown up. She was the only one who had never bought into the blame game for William Fletcher's death.

Good thing Jimmy was more determined to keep Martine safe than the killer could possibly be to claim her.

Flipping through the yearbook pages, he stopped at the faculty section. There he was, Fletcher the Letcher. Probably about forty, light hair going a little thin on top, dark eyes, white shirt, sport coat, printed tie. He could have sold insurance or used cars, kept books or managed personnel; he had that sort of remarkably average look.

But none of those other jobs would have provided him pretty much unlimited access to teenage girls.

Jimmy found the list he'd been adding to all day and wrote Fletcher's name at the bottom. Where had he taught before coming to Marquitta? Why had he left his last job? How long had he been married, and why had his wife chosen to go to prison without presenting some sort of defense? If he'd been abusive—always a possibility in domestic cases—she might have gotten off, depending on the degree of abuse, but she hadn't even tried.

The early start to his day was making itself felt. He rubbed his eyes, then stood and stretched out the kinks before putting the leftover pizza in the refrigerator, its empty gleaming surfaces reminding him to go grocery shopping the next day. He didn't cook much, but he knew from experience he could live on cheese and crackers, tortilla chips and salsa, and peanut butter sandwiches, and he always appreciated a cold beer from time to time.

Or maybe, as rain suddenly pounded the windows, a hot buttered rum.

The rain blurred the city lights that stretched as far as he could see and made him sigh. New Orleans, with its subtropical climate, was always a damp place, and he actually preferred humidity to drier weather, but this was too much. He had four or five pairs of wet shoes drying along the bedroom wall. Every day for the past week, he'd had the option of changing clothes when he got a chance or spending the day in some degree of wetness. He wanted to put away the overcoat and feel the sunshine on his face, the sooner, the better.

Besides, there was a hell of a difference between rain with subtropical temperatures and rain with the midthirty degrees they were having tonight. Another couple of bumps down on the thermometer, and New Orleans could wake up to snow and/or ice in the morning, and that would be the icing on a truly bad weather cake.

He was shutting off lights when his cell phone rang. He didn't glance at caller ID before answering it. He gave his number to so many people—suspects, witnesses, families and friends, lawyers, district attorneys—that the majority of calls came from people whose names he didn't always recognize.

"DiBiase," he said, heading past the kitchen into

the short hallway that connected to the bathroom and bedroom.

"Um…" The caller cleared his or her throat. With the next word, Jimmy recognized the voice. "Detective…"

His muscles tightened. "Martine. Is something wrong?"

"I'm sorry to bother you, but I, uh, got an envelope in the mail today. I just got around to opening it, and… It's a note that says… It says, *I know what you did.*" Her voice quavered on the last word, and she drew in a noisy breath. "There's something else in the envelope. It's stuck to the glue on the flap, and I didn't want to tear the envelope to get it out since I thought you might want it intact, but… It looks like a piece of fabric."

"Fabric?" he echoed. Executing a sharp turn, he went back to the island, switching on the lights overhead, shuffling through the papers there. He found the report from the Seattle detective, scanned through it until he reached the inventory of items found on Callie Winchester's body, and then he cursed softly. "About an inch square? Some sort of blue pattern?"

For a long time, she was still. He wasn't. He headed to the bedroom, shoved his feet into running shoes, threaded his belt and holstered weapon through the denim loops of his jeans, then grabbed his Taser in its holster and clipped it onto his waistband in back. "Martine? Are you there?"

After another moment of nothingness, she whispered, "Oh, God. It's part of the bandanna we used to make the voodoo doll, isn't it? And you found it on Paulina, too, or Callie."

"Callie." He opened the coat closet in the entry,

yanking on a rain slicker, shoving a canister of pepper spray into one of its oversize pockets. "I'm coming over now. Is everything locked up? All the doors, windows, the gate to the courtyard?"

"Yes, yes."

Tension came over the line in waves, tightening the knots in his neck, jaw and shoulder muscles. He was tempted to run down the stairs to the garage, but the elevator would be quicker. Its bell dinged and the door opened only seconds after he punched the button. "Stay on the phone with me. I'm not far away, and I don't have to worry about breaking any traffic laws."

"One of the perks of the job, huh?" She sounded a little more relaxed or, at least, as if she was trying.

"That, and parking illegally. That really comes in handy when you're picking up takeout." He stepped out of the elevator onto the bottom level of the garage and jogged to his car. "That's what I did when I picked up my dinner tonight."

"Of course you did. While we law-abiding citizens circle endlessly."

Though they'd never discussed it, he'd just known she would frown on any perks he got because of the job—free or discounted meals, a pass on traffic infractions, whatever else, but especially the easy parking. Grinning because he knew she would hear it in his voice, he pulled out of the garage, made a sharp turn and headed her way. "Aw, come on. Do you know what we get paid?"

"I hear you don't work for the city because you love the pay."

"You've been asking about me?"

For the first time in hours, she was back to her usual

scornful self. "I don't have to ask. You give everyone so much to gossip about that it's hard, when we know the same people, not to hear at least some of it."

There'd been plenty of gossip over the years, mostly about his ways with women, some about how an honest cop could afford his lifestyle. He doubted Martine cared about the money situation—though over the years, there had been plenty of people outranking him who did—but if she'd heard any of the talk about him and women before their second meeting, she never would have let him within arm's length of her. "Yeah, okay. I work for the city because I love the job. And I happen to have a bit of family money that helps smooth over the rough places." Like the apartment he'd just leased. The mountain cabin he rented once a year in Wyoming. The cars he swapped out for new ones every few years.

Before she could respond to that, he went on. "I just turned onto your block. Don't open the door until I ring the bell."

"Okay." The word sounded flat, the lighter moment gone. As he pulled into the empty space beside her car, he added his usual professional encouragement. "It'll be okay, Martine."

Martine listened to the bell, immediately followed by DiBiase's gruff voice. "Open up. It's pouring." She undid the locks, then backstepped to avoid the water running from him to puddle on the mat. She wasn't at all surprised that just one glimpse of his face sent her personal security rating zooming from *no one can save me* to *the big strong man will protect me* in half a nanosecond. It wasn't all Jimmy, either, she reminded herself. Any woman who was feeling vulnerable would gain strength from a man in uniform, even when he didn't actually wear a uniform. Being with Jack made her feel safe. Ditto for navy cop Alia, Jimmy's ex-wife. People who swore to serve and protect—and who carried big guns—always got two big thumbs-up from Martine.

But she couldn't honestly admit that if Jack or Alia was standing in her entry she would be thinking about how easily they filled the space, or about the warmth that just sort of radiated off them, or that they smelled incredibly fresh and green and musky.

She shook her head as she turned and started up the stairs. Shadows fell over her, one looming ahead, long and threatening, another sneaking along behind. New light bulbs, she reminded herself. At least three hundred watts each. She wanted this staircase to be visible from outer space.

When they reached the kitchen, he hung his slicker over the back of a dining chair while she took a clean towel from a drawer and handed it to him to dry his face.

"One of my homeless guys says the city's going to float away if this keeps up. They'll find us floating somewhere in the gulf, and the state will have to decide whether it wants us back. If not, we'll all be learning Spanish."

Maybe Martine was shallow, but she appreciated every moment she could think of something besides her own troubles. "Does he sleep out on nights like this?"

"He's got places. Back when I was in Patrol, I'd pick him up on bad nights and take him to a shelter.

He'd be all grateful—*Thank you, young James, you've saved my life*—and three or four hours later, I'd find him sneaking back to one of his hiding places." He shook his head, and a bead of water fell from his hair to his temple. He wiped it away with the towel before spreading it over the lip of the sink. "Some people really can't handle the shelters—the crowding, the rules, the conformity. Darrell's the nicest guy you'd want to meet under a bridge or in an abandoned warehouse, but put him in a shelter…" He shook his head.

Martine knew Jack helped homeless people and runaways and prostitutes and budding juvenile offenders beyond the scope of his job—she supposed she knew rationally that a lot of cops did. But to find out the same about DiBiase… She'd been quite happy believing the worst of him for practically the entire time she'd known him. She wasn't sure she was comfortable with giving up one of the constants in her normally comfortable life.

"You want coffee?" She gestured toward the counter as she picked up her own mug. She'd brewed two while on the phone, after he'd said he was coming over. Everything needed for the perfect cup was on the counter in easy reach: sugar, sweetener packets and cream, along with bottles of Bailey's, Frangelico, Kahlúa, bourbon, whiskey and rum. Every spirit she had in the house, in fact.

"I like variety in coffee," he said, a teasing note lightening his words.

"Yeah, well, the plain stuff wasn't making the chill go away." Wrapping her hands around her mug, she took a sip, and the rum fanned a tiny flame to life deep in her stomach. She wasn't much of a drinker, in part because booze always made her flush uncomfortably. Now that was her goal.

He added sugar and cream to his, bypassing the liquor as he faced her. "You okay?"

"Oh, sure. When my friend said someone was trying to kill her, I thought she was crazy. When she said someone wanted me dead, I thought she was freaking crazy, and now she's dead and some lunatic is threatening me." She held the cup tighter as she went down the hall to the living room and plopped in the chair closest to the gas fireplace, its flames dancing as they released heat into the air.

The second floor of her building had originally been a single-family home, then divided into two apartments before she bought it. She'd rented the other space occasionally, though Reece, then her employee, had been the last to live there. After she'd moved into her own place with Jones a few years ago, Martine had opened hers up again, knocking out walls, turning numerous small rooms into fewer larger rooms, exposing brick walls and ancient wood floors along the way.

DiBiase took a seat on the couch, set his cup down, and opened a small black bag that she hadn't noticed before. Or his truly disreputable running shoes, way overdue for a trip to the landfill. Or his sweatshirt, the angry wave logo faded but still proclaiming his loyalty to Tulane.

In the last twenty minutes, she hadn't noticed anything but the intense desire to break down into a sobbing, terrified heap.

From the bag he removed latex gloves, evidence bags and a marker, then turned his attention to the elephant in the room, sitting in the middle of the coffee table. The envelope was a regular business size, made of heavyweight kraft paper, and there were faded spots on it, likely splatters from the rain. The note, in contrast, was written on the cheapest of white paper, almost as flimsy as tissue. She'd slit the envelope along one short end, and when she'd turned it over, the note had fallen out. It had taken her a few minutes and a whole range of emotions to realize that something remained inside the envelope.

Despite the gloves, DiBiase handled the paper gently. "We'll need your fingerprints for exclusionary purposes. We can do that in the morning." He sounded intense even though he looked as if nothing else existed at the moment but the note. "'I know what you did.' Didn't put much thought into it, did he?"

Her hands began to tremble again, and she took a large drink of coffee and rum and decided her next cup would be mostly rum. "Enough to make my heart stop, which, I'm guessing, was the purpose."

He glanced sharply at her, then slid the note into an evidence bag and picked up the envelope. "No return address. Postmarked three weeks ago in Jackson, Mississippi. You know anyone there?"

"No." She was still having trouble believing she knew anyone capable of murder. Sure, she thought most people, herself included, could kill to protect themselves or someone else, but cold-blooded premeditated murder…to track down someone like Paulina or Callie, to terrorize them, kill them and discard their bodies in a cemetery…

Squeezing the top and bottom of the envelope made the sides push out, and DiBiase squinted inside, leaning closer to the lamp at the end of the sofa. "Blue bandanna. It's faded, looks old but not worn. Like someone's been saving it all these years." His gaze shifted to her again. "That's what you used to make the doll."

Sick deep inside, she nodded. "I told you, it was really crude. Callie, I think, or maybe Tallie, had her hair tied back with it. She said she would sacrifice it to the cause." Hearing the word *sacrifice* out loud made her cringe. They'd been so stupid and insensitive and naive.

But no one deserved to die for it.

Letting the envelope close again, he put it, too, in an evidence bag and labeled both before stripping off the gloves and turning toward her. "So either one of your friends told someone the details of what you'd done, or someone was watching you in the woods that night."

Lord, she was tired of shivers racing down her spine. Was it possible someone had followed them and spied on them that entire evening, two, three hours or more? That while they laughed and passed a joint and a bottle and acted their silly selves, someone who was truly evil had waited near enough to hear what they said and see what they did? Had he intended to confront them, hurt them, maybe kidnap or even kill them, or had he been satisfied at that time with being a simple peeping pervert instead of a murderous one?

"I can't imagine they told anyone. Like I said, it destroyed our friendships. It changed our entire lives." She worried the edge of her lip between her teeth for a moment before sighing. "I guess someone could have followed us. We weren't the smartest kids around. We thought the world pretty much revolved around us."

"Did you have any enemies?"

Though she'd watched enough TV shows to expect the question, it still seemed totally surreal to her. They'd been seventeen and eighteen years old—*kids*. Shouldn't developing enemies capable of murder have to wait at least until they were grown up? "I don't think Sybil Merchant waited twenty-four years to kill Callie for stealing her boyfriend."

DiBiase reached for his coffee. "You were pretty girls who liked to have fun. I'm guessing the guys liked you, and the girls wanted to be part of your group."

She'd really never given it much thought, but yes, they'd been popular. They'd all made friends easily, and boyfriends had come even more easily. And their little clique had been exclusive but not by design. They'd been best friends forever. They hadn't deliberately shut anyone out; they'd just had no reason to let anyone in.

"We weren't mean girls," Martine said at last. "Callie didn't really steal Sybil's boyfriend. He'd already broken up with her, and Callie only went out with him once. We were nice…enough."

"But you were the cool girls, and other girls wanted to be one of you. Other guys, besides Sybil's ex, wanted to be chosen by one of you."

"I guess. Yeah. But it was just high school. It wasn't the best years of our lives. It wasn't the wonder years that we would look back on with great fondness and relive at every reunion that came along. It just wasn't that important."

He grinned. "Maybe not to you, and definitely not in the greater scheme of things. But you'd be surprised how many people do consider it the best time, the wonder years. A lot of people are just older versions of who they were then. Life hasn't lived up to their expectations, so they live in the past. They still hold the same petty grudges and jealousies. They still envy the cool kids and are intimidated by the smart kids and scared of the tough kids. It made them who they are today, and they can't let go. So…any enemies besides Sybil?"

"Who went to college in Los Angeles, by the way, married and divorced a very successful movie producer and now lives on the beach in Malibu when she's not at her Paris flat. The boyfriend who broke her heart sells cars in Shreveport."

The liquor was doing its job. At least, she hoped it was the reason the chills had finally left her and at least some of the tension had drained from her body. She dearly hoped it had nothing to do with the fact that the biggest womanizer—heartbreaker—charmer—of the New Orleans Police Department was focusing all his attention on her.

Suddenly even warmer than before, she shifted away from the fire to get more comfortable. "Honestly, none that I can recall. The aftermath of our dabbling in voodoo was the only traumatic thing that had happened. Our parents were all still together, our families were close, we had friends and boyfriends, we made good grades, we were looking forward to college or moving away. Most people liked us. Some didn't, but even with the ones who didn't, it was no big deal. It was just normal life."

The humor that had lit DiBiase's face a moment ago faded, leaving the intensity back in place. "Callie and Paulina are dead, Martine, and their deaths are somehow connected to that night. It was a very big deal to someone."

* * *

Jimmy drained the last of his coffee. "I'm going to get this stuff to the lab—" or maybe have a patrol officer meet him somewhere and deliver it for him; his bed was still calling his name "—then I need to get to sleep. I'm going to Marquitta tomorrow to look around, talk to some people. You think you could go? Show me where you did the ritual if it still exists?"

As he stood up, so did she. "Okay. When will Jack be back?"

Hoping that if he got back overnight, he could be the one taking her for a drive tomorrow? Jimmy kept his sigh to himself. Whenever Jack did get back, he would defer to Jimmy on pretty much everything about this case. They may have started out sharing it, but his leaving made it primarily Jimmy's case. He wouldn't tell her that, though, not now. "He doesn't know. Bad weather, and the guy's lawyer is trying to keep him in Nebraska. Here he faces two first-degree murder charges. They've only got him on armed robbery there. Is your Jimmy fun-meter on overload?"

She didn't make the kind of caustic remark he'd come to expect. Instead, her mouth curved, nowhere near enough to suggest a smile, but it was a start. "Evie doesn't like for him to be gone."

"Why don't you spend the night over there? She'd be happy to see you, and the kids would scare away most of your basic stalker types."

For a moment, she looked tempted, but then the look faded. "If someone's watching me, I couldn't possibly lead them to Evie's door. When she and Jack were getting back together and she got caught up in that case of his, we agreed to keep our potential killers away from each other." Her face screwed up into part frown, part bewilderment. "Of course, at the time, I didn't think I would ever have a potential killer."

"And your killer doesn't know you've got me." She'd had him for a long time in one way or another: interested, attracted, intrigued. In the beginning, he'd considered her a possible friend with benefits, then an enemy whom he could surely convert if he made the effort, an acquaintance, a thorn in his side, an annoyance and, still, someone who drew him in a way no one else ever had. But that was his secret.

He forced what Evie called his crap-eating grin: big, broad and confident. "In fact, if he knew I had this case, he would probably just mark you off the list and move on out of town. I have a reputation, you know."

His words and action made her expression go dry. "I know your reputation. I doubt there's a woman in the city who doesn't."

"I'm talking about my reputation as a damn good detective." He went into the kitchen, rummaged through the slicker pocket and pulled out the pepper spray. "You know what this is?"

She nodded from the doorway.

"You ever used it?"

As she shook her head, she slowly closed the distance between them.

"It's small enough to carry in your pocket. Don't put it in your purse, then have to dig it out. Shake it up really good before you go out, and if you need it, make sure you're upwind and slide your finger right in here and press."

He held it out, but she didn't take it right away.

"Does the police chief know you go around arming citizens?"

"Who do you think put the idea in my head?" He pushed the can a little closer, and finally she wrapped her fingers loosely around the bottom part of it. "Hold it firmly. You don't want someone grabbing it out of your hand. Up here." He loosened her fingers, then slid them higher. "There's no safety, no on/off switch. You slide your finger under this little flap, you point and you spray, then run like hell the other way."

Her fingers were cool and unsteady beneath his. He guided her index finger along the length of the can, until the tip was resting lightly on the button. If she wanted, she would need only two seconds to tilt the can upward and blast him in the face. He'd seen her a time or two when she might have been angry enough to do it. That passion had surprised him. He'd figured a woman her age, not married, as independent as anyone he knew and open to a one-night stand wouldn't give a damn about that one-night stand's marital status.

He'd figured wrong. Vows, fidelity, infidelity— hers, his, anyone else's—were important to her. She believed they said an awful lot about a person—in his case, an awful lot that was bad.

And his attitude hadn't helped any. The next time they'd met, this time out to dinner with Evie and Jack, Jimmy, surprised by her disdain, had remarked, *So you almost slept with a married man. If it's okay with me, and I'm the one who's actually married, why is it such a problem for you?*

He should have kept his mouth shut and his hands off her and definitely his mouth off her. He should have thought, *Damn, she's gorgeous, and when I'm divorced and not with anyone else, I'm going to ask her out.*

And now he should keep his mind on what he was doing.

Slowly she removed her hand, and the pepper spray, from his. "Will you get in trouble loaning this to me?"

"It's mine, not the department's. No one will care. Same with this." Reaching behind him, he unclipped the Taser holster and set it on the table.

"I've never used a gun." Martine backed away, a bit of panic in her voice.

"It's a Taser. Less-lethal force. You shock the hell out of someone, knock 'em to the ground for a bit, and you run like hell. It's got a laser sight, so wherever you put the dot is where the barbs are going to go. You can shoot it from as far as fifteen feet, and the shock lasts thirty seconds, which gives you time to escape." He removed the weapon from the holster and showed her the power button, the safety, the flashlight and the laser. He removed the cartridge and showed her that, and how to reinsert it, and how to use the Taser without the barbs as a stun gun. Then he offered the black-and-yellow weapon to her.

"I'm not asking you to go around armed all the time. I don't believe people should carry weapons for self-protection unless they're absolutely committed to using them. A gun does no good if the bad guy takes it away and uses it on you." He shifted his gaze from the barrel of the Taser to her face.

"But you've got some wingnut out there who wants to hurt you for something you didn't do. He knows where you work and where you live. Now that Paulina's out of the way, he's probably watching you. Neither the pepper spray nor the Taser are going to kill him, but they will give you an advantage, and when your life is at stake, Martine, you take every advantage you can get."

He watched the emotion flicker through her eyes, from a clear desire to refuse to some degree of interest, from distaste to fear to resignation to relief. He rarely felt physically vulnerable; he'd always been big, strong, fast, more than capable of holding his own. He'd learned to fight in school and honed it on the job, and a pistol on his hip or in his hand was as natural as a cup of coffee to someone else.

But he understood how vulnerable people could feel, just going about their everyday life, and Martine was in a much worse situation than that. No one knew how the killer had gotten his hands on Callie or Paulina. They had no clue just how much he had known about their daily activities. Had they been safe at home when he took them? Had he persuaded them to meet him? Had he grabbed them off the street?

"When this is over, when we catch this guy, you can give them back. You'll never have to pick up a weapon again…unless you decide you like being prepared to defend yourself. But for now, Martine…please. I don't want anything to happen to you."

Again, emotion flickered through her eyes. Surprise at how serious his last words had sounded? Before she could give it too much thought, before *he* could give it too much thought, he grinned. "If you get hurt on my watch, Evie and Jack will give me hell every day of my life."

She took a breath, wrapped her fingers around the Taser grip and blew out a deep breath. "Okay. Run through this with me again."

* * *

Martine went to bed Wednesday night convinced she wouldn't sleep, but fatigue won out…maybe, with a little help from the pepper spray and the Taser hidden beneath the extra pillow on her bed. Less-lethal force, DiBiase had called them. She didn't want to kill anyone, but she didn't want to die, either. If his weapons could get her out of a life-or-death situation without having to kill someone else, she was happy to hoard them close.

He'd said he would be by around ten to pick her up for the trip to Marquitta. She didn't want to spend hours in a car with him. Didn't want to show him that spot out by Twins' Landing where she and the girls had their last big hurrah. Didn't want to see the town and the familiar faces, familiar places, that would remind her of them. She just didn't want to go, period.

But she owed it to her girls, to herself and to DiBiase. And who knew? The life she helped him save might be her own.

She'd called Anise, asking her to come in early to open, eaten a small breakfast, inhaled three cups of coffee and changed pants four times. She wasn't looking for the pair that flattered her most, she reminded herself with a scowl in the mirror. She needed pants with a pocket big enough for the pepper spray and with a substantial enough waistband to make wearing the Taser as comfortable as she was ever going to be with something stuck inside her pants. She settled on olive-drab cargo pants and, to go with them, sturdy boots and a white shirt with a khaki sweater over it. With the heavy sweater tugged over her hips, no one would notice the weapons adding bulk where she didn't have it.

When she saw DiBiase's car pull to the curb, she grabbed her purse and slicker and trotted down the stairs. The bell rang before she reached the halfway point, and she called, "I'm coming."

Hurry, Tine, Paulina used to shout, and she'd shouted back, *I'm coming!* All those years, constantly coming and going, never more than a phone call apart, so close they could finish each other's sentences.

All gone. All those good times, all the potential, all the promises. Vanished.

She undid the locks and stepped outside. Her breath misted in front of her face, but for once there was no fog, no rain. Still no sun.

From where he stood at the bottom of the steps, DiBiase said, "Anise says this is a temporary break. The fog will be back today, and we may see some snow before it's all over."

Martine wrinkled her nose. "I hope she's not dabbling in weather control."

"Nope." He opened the passenger door for her, then grinned. "She's watching the Weather Channel."

"Did you go inside the shop?"

"No, she was turning over the Open signs when I got here. She opened the door to speak."

Martine was faintly relieved that he hadn't gone into the shop. It just really wasn't a good time to find out that he'd gotten another static shock from the doorknob.

"I called the police department in Marquitta," he said as he pulled away from the curb. "I want to talk to the detective who investigated Fletcher's murder. Find out what their case looked like before the wife confessed."

"What does that matter? She admitted she did it. Case closed."

"You'd be surprised how many false confessions have resulted in convictions. People trying to protect somebody else, people trying to take credit for someone else's actions, people who have mental issues that cause them to confess to just about anything. And that's not including the ones who are coerced into a false confession by cops."

"You could never make me confess to something I didn't do."

"Of course I could. It's called the Reid technique." DiBiase glanced at her from the corner of his eyes. "Given enough time, I could get you to confess to killing Paulina and Callie yourself. It's trickery, deception and psychological manipulation at its finest. You break down your suspect and build them back into someone who believes you'll help them if they just tell you what you want to hear."

"It sounds unethical."

"It can be with the wrong cop."

She hesitated, then asked, "You ever settle for a confession you knew wasn't true?"

"No."

He said it simply, normally, and she believed him. He might not grasp the meaning of things like *forsaking all others* and *until death do us part*, but her problems with him were with the man, not the cop.

A man she hadn't seen much of the past two days.

A cop who'd impressed her with his dedication to the job, with his patience with her, with his need to protect people and find justice for people he'd never known.

A cop who'd come out last night after a hellishly long day, in pouring rain, to pick up evidence and to make her feel safer. Who'd brought her ways to negate her overwhelming sense of helplessness.

They drove a few miles in silence, those last thoughts replaying in her mind: impress, dedication, patience, need to protect. A few days ago, she would have claimed Jimmy DiBiase could never impress her on more than a superficial he's-damn-hot level, and she wouldn't have believed he could even define the other things.

What a difference a murder made.

As he merged onto the interstate, he glanced her away. "Did you ever meet Fletcher's wife?"

Eyes narrowed, Martine focused on the past. In elementary school, she'd adored her teachers and cried each time she'd passed to the next grade and a new teacher. By senior year, all she had cared about was the easiest classes that would fulfill her graduation requirements, going to the dances and staying out of Fletcher's reach. "If I did, I don't remember."

"Did they have any kids?"

Their school hadn't been huge; she'd known either names or faces for pretty much everyone, but she couldn't recall a Fletcher son or daughter. "Not that I can think of. Maybe a younger kid?"

"How much do you remember about the case?"

A shudder rocketed through her, and she moved uneasily to hide it, shifting her weight and tugging at her seat belt. There wasn't much room in the passenger seat with the computer extending into her space, and she felt she needed it right now.

"I was the last one to leave town. Robin and the

twins were gone practically before the police started their investigation. Paulina took off next. At first Mrs. Fletcher denied having anything to do with it. She swore she hadn't seen him since the night before, that she'd fallen asleep on the couch. Then, after a couple days, she stopped crying, got all stiff-backed and stony-eyed—that was how my mom described her— and apologized for lying. She said he'd made a fool of her one time too many, that she'd snapped and shot him while he slept. She said that wasn't the life he'd promised her, and people had to pay when they broke their promises."

She considered that a moment. "I don't understand… When my dad decided he didn't want my mom anymore, she hired a lawyer and made sure she was taken care of. She didn't for a minute think about taking out his rifle and killing him. I didn't consider killing my ex. Alia didn't consider killing you."

"Sure, she did," he said with a grin. "Granted, she's a highly capable federal agent. She probably could have gotten away with it easier than you or your mom could."

Martine appreciated the smile his response brought her. Alia often said things to or about DiBiase that seemed really harsh on the surface, but it didn't take anyone long to see that they still shared an affection few divorced couples managed. It was probably because they *were* divorced. They hadn't dragged the marriage out long enough for Alia's love to turn to hatred.

Jimmy's infidelity probably meant more to Martine at the moment than it did to the woman he'd cheated on. There was a lesson in that, but not one that Martine wanted to look closely at now.

And she wasn't going to start calling him Jimmy. *DiBiase* had worked just fine for years. It would continue to do so now.

The drive to Marquitta would always be familiar, not that she'd made it very often since her mom started her travel career. When they visited, it was usually Bette stopping in New Orleans on her way someplace else, and visits with her father... Well, she'd always been more of a mama's girl. She saw Mark at Christmas, on both their birthdays and Father's Day but not very regularly other than that. He'd changed from the father she'd grown up with, and she didn't have much in common with the man he'd become.

"Did you grow up dreaming of leaving your hick hometown in the dust?"

The question drew her glance across the car. DiBiase sat in a comfortable slouch behind the wheel, one hand resting at the top. His suit today was dark gray, the shirt white, the tie black-and-silver stripes. Evie had once shown her Jack's half of the closet, and they'd snickered together over the seven dark suits, seven lighter suits, seven white shirts and the rack of similarly dark ties. Now she wondered if DiBiase's closet looked the same. As far as contents, probably, though she didn't imagine his would be nearly as neat as Jack's. Jack was always more put-together, while Jimmy, no matter how squared away he was, always gave a bit of a tousled impression. It was too easy for comfort to imagine him in a looser, more relaxed setting.

A more intimate setting.

Even, if she relaxed her guard, in no clothes at all.

Martine scowled. Apparently, her brain *was* going to start calling him Jimmy, with her permission or without, and thinking all sorts of things about him that she'd sworn off that night she found he was married. Damn.

She forced herself to concentrate on his question. "Aw, I wouldn't call Marquitta a hick town. It's got at least eighteen thousand people." Then she shrugged. "I loved New Orleans from the first time I saw it. I was convinced God had intended for me to live there but dropped me in Marquitta by mistake. Getting there was the goal for the first part of my life, and staying there has been the goal since. What about you? Could you not wait to get out of your hick hometown?"

"I would have moved away in seventh grade if I could have. My hick town is Cypress Hill. Back that way." He gestured vaguely toward the west.

"I've been there. When my mom first started her travel blog, she mostly focused on local places. She did a story about the plantation the town is named for, and I went along. Gorgeous place." A *Gone with the Wind*–type place, huge, white, gracious—a real step back in time. Massive columns, immense live oak trees, regimented gardens, lush velvety grass and more antiques than all the shops in the Quarter could hold. A tribute to a time long past. Lovely to visit, but she wouldn't want to live there. "Have you toured it?"

He didn't meet her gaze. "Yeah, I've, uh, seen it."

"Of course. You live that close to a historic site, you probably see more of it than you want, between school field trips and showing family guests around town."

"Uh-huh."

Still he didn't look at her, and her gaze narrowed as she identified discomfort in the set of his jaw. His fingers were tighter on the steering wheel than they'd been moments ago, and his slouch didn't look so comfortable now.

I work for the city because I love the job, he'd said last night, then added, *And I happen to have a bit of family money that helps smooth over the rough places.*

Cypress Hill was a decent enough little town, though dusty and sleepy, one of those rural places where the population dropped steadily every decade as the young people went off looking for jobs and careers. Not the sort of place that attracted a lot of businesses or families of a lot of wealth. In fact, all its wealth, if she recalled her mom's research correctly, pretty much belonged to the family that owned the plantation. She was certain they had been mentioned in the article, as well—when Bette did a story, she did it justice—but all Martine remembered was that the property had come down through the wife's family so there were two surnames involved.

A bit of family money... "I don't remember Cypress Hill having much in the way of opportunities. A couple of convenience stores, some churches, a bank, a few bars." She couldn't be sure of any that, but she knew from Bette's travels that the description covered a great many small towns.

"Yeah. We went to school in the next town over. And to the doctor, the dentist, the grocery store…"

She was enjoying being the one asking questions that he hadn't expected. Turnabout was always fair play, even when it was on a much less important subject. "Did you ever ask your parents to move to the next town?"

"They couldn't do that."

"Why not?"

Finally he looked at her and lifted one shoulder in a careless shrug. "Their income was kind of tied to Cypress Hill."

"Cypress Hill the town? Or Cypress Hill the plantation?"

He slowed to take the next exit, the signal light blinking, then came to a stop at the highway where he needed to turn. "Okay. My DiBiase father married my Ravenel mother, whose family built Cypress Hill back in 1820. She grew up in the house. So did my sisters and I. After my sisters left home, my parents had a smaller place built way out back and opened the house up for tours, weddings, overnight stays, etcetera. It's been very successful for them."

"Wait a minute. I'm trying to picture this." Martine closed her eyes, imagining a beautiful, refined, beloved mansion and Jimmy at eight, twelve and sixteen, sitting on furniture fit for a castle and eating off dishes fit for a king. Jimmy, being polite, well-mannered and behaved, as generations of Ravenels before him had always been.

Opening her eyes again, she smiled smugly. "The image just won't form."

The look he gave her was grumpy. "Where did you think I grew up? In a home for juvenile delinquents? On a farm, with the animals?"

"Don't get annoyed with me. I didn't know you even had parents until last night." She pointed helpfully to the right. "Marquitta's that way. Just follow the road to the middle of nowhere."

Her mood significantly better, she returned to gazing out ahead of them, this time with a smile easing the tension on her face.

After a moment, she caught a tiny glimpse of a smile on Jimmy's face, as well.

Chapter 5

Marquitta had so much more to offer than Cypress Hill that if Jimmy had grown up there, he might have gone back after college. It had all the businesses he needed to survive: grocery stores, convenience stores, liquor stores and restaurants. Its police department was of a decent size, around thirty-five officers, and there was enough crime to keep them busy, though homicides were rare. For a homicide detective, that could be good or bad, depending on the week.

"I've got an appointment with the detective in charge of the Fletcher case in fifteen minutes at a coffee shop up here," he said as he drove along the main drag downtown. "I'll ask if he minds you listening in, but if he says yes, you'll have to have your coffee alone."

"Or I could walk around downtown."

"Or you can sit at another table and have your coffee alone. Come on, Martine, this guy who's very upset with you and your friends probably lived here when you did. He knows your face, and he knows his way around if he followed you into the woods, so you don't get to go off anywhere without me."

"Okay."

Her easy acceptance made him shake his head. Just a few days ago, the idea of her agreeing to something he suggested would have seemed impossible. All she'd seen when she looked at him was the cheater, the betrayer, the liar who had almost seduced her.

Damn, he regretted that he'd failed. Regretted that he'd even tried. Wondered what would have happened if he'd waited until he was single again.

And while she was cooperating at the moment, he wondered what it would take to make her forget that guy completely. To convince her that he'd changed.

Yeah, he heard that line a lot from people he'd arrested, and he rarely believed it from them. He'd gotten cynical enough over the years that he wasn't sure he would believe himself.

The coffee shop was located on the corner across the street from the police department. Jimmy found a parking space on the adjacent street, met Martine on the sidewalk, and they headed back to the corner. "Are you armed?"

She held her arms out from her sides. "Can you tell?"

He gave her a long, attentive look, from her shoulders to her knees, then back again, even though he knew exactly where the pepper spray and the Taser would be. "With all those clothes, you could be packing an AR-15 under there for all I know. Are you comfortable wearing them?"

"They don't seem as weird as I thought they would."

"Hopefully we'll get this guy before they become second nature." He opened the coffee shop door, and heat rushed out, carrying the aromas of coffee, sugar and cream on the air.

A white-haired man stood up at a table in the center, surrounded by other older gentlemen, with enough empty sugar packets and creamer tubs to indicate that they'd been at it awhile. "You DiBiase?"

"Yes, sir, I am." *You'll recognize me*, the guy had said, *because I'll be sitting at the old cop farts' table. Bunch of retirees that have nothing better to do than relive their glory days.*

Much as Jimmy appreciated a hot cup of coffee or three in the morning and swapping stories with other cops, when he retired, he sincerely hoped he didn't find himself hanging out in a cop coffee shop or bar, rehashing old cases. He intended to have more in his life than getting old and nostalgic.

The older guy met him in the aisle, a brown expandable folder tucked under his arm, shook hands, then smiled at Martine. "Do you know we didn't get our first female officer until eight years ago? I bet you brighten up the office. I'm Carl Taylor."

"Nice to meet you, Carl. I'm Martine Broussard."

"Martine's not an officer, Detective," Jimmy said. "I wanted her to sit in because she knows some of the victims involved in my case, but if you'd prefer she didn't, that's fine."

Taylor's gaze shifted back to Martine, shrewd and evaluating, before he smiled again. "If DiBiase trusts you, who am I to object? It's his case. And it's Carl, son. If I get used to being called Detective again, my wife's gonna pitch a fit. She says it took the first ten years of retirement for me to remember what my first name is."

They took a table for four in the back, Jimmy sliding out the chair in the corner for Martine. He hadn't realized exactly how uncomfortable he was going to be with her visiting her hometown until they'd crossed the city limits. He didn't know enough about the suspect's pattern to know whether bringing her here increased the danger or provided a bit of safety over leaving her in the shop and the home that the guy already knew about.

At least they were in a room with a bunch of retired cops, and the police station was only a ten-second run away.

Taylor waved to a waitress who took their orders for coffee, then set the folder on the table. "So you were asking about the Fletcher case. Easiest murder case we ever closed. Not that we have very many murders around here. Do you mind if I ask why you're looking at it now? It's been over twenty years."

"I have a new case that appears to be tied to that one."

"Tied how?"

Jimmy had been debating how to answer that question since making the appointment. In general, he didn't like sharing with outside agencies, but sometimes there wasn't much choice. Other cops didn't like it when he asked all the questions and gave them nothing in return, even if it was only to satisfy their curiosity.

"Can I get into that later?" he asked as the waitress brought three steaming cups of coffee.

"Sure," Taylor agreed. "I won't forget. So… I'll just start at the beginning. Police got a call around eight fifteen on a Sunday morning. Katie Jo Fletcher, in hysterics, screaming that her husband was dead. She was so shaken, she couldn't even get her address right. We found him in bed, shot once in the chest and once in the groin. No sign of a break-in, no struggle and no weapon."

"Any neighbors hear the shots?"

"Nah. They lived back a good ways off the road. Katie Jo, she was wailing and keening, going on about how he didn't deserve that, that he'd been a good husband and a good father—"

"Father?" Jimmy glanced at Martine. "How many kids did he have?"

"Just the one, Irena. Stepdaughter, really. Used her daddy's name—Young."

Martine's brows narrowed in the way that meant she was concentrating. "I think… Do you have a picture of her, Carl?"

Taylor thumbed through the files in the thick folder and pulled out a thinner one. All it held was a school photo and a single sheet of paper with minimal information.

When Martine took it, Jimmy leaned close to see it better. A strand of her hair brushed against his cheek, and the scent of her perfume drifted on the air. Not the time to think how good she smelled or how good she'd felt all that time ago.

He barely managed to keep himself from rolling his eyes. *Any time* was a good time to think those kinds of things. Life was too short and uncertain to limit pleasures to certain times or places.

Irena Young was a pretty enough girl, though her hair was overstyled, her makeup overdone, her outfit overmatched. The effect was desperation—to fit in, to be accepted—and the fear that it wasn't going to happen shadowed her eyes.

Resettling in his chair, Jimmy asked, "You remember her, Martine?"

"I… I do. She was new that year, and she didn't seem to like it. We felt bad for her, having to start her senior year at a brand-new school. But we had no clue she was Mr. Fletcher's stepdaughter."

"Would you have wanted anyone to know if you were her?"

"No, of course not." Her fingers trembled slightly as she returned the folder to Taylor.

"So you're from here." Taylor's gaze narrowed. "Are you Bette and Mark Broussard's daughter?"

"Yes, sir."

"You look like your mom, but you've got your daddy's coloring. What remote part of the world is she in now?"

"London. Not too remote."

"Our hometown girl made good. Not that we see much of her anymore. She tells my wife life's too short to waste."

"Smart woman," Jimmy said, grinning at the coincidence before returning to the subject. "You said this was the easiest murder case you ever had. Did you suspect Katie Jo from the beginning?"

"She was the wife. We always suspect them. But no more than usual. They seemed to get along fine, though there were rumors that he ran around on her. Also rumors about what went on behind closed doors. They didn't socialize, didn't go to church, he wouldn't let her get a job. According to her, he was pretty controlling. But she was truly grief-stricken. I've seen a lot of people at the worst times of their lives. I can usually tell if they're playing a part or if they're sincere, and that woman was sincerely in shock at her husband's death."

"But?"

Taylor tore open three packets of sugar, dumped them into his coffee and stirred it, the spoon clinking against the porcelain. "But the next day, she was all calmed down, like she'd cried every tear she had. She walked into the police station, quiet, head held high, told us she'd shot him and where she'd hidden the gun."

"Did you believe her?"

Again, Taylor took a moment before answering. Jimmy knew from his own experience that the detective was replaying the scene in his head, looking at it from every angle. Finally, he shrugged. "No reason not to. She knew where Fletcher kept the gun. He'd taught her how to use it in case she ever needed to defend herself. He'd moved them around an awful lot— never stayed at a job more than a year. He took her and the daughter away from their family and friends, the girl had trouble fitting in at new schools over and over, they had money problems, and there were those rumors. Plus the gun, and her prints were on it and the bullets still loaded. We couldn't ask for more."

With that evidence, Jimmy would have believed her, too. "Why did he change jobs so often?"

"We checked with the schools where he used to work. Never fired, just resigned at the end of each year. Wife said he wanted to experience life elsewhere. Not something she was aware of when she met him." Taylor shrugged again. "I got the impression she wouldn't have married him if she'd known he was going to up-root them every year."

Wouldn't have married him. Not the sign of a happy marriage.

And never fired meant nothing. Jimmy had heard of too many problem teachers who'd never been fired—just forced into resigning by a school district willing to keep silent as long as they got to pass the problem on to someone else. Thieves, dopers, philanderers, abusers, pedophiles. Fletcher appeared to qualify on at least two counts.

What better motivation for killing a husband than his messing with her kid? Whether Fletcher had gotten too friendly with Irena, like he did with the girls at school, or had just made her life miserable because of his choices, Katie Jo might have felt drastic action was necessary.

Beside him, Martine spoke up. "Why didn't she want a trial? It seems she might have gotten some sympathy from a jury."

Taylor shifted in his chair, crossing one ankle over his knee. He didn't have to consult his notes. He'd probably refreshed his memory after Jimmy's call yesterday, but a lot of cases stuck with a cop, and this was probably one of Taylor's never-forgets. "She didn't want her girl to have to go through that. She'd done the crime, and she was willing to do the time. She said the sooner it was over, the sooner Irena could get on with her life. I suspect she also didn't want anything coming out at trial that would tarnish Irena's memory of her stepfather, or maybe she didn't want her to hear the details of what she'd done herself."

"Maybe she was a killer with a conscience. I've run

into a few of those over the years." Jimmy hesitated, glanced at Martine, then quietly asked, "Did you know the victim's nickname at the local high school was Fletcher the Letcher?"

The detective had not known that. An hour later, back in the car and buckling her seat belt, Martine marveled over the fact. As Jimmy stowed the detective's folder—including Taylor's own personal investigative notes—in the back seat, then fastened his own seat belt, she sighed. "Every girl in high school that year knew about Fletcher. It was about as far from being a secret as anything could be. With that many people who knew, how is it possible that not one of them ever said anything to a mother, a sister, another teacher or a counselor?"

He gave her a steady look. "You were one of those girls. Did you tell your mom?"

Slowly, regretfully, she shook her head. "I never considered it."

"Your parents would have been upset. They would have wanted to know if he'd touched you, and when and where. They would have made a big deal of it, invading your privacy, making you feel guilty or dirty or somehow responsible. And you didn't want anyone thinking, even for a minute, that you might have been Fletcher the Letcher's victim. So you stayed quiet. So did your friends, for the same reasons. So did all the girls, and the boys who knew."

She pressed her fingertips to her temples, rubbing to lessen the tension gathered there. "Poor Irena knew."

"And she stayed quiet, too. That's how these guys get away with it. In the beginning, no one wants to believe they're capable of it. No one wants to believe it's serious, that it wasn't just a bump or an accident, and when they figure out it is serious, no one wants to be the one to complain. No one wants to be labeled a victim. No one wants to face the scrutiny and the questions and the gossip that come with speaking out."

He was right on every point—he had a good grasp of the way teenage girls thought—but she couldn't help but feel ashamed. "It was a really crappy thing for us to do." If they'd come forward, told their parents, made complaints, how different would Katie Jo's and Irena's lives have been? How many girls would have escaped the letch's attention?

Jimmy twisted in the seat to face her. That intensity had returned to his face and his voice, strong with emotion and understanding and an expression she was beginning to think of as his driven-to-get-justice look. "Would it have been nice if you'd all stormed the principal's office the first time he touched one of you? Sure. Are you somehow culpable for what he did because you didn't? Of course not. You were kids. You'd be surprised how many adults can't or won't speak up. I can't count how many murders I've investigated that took place in restaurants, bars, crowded places, and nobody saw nothin'. I work months to solve cases where all the victims' families and friends know who killed them, but they won't tell me a damn thing. That's the job."

"Sounds frustrating."

"It can be."

"So why do you do it?"

His grin came unexpectedly, lightening the tension in his face, making his eyes dance with smug macho arrogant sweet-talking pretty-boy satisfaction. "It's not what I do. It's who I am."

Last week she would have scoffed at that. He was a legend in his own mind, she would have said. Pity the people of New Orleans, she would have added.

This afternoon, she took it at face value. He was a dedicated cop with a better understanding of people than she'd ever given him credit for. And not just understanding but acceptance, too. He knew what motivated people, what scared them, what drove them and what held them back, when she'd thought he was just a complete and total jerk.

Now she was coming to realize that he was just a partial jerk, and since the same could be said of her…

He started the engine, then pulled out of the parking space. "How do we find these woods of yours?"

"Go straight." She gazed out the side window at familiar old buildings, most occupied by unfamiliar businesses. The dress shop on the corner was now a bookstore; the mom-and-pop pharmacy that still had a soda fountain into her teens was an insurance office; and the shop where her dad had gotten his hair trimmed every few weeks was empty, the striped barber pole still in place outside, its glass cracked.

But the diner where the Broussards had eaten breakfast every Sunday was still in the same spot with the same specials advertised on the windows. She looked longingly at it even after they'd passed, wishing they were going there instead of to the woods.

"I don't know if the woods are even there anymore," she said as the diner faded from sight. "The property was owned by the Winchesters. They might have sold it when they moved away. It had waterfront access, sort of. There's a creek that leads to the lake where they'd built a dock, and Mr. Winchester took his boat out from there. We used to picnic and play and swim there, though as we got older, we mostly just laid in the sun. They called it Twins' Landing after Callie and Tallie."

Her chest burned, and she realized she'd run out of air. She filled her lungs, then let the breath out slowly. The burning from the lack of oxygen eased but moved instead to her throat and made her eyes go damp. It was one thing knowing that Paulina and Callie were dead, to even see the picture of Paulina, pale and still, but being in Marquitta made it worse. Made it more real. She'd ridden bikes down these streets with them; they'd gone to movies at the theater just ahead; they'd attended that elementary school together and played in that park. They'd learned to drive here, had their first dates, first kisses, first sex here.

They'd *lived* here—still lived here in her memories, a little fuzzy and distant but here.

Would it still be the five of them here after she returned to New Orleans today, or would only three of them remain in those fuzzy, distant images?

When Jimmy's hand took hold of hers, she startled, her eyes jerking open, her breath catching. For just an instant she'd forgotten him, had been so lost in the past and the sadness and the regrets. He didn't say a word but curled his fingers, warm and strong, over hers, and held on tightly.

She held back just as tightly.

When their turn appeared ahead, she had to clear her throat to speak. "Turn right at the light." That would take them to the neighborhood where her and Paulina's families had lived since before they were born, where the other three families had moved in and completed their tight-knit little circle.

Jimmy made the turn before he began talking in an idle manner that struck her more as thinking out loud than actual conversation. She was happy for the distraction, though.

"So…as far as Taylor knows, Katie Jo is still in prison, and Irena went to live with her mother's sister in Idaho. Irena probably wasn't crazy about her stepfather, given that he created so much disruption in her life and that she managed to hide the fact that he *was* her stepfather for the entire school year. She probably came back to Louisiana to visit her mom—maybe even moved here when she was able, so I'll check on her and Katie Jo when we get back. I'll go through Taylor's notes, too, see if there was any evidence of the affairs."

"Turn left here," Martine said absently. Katie Jo Fletcher had gotten a life sentence, according to Detective Taylor. She hadn't negotiated, hadn't tried to get herself any kind of deal whatsoever. Martine couldn't imagine giving in so completely.

But it was even harder to imagine being in a marriage so bad that murder seemed the only way out.

"Do you think she planned it? Practiced her grief-stricken widow routine until it came naturally? Waited until graduation so Irena wouldn't have to change schools again? Slept on the couch because she couldn't bear to lie in bed with him one more night? Got up and checked on her daughter to make sure she was still asleep and wouldn't see anything? Walked into the bedroom and shot her husband, went out into the woods to hide the gun, then came back and called the police?"

"Maybe. Probably. Though the grief-stricken part might not have been such a stretch. Some people don't realize the impact of killing someone until they've done it. They've been exposed to so much violence on the streets, in the news, on TV shows and in movies, and they think it's no big deal. You point the gun, pull the trigger, and boom, it's over. But once it's done, once they see the blood, once they realize that person is truly dead and is never coming back, it can haunt them.

"I suspect Katie Jo falls into that group. Whether it was one moment of rage or a calculated plan, it changed her whole life. It changed Irena's whole life. Katie Jo didn't want that much out of life, and all she got was prison. The sad fact is that if she believed murder was her only option—and she must have, since that's the one she chose—then prison was probably better than what she had before."

It was way beyond sad, but Martine didn't want to focus on that now. "Stop here," she said, leaning forward to look past him at the house across the street. "That's my house. My mom's house. I grew up there."

He glanced at her, then the house. It was a great place, big and white with deep green trim, new enough to lack the headaches of a truly old home but built to look as if it had been there a hundred years. She'd spent entire chunks of her life on that broad front porch with her girlfriends, her boyfriends, her mom's cats, her parents and other family when they visited. This house had been the center of her life.

A life she wanted desperately to distance herself from.

She pointed out the four other houses as they followed the winding streets to the back of the neighborhood. The Winchesters' house was last, set in the middle of a lot twice the size of the others, a mini-mansion, bordered on three sides with woods.

"We'll have to walk from here," she murmured, huddling deeper into her jacket. Jimmy pulled to the curb and shut off the engine. She got the impression he would let her linger if she wanted, but she opened the door immediately. Any lingering she did today would be at home, in the comfort of her secure little apartment, herself locked in and the world locked out.

The idea of Martine Broussard going into hiding would make most people who knew her snort…but most people who knew her knew nothing about the voodoo ritual or Fletcher's death or Katie Jo's life sentence or the harshness of Irena's life. They didn't know about Callie or Paulina. They didn't know that for the first time in her entire life, Martine was scared. If it wasn't for Jimmy, she would be too scared to set foot outside her apartment.

Jimmy DiBiase making her feel safe. Now, that was a thought worthy of all the snorts in the world.

Maybe it was the cold, the gray, the surrounding dampness, but the clearing Martine led Jimmy to in the woods seemed an unlikely haunt for five teenage girls. The thick carpet of pine needles dampened sound, and there were enough leafy trees and shrubs to provide a barrier outside of which anyone could hide, especially after dark, and spy on them. A thought that had likely never crossed their minds.

Had Katie Jo done just that? Had she come upon them out here and watched, listened, wished for her daughter to have that kind of friendship? She'd wanted a happy, normal life for Irena, for herself, and thanks to her husband, neither of them had it.

"Do you think he molested Irena?" Martine asked.

Jimmy turned to her, standing at the edge of the clearing, huddled in her slicker. She looked cold and miserable, and neither had to do with the weather. A drop of rain plopped on her forehead, and she looked at the sky with annoyance before pulling the hood into place.

"He could have married Katie Jo with the idea of having his own little victim in-house. Or he could have discovered the joys of perversion after they married and turned to the girls he had easy access to at school rather than the one who lived in his house. Some guys like to keep it in the family. Some don't take it any-where near them."

But Katie Jo's willingness to give up her right to a trial... Protecting Irena from knowing ugly stuff about her parents, Taylor had thought. It could just as eas-ily have been protecting Irena from having to divulge ugly stuff about how her stepfather had abused her.

"Do you know where the Fletcher house was from here? Pickering Road?"

Martine's brow furrowed, then she pointed down-stream. "A mile or so that way. You can't get there from this neighborhood. You have to go back to the main road, turn left, then turn left again after a ways. It's a dirt road, maybe a thousand feet before it dead-ends."

An easy enough walk for Katie Jo if she'd needed to get out of the house for a while. She could have stumbled on the girls here and stayed hidden, making silent wishes for her daughter. She could have heard them talk about her husband's behavior at school with shock, if she hadn't known before, or disgust if she had. It could have been the breaking point for her, and the ritual could have inspired her.

Jimmy wasn't about to share that last thought with Martine. The other four had believed all along that they were somehow responsible for Fletcher's death. If Martine thought Katie Jo might have gotten the idea from their game, the guilt would embrace her as surely as it had the others.

And it would be so much crap. You could put an idea into a person's head, but the responsibility for acting on it belonged entirely to that person. *The teenage girls down the street made me do it* just wouldn't fly as an excuse.

He looked around one last time. There was really nothing to see, just a spot where for years kids had sneaked off to do the things kids did: Martine and her friends two decades ago, the current neighborhood kids today if the small collection of empty beer cans and used condoms behind a fallen tree was anything to judge by. Kids who had friends and drinking buddies and hookup partners.

He started to turn, but something held him there, his gaze shifting over the live oak that sheltered the clearing. Its branches were huge, some dipping down to rest on the ground before arching back up into the sky, all of them capable of bearing the weight of anyone who wanted to spy.

Any teenager not invited to the party. Any jealous, lonely misfit who wanted desperately to have just one friend. Any awkward, shy kid who couldn't imagine much better than being welcomed into the coolest group of girls at the school. Anyone who knew they hung out here, who lived near enough to walk along the creek under cover of darkness and watch and wish and want.

Maybe Katie Jo Fletcher hadn't killed her husband. Maybe she had been genuinely horrified by his death. Maybe she'd known where to find the gun because someone had told her. Maybe she'd been willing to go to prison because she hadn't wanted to ruin her daughter's life any more than William Fletcher already had.

Maybe it had been Irena Young standing next to her parents' bed, gun in hand, guided by the ritual she'd just witnessed, killing the bastard who'd made her life so hard.

Justification, Jimmy thought again. It would have been easier for Katie Jo to spend her life in prison— her punishment for bringing Fletcher into their lives— than to stand by and let her daughter go. The best of Irena's life could still be ahead, while the worst of Katie Jo's would end.

Jimmy blew out a deep breath, then refilled his lungs, the air heavy with the smells of the creek, the trees, the decay. If Katie Jo had gone to prison for the crime her daughter committed, the guilt must have eaten at Irena every single day. Had she honored her mother's sacrifice by living the absolute best life she could live? Or had she let resentment and anger slowly destroy her until she latched on to someone else, anyone else, to blame for losing Katie Jo?

"I'm going back to the car to wait."

By the time Martine's words registered in his brain, she had a fifty-yard head start, enough that her pink-and-yellow slicker was starting to fade into the gloom. He jogged to catch up to her, wondering if anything he could say would take the edge off her emotions. Not likely, so instead he concentrated on ignoring the cold and damp that had seeped into his clothes and the fact that when he breathed out again in a sigh, his breath formed a little cloud. This crap wouldn't be so bad if it would just get cold enough to snow. He liked snow, and New Orleans had had precious little of it in the city's history.

But as long as the wet stayed in liquid form, it was just damn dreary.

Neither of them spoke until they were in the car, heater running on high, windshield wipers working rhythmically, and he was turning the car around to leave the neighborhood. His stomach grumbled, reminding him breakfast had been a long time ago. "You want to get something to eat?"

"Not in this town."

"Okay." There were plenty of places on the way back to the city, and he wasn't particular. Though he wouldn't have minded hitting that diner she'd looked so longingly at downtown. He had a fondness for diners, strong coffee and fried eggs. But New Orleans had plenty of places like that, and he couldn't blame her for not wanting to spend any more time here than necessary.

"You mind talking?" he asked after a while, once they'd left the city limits and were traveling along the highway.

Though her head was turned so she could stare out the side window, he saw her lift one hand to rub her eyes before grimly asking, "Any chance it could be about anything in the world besides this case?"

He grinned. "A couple of days ago, you wouldn't have talked to me about anything in the world *except* a case." A couple of days. Less than two days ago, he'd still thought of Martine primarily as the one he hadn't been able to charm and she'd still looked at him as if she'd caught a whiff of something particularly nasty. He could have easily imagined spending this much time with her but for damn sure not in this way, and she would have been horrified by the idea of spending time with him, much less letting him into her apartment and her life.

Big changes. And all it had taken was for Paulina to give up her life.

"What do you want to talk about?" Feeling the need to draw her out of the funk she'd sunk into, he injected the smug note into his voice that had always driven her crazy. Better to have her crazy than so lowdown blue. "How about how much you regret not sleeping with me that night?"

Slowly her head turned, and on her face was the scathing look he'd come to know so well. "Thank you for reminding me you're a jerk." That was better, that spark that flared in her eyes.

"I'm a good cop," he protested.

"Who's a jerk."

"But not on the job."

She opened her mouth as if to debate that, then closed it again. It was a source of pride to him that his reputation was for solving ugly cases while being relatively fair and courteous to everyone involved. Suspect, person of interest, family or witness—cooperating or not—he treated them the way people deserved to be treated. Granted, he didn't have huge amounts of patience with people who lied to him, but that was one of his people qualities, not a cop quality.

Though Martine's dislike for him stemmed from the fact that she considered him a liar, because he had come on to her without telling her he was married. At the time, he'd defended himself by pointing out that he hadn't said he wasn't married; he just hadn't said he was. It hadn't been much of an excuse, not in her eyes, not even in his own. *Of course* he shouldn't have been flirting with any woman other than Alia. *Of course* he shouldn't have tried to seduce Martine. *Of course* being an unfaithful bastard had been wrong, and he didn't blame her for holding it against him.

But that was a long time ago. He'd learned since then. He'd changed.

She moistened her lips. "You're actually not as… You're a better…detective…a better per-per—" With her cheeks flushed deep red and her inability to finish *person*, she rolled her eyes, shook her head and looked away again.

Jimmy's impulse was to make light of it. To tease that, along with New Orleans, hell must have frozen over because Martine Broussard was actually complimenting him. To grin his crap-eating grin and make another over-the-top, guaranteed-to-piss-her-off comment. But he didn't. That was the stupid Jimmy from before. The Jimmy he was today didn't even want to.

Instead he swallowed hard and quietly, sincerely said, "Thank you, Martine. You don't know how much I appreciate that."

Then stupid Jimmy just couldn't resist it. His most

obnoxious smile stretching across his face, he added, "Hell has officially frozen over."

After burgers at a little hole-in-the-wall place just off the interstate and more rain, dear Lord, than Martine could bear, they were finally back in the French Quarter, driving slowly along Royal Street. Water rushed along the street, some diverted into the city's overtaxed drainage system, the rest running where it could, puddling where it couldn't. When her building came into view ahead, a great sense of relief flooded through her, easing the muscles cramping in her neck, her shoulders and her back. Funny, that after spending part of the day in her hometown, she felt as if she was finally home, but that was exactly the feeling warming and brightening her.

They'd been gone not quite four and a half hours, but she felt as if she'd risen with the nonexistent sun and trekked the whole way on foot. All she wanted was to crawl into bed, turn the TV on to something frivolous and funny and not come out until morning to bright sunlight, fabulous early-spring weather and the last few days erased from her memory.

Hey, if she was going to wish, she would wish big.

Jimmy stopped in his usual spot. "You okay?"

"I'm adapting."

He nodded, apparently remembering her mother's words about that. "I have an appointment at five with Mr. Bradley."

"Mister— Oh." Paulina's husband. "I don't envy you."

"Yeah, if Jack were here, I'd be passing it on to

him. Bradley got in about an hour ago. He has paperwork to take care of to transfer his wife's body home
for the funeral as soon as the coroner releases it." He
drummed his fingers on the steering wheel, gazing
past her. "Everything look okay?"

She turned, saw nothing suspicious at her front
door, then saw Ramona and Anise watching from behind a display of T-shirts. Ramona, as always, was
smiling; Anise, as often enough, was glowering. Martine might have to clarify her comments to the girl
about Jimmy so she didn't try any new methods of
keeping him out.

"It looks the same. Except…" She'd just flitted a
look over her car in the driveway, but now she studied it closer. Climbing out of Jimmy's car, she crossed
the sidewalk to walk inside the arch that covered her
parking space. His footsteps sounded right behind her.

A few pieces of trash had blown inside; she picked
those up and dropped them into the can in the corner.
As long as she was at the front of the car, next to the
tall wrought iron gate that led into the courtyard, she
rattled it to make sure it was secure. The chain jangled
before uncoiling and landing on the bricks below, the
still-closed padlock making a *thunk*.

Jimmy took her hand from the gate and began pulling her backward. "Someone cut the chain instead of
the padlock to make it less noticeable that they'd tam-
pered with it. When was the last time you checked it?"

Weariness made her eyes ache. "I don't know. I always look when I get in my car, but as far as actually
touching it…"

Still holding on, he steered her back to the sidewalk and up the stoop. He found her keys in her jacket pocket, unlocked the door and ushered her inside. "I'll call someone and have them check it out. I'll get someone to replace it, too. Right now we'll take a quick look at this, then go from there."

This was the reason she'd gone to the car in the first place; she'd just gotten totally distracted. It was the same kind of kraft envelope she'd received in the mail the day before, and it had been tucked under the windshield wiper on her car. It looked heavier than the other, and whatever was inside, she didn't want to see.

But how could she *not* look?

On the way up the stairs, Jimmy called in and requested a patrol officer. Once he was off the phone, he seemed quite at home in her apartment. He turned her in the direction of her workroom, flipped on the lights and switched on the space heater. After pulling on a pair of thin gloves from his coat pocket—"I never leave home without 'em"—he took a seat and carefully cut open one end of the envelope.

Inside was a piece of typing paper, folded in thirds, with photographs taped to it, the folds made to avoid bending the pictures. Martine stood behind him, looking over his shoulder, vaguely detailing things she shouldn't be noticing, like the dark sheen to his damp hair, the scent of his cologne, the breadth of his shoulders. Other things, too: the silence in the apartment, the loud hollow whoosh of her breathing, the awareness that if someone had trespassed in her courtyard without her knowledge, they could have trespassed in her apartment, too. Maybe they were just that good, that there were no visible signs.

Maybe she wasn't so safe here, after all.

Jimmy cautiously unfolded the paper, resting his gloved hands on either side to hold it flat. Across the top in thick black print, someone had written *Actions have consequences*.

Underneath that was Callie's senior picture, cut from the yearbook, the slashes careless and including portions of the pictures around her. A thick black X blocked most of her face. Beneath it was Paulina's picture, again including portions of the nearby shots and another X. On the bottom row were pictures of Tallie, Robin and Martine. A question mark was scrawled onto the paper above each of them.

"Actions have consequences." Martine sank into the chair next to Jimmy. "Actions have… That was something Fletcher said all the time. He got a kick out of enforcing the rules. He was rigid about it. I think he just liked having the kids plead with him not to get them into trouble, plus it gave him a chance to get alone with the girls to discuss their infractions."

"So pretty much anyone in one of his classes would know he said that a lot." Jimmy folded the paper again and slid it into the envelope. "Katie Jo and Irena would have known, too."

"But Katie Jo's in prison—"

"Maybe."

"And Irena… She was just a kid."

"You were all just kids then. If Paulina and Callie could be killed for what they did as kids, then the killer could be the kid they did it to, loosely speaking."

Martine recalled Irena's image, a scared teenage girl trying too hard and having a tough time of it. Being a high school student wasn't supposed to be so hard, but it was for so many, and they took it so very seriously.

But she couldn't imagine Irena, or anyone truthfully, resorting to violence twenty-four years later. That was a long time to nurse wounded feelings and letdowns, time where there had been so much more important stuff going on in life: college or a job, a career, falling in love, marrying, having children, travel.

Unless the consequences of their actions had robbed her of all that.

Martine stubbornly shook her head. "I've just got it in my mind that it's a man. A man would find it so much easier to grab a woman off the street, to contain and control her, to bash her skull in and dump her body in a cemetery."

"But a woman doesn't need physical strength. Typically, women aren't seen as threatening, and people don't expect them to be armed. A skinny little girl could walk into your store, chat you up when you're alone, pull a gun and do whatever she wanted with you. Take you where she wanted. Dump you where she wanted." He looked up at her, his expression grim. "Women are resourceful, Martine. Don't ever underestimate them."

To think that a woman, a girl they'd gone to school with, was capable of murder…

A girl they'd gone to school with for an entire year and Martine had barely remembered. She must have had classes with Irena Young, must have passed her in the hall, must have seen her on an almost daily basis, and she'd completely forgotten her. Couldn't recall a single conversation with her, not one friendly exchange.

She pulled a chair to the heater, where she could absorb most of the warmth it put out, and sank down. Wishing her voice sounded more like a capable adult's and not a frightened girl's, she wistfully asked, "Do you really think it could be Irena? Blaming us for breaking up her family, getting even because we weren't friendly enough?"

Jimmy pulled a plastic shopping bag from the box on the shelf and put the envelope inside. He definitely felt at home there.

The odd thing—as if that wasn't odd enough—was that she didn't mind. She had no desire to drag the table and chairs and sofa into the street, douse them with gasoline and burn the DiBiase cooties until not even ash remained. She didn't want to do a cleansing ritual to rid the space of his germs and scents or to meditate the memory of him within these walls right out of her mind.

"I have a list of suspects," he said after tying the bag's handles into a loose knot. "Katie Jo might have gotten an early release. Twenty-four years is a long time to think about the choices she made. Irena might have gone on with her life, or she might have spent those same twenty-four years wondering why the hell you and the others were so special that you got to be pretty and popular and have best friends and parents who loved you and normal lives while she was stuck with her nightmare.

"Fletcher might have had a friend who shared his tastes—another teacher, a neighbor, someone at his church. Irena's father might have resented Fletcher for taking his place in his daughter's life, taking her away from him. Fletcher could have gone a lot further than just touching with some girl, who would resent everyone who knew what he was doing and didn't tell, or that girl's father could be playing the avenging angel. Or one of your friends could have told someone who felt compelled for whatever reason to punish whoever they could."

His smile was tight-lipped, not showing his teeth, and disappeared quickly. "There's no shortage of people on my list, Martine. The only thing I'm sure of right now is that you're not on it."

Relief seeped into her, thawing some of the ice that had settled in her stomach. And more: gratitude. A little bit of security. Comfort.

And a little too much of the desire that had almost led her to break her number-one relationship rule and jump into bed with a married man.

Who wasn't married now and hadn't been for a long time.

He crouched in front of her. "I've got to drop this off for the lab guys and make a couple calls before I meet with Mr. Bradley. Don't answer the door unless it's someone from your life here." He emphasized that with a tap of his fingers on the wooden arm of her chair. "Don't go out. Don't talk to any old friends or acquaintances. If you go to the shop, don't stay there alone. When the others leave, you leave, too, and ask them to wait outside until you get yourself locked in here. Don't open any windows, don't unlock any doors. Just pretend you're a bear and hibernate."

The obstinate part of her wanted to argue with him, even though she intended to do exactly as he said, but she didn't have the energy. Instead she nodded mutely, then roused herself enough to say, "So when the officer comes to look at my gate?"

"I'll talk to him. Don't open the door even to a cop unless it's Jack or me."

Again she nodded.

He pushed to his feet, reached for her hand as if it was the most natural thing in his world, and she let him take it as if it was the most natural thing in hers. Together they walked down the stairs to the entry, where he squinted up at the light bulb, then gazed down at her. "We'll get this guy."

"Or girl."

He acknowledged that with a grimace that she privately echoed. What did it matter whether it was a man or a woman? Dead was dead, no matter whose hand accomplished it.

Shaking off the thought, she focused on Jimmy. "I can't say it's been a fun day, but…thank you, Jimmy."

The look that flashed across his face was…sweet. Not his sweet-talker look, either; that was always smug. No, this was just plain sweet, and it hurt her heart just a little. She'd spent a lot of time wishing she'd never met this man, and here he was now, trying to save her life. No matter what happened, she would always be grateful for that.

Unless, of course, he failed. Then she would haunt him.

Ah, there was the old Martine.

And with his grin, the old Jimmy appeared in front of her. "Like I said, hell has officially frozen over. I'll see you."

After locking the dead bolt behind him—and the chain lock—and shoving the concrete planter in the corner over to block the door—Martine headed back up the stairs. It wasn't until she reached the top that she realized she was still smiling.

Chapter 6

Jimmy didn't have an office, just a desk in a room shared with other desks, so he met Shawn Bradley in one of the interview rooms. The man was about his age, his skin sallow, his face hollowed, the last few months having worn hard on him. His tone varied from quavering to flat and blank, as if he just didn't have the emotional reserves to keep up the inflection.

Jimmy offered his condolences, asked about the transfer arrangements and if he needed anything while he was in town, then, hiding his reluctance, went straight to his main interest. "You filed a missing person report on your wife three months ago. What happened?"

Bradley drew a deep breath and held it, his shoulders shaking when he released it. "Everything was fine. Honestly, I'm not stupid. I didn't see anything unusual. Her job was normal, my job was normal, money was good, we were getting along fine with family, she doted on the cats like she always did. We were even planning a vacation—a few days after Christmas in Bermuda. Then one day I kissed her, told her I loved her and left for work, and…I never saw her again."

Even after all this time, his tone was bewildered. He still couldn't understand how everything could change so drastically in a single moment. Jimmy had never experienced it, but he'd spent a lot of time with people who had. Some of them never understood it. Some never accepted it.

"She didn't leave a note?"

Bradley shook his head. "Her purse was gone, her keys, her car. So was a suitcase of clothes—jeans, T-shirts— and her personal savings account was cleaned out. She left her cell phone, her wallet, all her jewelry. Video from the bank showed she was alone when she got the money. Traffic camera videos showed her alone in her car, which was found the next day in Montgomery. There was no sign of her."

"Was there anything unusual on her computer? Anything personal in the mail? Text messages or phone calls?"

"No. I tore the house apart a dozen times, looking for something that seemed wrong or out of place. Her parents and I even hired private investigators, but there was nothing."

Jimmy found it easier to look at his notes than to see the loss and grief on Bradley's face. He would bet this month's rent that Paulina had gotten an envelope in the mail, maybe at work, like Martine, so her husband wouldn't have been aware of it. Already susceptible to the guilt from their teenage prank, the note and the small bit of voodoo doll/bandanna had certainly freaked her out. Had that made her flee, or had she held out until the second letter arrived?

Actions have consequences. A marked-out photo of Callie. Maybe an internet search to find out that Callie was indeed dead, and at some point Paulina had made the effort to contact Tallie and Robin, either before her flight or while on the run.

"Did she talk much about high school?"

Bradley's frown tightened. "High… That was a long time ago."

Jimmy waited.

"Uh, not much. She grew up somewhere around here. Moved to Mobile first chance she got. That's where we met, at the University of South Alabama."

"Did she stay in touch with any of her high school friends?"

His brows arched, his gaze lifting toward the ceiling, while he considered it. "There were a couple— sisters, I think. Sometimes they traded Christmas cards, not every year but from time to time. Paulina never said much about them. 'Just someone I used to know.'"

Jimmy made a note of that, wondering more defensively than he should why those three had maintained any contact while cutting Martine off cold. She had been one of them. She and Paulina had been the first friends, the best.

And she had been the odd one out at the end, the only one who didn't accept any blame for Fletcher's murder.

"Did your wife ever mention William Fletcher? He was a teacher her senior year."

Bradley thought about it, looking as if he'd just about exhausted his supply of answers. "No, she never talked about school. She never kept any yearbooks, pictures, dried corsages, nothing. She never even casually said anything like, 'Oh, yeah, back when I was in school…' That time didn't exist for her anymore. I never asked why. It was just the way she was."

"One last question. Did she ever mention Tine or Martine Broussard?"

"No. Who was she?"

"Her best friend through high school." Jimmy hesitated, then went on. "She came to New Orleans to see Martine. She met with her for a few minutes Tuesday afternoon."

For a moment Bradley was unmoving. Finally, with a deep exhale, he slumped back in his chair. "My wife just disappears like she never existed, then pops up three months later in a city she refused to ever set foot in to visit her best friend I never heard of and is murdered that night. Why? Where was she in the meantime? What was she running from? What the hell was going on? Is this Martine person involved? Do you think she killed Paulina?"

"No, absolutely not," Jimmy said firmly. "As for the rest of it, we're trying to find out, Mr. Bradley. We'll find this person and see that he pays for Paulina's death." He didn't promise; he knew promises could be impossible to keep, but he did have every intention of stopping Irena/Katie Jo/Mr. Young/whoever the hell was responsible for this man's sorrow.

He damn well intended to keep them from hurting Martine.

After getting an officer to take Mr. Bradley back to his hotel, Jimmy returned to the computer on his desk, working his way through the questions in his notes. Police work was so very different with the internet and computers. He still did a lot of legwork, but a lot of information that in the past would have required visits to various offices and endless phone calls or faxes was often quick and easy to access.

It took only a couple of minutes to strike one suspect off his list: Katie Jo Fletcher had died of natural causes—complications of pneumonia—at the Louisiana Correctional Institute for Women in St. Gabriel last September. The news made him sad for a woman he'd never met, a woman who'd spent half her life in prison for a crime his gut instincts insisted she didn't commit. All she'd wanted was a normal life for her daughter, and all she'd gotten was disappointment.

Jimmy took a break to get a fresh cup of coffee, then returned to his computer. It took longer to get information on Irena Young, and it was no help at all. The address on her driver's license came back to a Baton Rouge apartment, but a phone call to the manager said she'd moved the year before. The woman who answered at the work number she'd given said she'd quit her job as a salesclerk about the same time, and the cell phone Irena had listed went to a generic voice mail message. He would have to get in touch with the provider to find out if the number was still hers.

"You're working late."

Jimmy glanced up, a smile forming automatically. The petite blonde standing there worked with Alia over at NCIS, and they'd met a number of times over the past year for dinner or drinks—not dates, just evenings out with Alia and Landry. She was smart, pretty, had too nice a body to hide in plain gray pants and a matching jacket over a black shirt, and her name was Delaney, but damned if he could remember whether that was her first name or last.

Holy crap, Jimmy, you never forget a woman's name.

Hey, he'd been insisting he'd changed, hadn't he?

"I'm a dedicated officer of the law," he replied, gesturing toward an empty chair nearby. "Why aren't you home where it's warm and dry?"

"That's where I'm headed. I needed to talk to one of your fellow detectives first." Delaney—first name, he was pretty sure—sat down, crossed her legs and clasped her hands. "Alia tells me you're looking for a lonely heart. Any idea where it got off to?"

He rolled his eyes at her teasing note, but not at the subject. The heart's location was a question that had stayed in the back of his mind. He could too easily imagine it in the killer's home, wrapped in foil in the freezer or floating in liquid in a glass jar on a shelf, ghastly and creepy and giving the killer a jolt of pleasure every time he or she saw it. "I hope it's buried somewhere."

"Or eaten. 'The heart of your enemy…' Maybe used in medicine or offered as a gift to the spirits."

He grimaced at her matter-of-fact response. He could stomach a lot, but some things he would really prefer to remain uninformed about. Nevertheless, he flipped open his notebook and picked up a pen. Finding someone knowledgeable about such things was still on his to-do list, and he was never one to turn his back on freely offered information. "You familiar with human sacrifice?"

"It's an interest of mine. I can probably answer your questions, and if I can't, I know people who can."

"Okay, the heart of your enemy…people really do that?"

"Since the beginning of time. It's been reliably reported that it's happened recently in the Middle East. People believe it's the ultimate revenge on their enemy but also that they gain whatever power or strengths the enemy had. The fresher the heart is, the more power it holds."

"So they like it still beating?" His stomach flipped at her nod. He'd been thinking a rare steak and baked potato sounded pretty good for dinner, but he could forget that for a week…or two or three. "Is it a thing in voodoo?"

"No. Not legitimately. One of the central beliefs of voodoo is reincarnation. They believe that a person will be brought back in the same body, the same form, and so if the body has been mutilated, the mutilations remain, so it's taboo."

"But in every group there are extremists who twist the religion or the beliefs to fit their own needs."

She nodded. "Voodoo has been misappropriated by some practitioners not out of deep devotion but to frighten off competitors, to gain fame, to build a fortune or just out of a sense of fanaticism, and those people tend to do things their religion forbids. Medicine murder is one of those things. Practitioners of a lot of religions, not just voodoo, believe that the sacrifice of a living creature empowers and protects them. Animal sacrifice is common, but among the extremists, humans are believed to give the most power. Their organs are used to make medicine. Some body parts—eyes, fingers, genitals—become charms, and heads are buried to keep evil spirits from the house."

"Damn," he muttered, wincing at the thought.

"It's more common in Africa, though there have been cases worldwide. It most likely has absolutely nothing to do with your murder." Delaney smiled the way only a cop could, as if she hadn't just talked about cutting off private bits and stringing them up to wear. "Are there any other ritual aspects to your case? Any other body parts missing? Any sign of a ceremony taking place?"

He shook his head.

"Then three possibilities come to mind. First, a healthy heart is worth around one hundred and fifty thousand dollars on the black market for transplant. It would be a pretty sophisticated process, though, removing it, transporting it, keeping it usable, and if you're going to kill someone to steal a heart, why not take the liver and a kidney or two? Why settle for a hundred fifty grand when you could get nearly seven fifty?"

She raised her hand, ticking off another finger. "Second, taking the heart could have been an attempt to throw your investigation off track, to make you think voodoo or witchcraft was involved, but the guy didn't know enough about either to make it look realistic. Third and most likely, taking the heart was symbolic. You've got a really angry person, holding a hell of a grudge, believing the victim was coldhearted or heartless in her treatment of him. Not only did he kill her, but now she really is heartless. In that case, he probably threw it in the river, tossed it in a Dumpster or, who knows, fed it to a gator. It wouldn't have any real value to him."

"Isn't that a lot of work to punish someone who's dead?"

Delaney shrugged. "I'm no doctor. I would imagine, though, that getting through the rib cage is the hardest part, and a pair of bolt cutters would do the trick. Maybe even garden loppers."

"Holding a grudge fits with my theory. You know there's a second victim in Seattle? And the two women grew up together."

She rolled her blue eyes. "Gee, Jimmy, if I'd known that, I could have saved myself climbing a flight of stairs to see you." Her smile softened the words. "But you have to cover all the bases, don't you? I know it hasn't been long, but are you making any progress?"

"I've managed to take one person off the suspect list."

"You do have other cases, don't you? Or are you NOPD guys so pampered that you only take one case at a time?"

"Hey, at least we don't need a TV show for people to know who we are. If it wasn't for that, the average citizen wouldn't have a clue what NCIS is."

She stood, adjusted her jacket over the gun on her hip and gave him a recruitment poster–worthy smile. "The people I put in prison know what it is, and that's all that matters to me. Good seeing you, Jimmy. Get home before the temperature drops another degree and that wet stuff turns to ice."

"Thanks, Delaney." He watched her walk away, admiring the way she sashayed, then dropped his gaze to his battered notebook. He always had multiple cases going, but it was typical of the job: the most recent case took precedence. The longer an investigation dragged out, the slower the leads developed and the less active work it got. Keeping Martine and her friends alive was more important at the moment than finding out who killed the victims in his other cases, and not just because he had a thing for Martine. Even if she was a total stranger who didn't spark a bit of interest in him, the living still counted for more than the dead.

Besides, his other open cases were all of the *I didn't see nothing, I didn't hear nothing, I didn't do nothing, I'm not saying nothing* variety. The witnesses would still be just as uncooperative in a few days or a few weeks as they'd been so far.

His priority now was keeping Martine alive, not for a few days or a few weeks but for good.

There was nothing like being stuck somewhere to make Martine want to go elsewhere, even if she had no destination in mind. After closing up the shop with Anise and Niles, she'd had a long soak in a hot bath filled with her favorite scented bubbles, drunk a glass of wine and spent a little time on the internet before edginess made her set the computer aside. She'd been wandering the apartment for the past hour, the television turned on for background noise. A trip downstairs reassured her that the front door remained secure, and a few rounds of the apartment confirmed that every window, along with the rear door that led to the court-yard, was also locked.

She stood at the kitchen sink, gazing down into the

dimly lit square, envisioning it in summer when the color and fragrance of the flowers were almost overwhelming. At the first sign of spring, she would drag out her patio furniture and prepare for eight months or more of sitting by the fountain, sipping tea, chatting with Evie and Reece and watching their kids play. The store staff would eat lunches there, and she would have dinners there, too, in her own private little paradise.

That someone had invaded.

Even now, safe inside, she shivered as the sound of the chain and padlock falling echoed in her memory. Now she wondered if she would ever feel as safe in the courtyard as she had before—if she would feel as safe in her life as she had before.

Distantly through the floor, she heard a clang, similar to the chain falling but stronger, more menacing. She was standing directly above the gate. Had someone bumped it? Opened it the wrong way and hit her car or opened it the right way and banged the giant cast-iron urn at the edge of the garden?

Her heart pounded, and her chest grew tight, making a deep breath impossible. A shudder raced through her, momentarily leaving her unable to think, to reason, to figure out what to do. The Taser was on her belt, the pepper spray in her left jeans pocket, the cell phone in the right, but she didn't reach for any of them, not until the cell rang, its jangle making her gasp and literally jump, her toes clearing the floor by a fraction of an inch.

With trembling hands, she pulled it from her pocket, clutched it tightly and stabbed at the screen. Her *hello* was tiny and shaky, barely more than a squeak.

"Hey, Martine, it's me." It was Jimmy, and he sounded concerned. "Are you okay?"

"That depends. Are you downstairs?"

"Yeah, I am, putting a new chain on the gate."

Oh, thank God. Knees wobbling, she leaned against the counter and pressed her free hand to her face. "Then I'm fine. Just—" She filled her lungs with air. "Just overreacting to everything."

"Sorry. The end of the chain slipped when I was pushing it through the gate. I'm locking it from inside the courtyard, so can I come in the back?"

"Yeah, sure." Trying a slow-breathing exercise to calm her heart, she fumbled the few feet to the door and undid the locks. A moment later, heavy footsteps sounded on the stairs.

"I'm coming in now. No force, please, less-lethal or otherwise, okay?"

"Okay." As she put away her phone, the door opened with a slow creak, letting in cold damp air and the scents she was starting to associate with him: cologne, shampoo, *man*. They were accompanied by amazing aromas emanating from the bag he carried.

"Are you hungry?" he asked as he set the bag on the counter, then shrugged out of his overcoat.

Two minutes ago, she hadn't been. She hadn't even thought about food since lunch. Now her stomach rumbled as gracelessly as possible, and her mouth began to water. "I'm starved. What did you bring?"

As he unpacked the bag, her stress washed away. Sure, there was still some of that *I'm the target of a crazed killer* fear knotted in her stomach that wasn't going away, but at this moment, Jimmy was here, and if anyone could keep the crazed killer away, it was him.

If anyone could make her feel safe, it was him.

And all that aside, she was glad to see him.

He'd brought comfort food, exactly what she would have chosen herself if she'd remembered she was hungry: fried chicken, potato salad, macaroni and cheese, coleslaw and, sweet mercy, yes, two slices of apple pie and a pint of vanilla ice cream.

Her mood improving 100 percent, she began gathering dishes, napkins, utensils and sodas. Without much discussion, they each filled their own plate and went into the living room, where she unfolded two TV trays from the corner. "They may be old-fashioned, but it beats spilling good food in your lap." She settled in her favorite chair, leaned forward to inhale deeply of the aromas, then sighed happily. "You've got good taste."

"You know, for the last however many years," he warned, "I've only gotten insults from you. If you stop being hostile *and* start paying compliments, I won't know how to act."

Though her cheeks flushed, her mouth was too full of hot, tender, juicy chicken with the perfect amount of crispy crust. When she swallowed it, she wiped her fingers delicately. "You can't deny you trolled for women while you were married."

"I'm not proud of it, but I don't deny it." His eyes twinkled. "You were much nicer before you knew."

"You weren't a cheat before I knew."

"Did one of your ex-boyfriends cheat on you?"

"Not that I'm aware of. Not my ex-husband, either, and not my dad on my mom or vice versa. I just grew up believing that there were certain things you honored, and marriage vows were high on that list. I know people get married for a lot of reasons, but done right, it's supposed to be a commitment, a partnership, giving and taking and growing together." She chewed a bite of potato salad, savoring the sweet mayo, the tang of the mustard and the bite of the pickle juice in the dressing. "I sound really old-fashioned, don't I?"

"You sound like my sisters." He waited a beat before continuing. "Who are really old-fashioned." After a moment, though, with a drumstick in his hand, he gestured. "You were right, Martine. It was a really crappy thing to do. I knew it then. I know it better now. I can't change what I did then, but I can say I wouldn't do it now."

Martine found herself entirely too tempted to believe his words. She managed a smile, but it wasn't as light as she'd hoped for. "Aw, Jack tells me that your fellow detectives rate the odds of you and monogamy ever being mentioned in the same sentence at somewhere around one in a billion."

His smile was designed for sarcasm. "Jack should keep his mouth shut. I believe in monogamy. I really do. I think people who claim it's an unnatural state just use that as an excuse for their own behavior."

"I think you're right," Martine said, and his brows arched as he leaned closer.

"What was that? Could you repeat it?"

She laughed. She actually felt good enough to laugh. Oh, how she'd missed it.

Before the thought of asking what he'd learned about the case could even fully form in her brain, she said, "Tell me how you terrorized your sisters growing up."

"Why does everyone think that? I was their favorite brother."

"And only brother. You told me you had advanced training in making them hysterical by the time you were ten."

"Oh, yeah, I did." He finished his chicken and picked up a spoonful of macaroni and cheese. "Imagine the kind of things you and your girls got into, only ten times more complicated. That's Dani and Rebecca. They were regular little generals of chaos, enlisting all the kids in town and half the adults in their mischief. And they always looked so innocent, with pigtails or braids, big eyes and the sweetest, most adorable smiles. They were a menace to the parish, only no one really believed they were capable of the pranks they pulled. People always thought I was behind most of them, but truthfully, no one could get you like Dani and Becca could."

Discovering that her plate was clean, Martine considered getting a refill, then decided she was good. Tucking her feet into the seat, she held her glass in both hands and settled in. "What about now? Are they still master manipulators?"

"Pretty much. Dani runs marketing at Cypress Hill, and Becca's in charge of everything else. They've got five kids between them who are being homeschooled and get to do things that are cool and actually make school look fun. The kids also help out at the big house. Everyone's got chores, even me, and the conse—" he hesitated so briefly over the word that she doubted anyone else would have noticed "—um, consequences of not doing them can be severe."

That was the way to handle it: just let the word and its ugliness slide away, out of her mind. There would always be time to face up to her situation, but pleasant, easy moments like this had been hard to find lately.

"It's funny to think that I might have met your parents or your sisters when my mom and I toured the place."

"You might even have met me. I haven't lived there since high school, but I've gone back for plenty of visits."

She might have seen him—younger, less polished, still too damn good-looking for his own good, charming and brash—but she doubted she could have met him and forgotten. She'd always had a fine appreciation for handsome, sexy men.

Then he said, "Nah. I would have remembered meeting you." Adding with unshakable confidence, "And you would have remembered meeting me."

She smiled sweetly. "I love modest men." She studied her glass, shaking it just enough to make the ice cubes clink, before lifting her gaze back to Jimmy. She didn't want to ask, didn't want to leave this comfortable moment for the darkness that her life had become, but the question slipped out despite her best intentions. "How did your meeting with Paulina's husband go?"

His humor giving way to seriousness, he gave what she was sure was an abbreviated version. She wondered what kind of guy Paulina had chosen to marry—her tastes in high school boys had varied widely—and sadly recalled their old promises that they would each be maid of honor to the other. But that night had happened, and Martine's maid of honor had been a roommate she'd lost touch with before her first anniversary rolled around. Who had been there for Paulina? Had the other three girls been invited, or had she left out everyone from the first eighteen years of her life on the big day?

"I haven't located Irena Young yet, but I did find out that Katie Jo Fletcher died in prison last fall."

The news gave her a bit of a jolt. "I'm sorry, for both her and Irena. She had a sad life." After a moment, she gestured to her laptop on the coffee table. "People say you can find anyone and anything on the internet, but it's not true, is it? I've Googled and Binged and searched every other way I could think of for Tallie and Robin, but I haven't found anything of use."

Finished with his meal, he settled more comfortably, too. Even sprawled back on the couch as he was, there was no mistaking the fine quality of his suit or the high price of his shoes. A public servant with a private fortune—or, at least, enough for occasional splurges.

But he looked just as good in jeans and a T-shirt.

Probably even better in nothing at all.

"Internet or not, if someone doesn't want to be found and is reasonably intelligent, they can hide as easily as ever. You ditch your credit cards, your cell phone, your email and your vehicle, you use public transportation, you pay cash, and you're officially off the grid. Look at Paulina. Three months on the run, police and private investigators looking for her, and they couldn't trace her beyond the first twenty-four hours. All we know about the time she was missing is that she bought a burner phone and used cash."

"And that she came here. And she was scared." Martine did her best to ignore the shiver of her own fear. It was futile when Jimmy, his voice grim, finished.

"And now she's dead."

* * *

After taking their dishes into the kitchen, Martine cleaned up quickly, brewed coffee for Jimmy and poured another glass of wine for herself, then glanced out the kitchen window. The rain shimmered in the air, falling in slow flat drops…that were actually snowflakes. For an instant, she brightened inside with just a hint of the wonder she'd always felt as a child when they'd been blessed with snow. Now she liked it mostly when it disappeared overnight, but it was gorgeous in its pristine falling state. Tourists didn't like snow in New Orleans, either, and business had been off enough the past week.

She used a small plate to make a tray for Jimmy, holding coffee, cream and sugar, and carried that and her wine to the living room. "It's snowing."

"Oh, boy," he said sourly. "Police work is so much fun when you add slick roads and ice and inexperienced drivers."

Martine sat, sipped her wine, then returned to their earlier conversation. "Why didn't Paulina tell her husband? Why not call the police? She had resources. Why didn't she use them?"

Jimmy tilted his head to one side, then the other, as if releasing the tension gathered there, before lifting both shoulders in a weary shrug. "Maybe she thought running away would protect her family from the danger. Maybe she was too ashamed to admit what you guys had done, or maybe she'd lived with the secret so long, she believed it more than ever and just couldn't face the con—"

Consequences. It wasn't as easy this time to just let the word slide away.

"I don't know if I showed good sense in not believing we were responsible for Fletcher's death or if I've just been selfishly going along in my own little world, refusing to acknowledge the impact of what we did."

His dark eyes narrowing, Jimmy patted the sofa cushion beside him. "Come here."

Something warm and promising curled in her stomach, even as some smidgen of lingering wariness warned her against it. He was here only because of his job; she was a subject in his investigation, nothing more. It wasn't supposed to be anything more. How could it ever be? As he'd pointed out, she hadn't spoken a civil word to him since that party, in a quiet dark nook in Evie's garden, his arms wrapped around her, his tongue halfway down her throat, his hands doing incredible things to her body and her willpower, when his phone had rung. Her dazed brain had been stunned when he pulled away to check the screen, then put it away again. *My wife*, he'd murmured carelessly. *I'll call her later.*

Even now, she felt a flare of that old dismay, disgust, scorn…and disappointment, because up to that point, she'd been thoroughly captivated by him. She would have followed him anywhere, would have plastered herself so firmly against him that she might have absorbed at least parts of him into her soul. She'd thought he might be…*special.*

That had happened six years ago, but since then he'd never made any secret of his attraction to her, even when she'd found it annoying rather than flattering. He was waiting, he'd told her once after the divorce, for her to give up her grudge so they could pick up where they'd left off. She'd suggested he would burn in hell first.

The wary voice in her head wasn't trying hard enough to warn her away. Without permission from her brain, her feet slid to the floor, her hands gripped the chair arms to push herself up, and she eased around the corner of the coffee table to sit down, half a cushion between her and Jimmy.

"Big step," he teased as she turned to face him. "No kitchen knife handy, my dinner fork is out of your reach, nothing to crack my skull with."

Her smile felt steadier than she'd thought it would be. "I still have your Taser and pepper spray. Having watched a few episodes of *Cops*, I've always wondered how much fun it would be to Tase someone in a non-dangerous situation."

"I'm not volunteering. Though on a busy night on Bourbon Street, offer fifteen bucks, and I bet you'll get plenty of takers, especially if you video it and promise to put it on YouTube."

She smiled, thinking of the foolish and reckless young men she'd known. Some outgrew it in their twenties; some took until their thirties; and some, she supposed, never outgrew it at all. Jimmy, she was pretty convinced, was a bit of a mix. He took his job seriously as hell, the rest of life not so much. He could be grown up when the situation required it, but he enjoyed the rest of his life as if he didn't have a care in the world.

Could he enjoy the rest of his life with the restrictions imposed by a monogamous relationship?

The question faded away when he moved, and her heart increased its steady beat. This close, she could better smell his cologne, could see the stubble of beard dotting his jaw and the tired lines etching the corners of his eyes and mouth. He'd had a couple of long days and was planning to have a few more, she suspected, until he caught the killer or at least scared him—or her—off.

His strong, comforting hand claimed hers, his fingers lacing with hers, the pad of his thumb rubbing firmly back and forth over the heel of her palm. "Fletcher's death wasn't your fault, Martine, and there's nothing selfish about acknowledging that. The fact that the other girls believed it didn't make them right. The fact that the killer might have gotten a couple ideas from you still doesn't make you responsible. You didn't know you were being spied on. You didn't put the thought of murder or the capacity for it into Katie Jo or Irena or anyone else. You know human nature. People don't become violent because they overhear girls playing. William Fletcher died because he was a lousy husband and stepfather and a teacher with a fondness for doing God knows what to kids. Period."

She must not have looked convinced, because he squeezed her fingers lightly. "You ever see a movie where a woman fakes her own death to get away from an abusive husband, he finds her and she kills him? What if someone else who sees it uses that as a blueprint to escape her own abuser, right down to the murder at the end? Does that make the screenwriter or the producer or the actress responsible?"

"Of course not," she murmured.

"And you're not, either. There's nothing original, Martine—not one single action in the history of mankind that hasn't been done before. Every good thing you can think of, every bad thing, millions of other people have already thought of them. And in my experience, most murderers don't need inspiration. They just need opportunity."

She sighed, tilted her head to one side to study him and bumped his arm, resting on the back of the sofa. Automatically, he wrapped his arm around her shoulders, scooted her closer and guided her head to his own shoulder.

Damn. The closer she got, the better he smelled. The better she felt. And oh, hell, yes, the better *he* felt. Hard muscle, soft skin, power, courage. He was a protector—her protector, for the moment—and she reveled in it in a way she never would have thought possible. Even the *crazed-killer* fear was calmer, almost dormant. For the first time in two days, she could relax, close her eyes, turn off the worries and feel normal again.

She would never undervalue feeling normal again.

She lost track of how long they sat there, warmed by his body and his presence, feeling a sense of ease seep through her with each breath, thinking that grudges became burdens after a while and when the wronged person—in this case, Alia—didn't hold a grudge, wasn't it presumptuous of Martine to?

You just want to have sex with him, her wariness pointed out. *Just like you wanted that night and practically every time you've seen him since.*

A faint smile curved her lips. Her wary nature knew her well, probably because they'd kept such close company all this time.

"What are you smiling about?" His voice was soft, his mouth close enough that she felt his breath on her cheek.

She fibbed. "You smell like apple pie."

"Nah, you smell the apple pie in the kitchen." After a pause, he shifted his shoulder, gently nudging her cheek, and repeated, "Hey, there's apple pie in the kitchen."

His boyish tone made her laugh. "Dessert coming right up. I'm guessing you like it warm with ice cream melting over the top."

"Hell, yeah."

She started to push up from the couch, but his hand stopped her. His eyes were dark, the familiar intensity back in place, but this time it wasn't for the case. It was for *her*, and the same sharp awareness sliced through her. His lips parted, and she wondered—anticipated— what he would say, but she would never know because, after a moment, they curved into a smile. His fingers stroked hers gently, lightly, before he stood up, then pulled her to her feet.

"I'll help you."

He'd been doing that all along—helping her to feel secure, helping her deal with Paulina's death, helping her find the answers to the million questions that plagued her. Given the way things had been between them before, she was impressed. And grateful. And regretful. And hopeful.

Her work and her friends had exposed her to a lot of mysteries in life, but this might be the biggest surprise of all.

Jimmy DiBiase had become the light in her life.

By the time Jimmy motivated himself enough to get off the couch one last time to go home, the snow was falling harder, accumulating thickly on all the flat surfaces except the middle of the street. Only a few tourists were on the sidewalks, warmed by spirits, he would bet, and traffic was almost nonexistent. His car gleamed white in the light from the street lamps, with enough of the cold stuff piled on it that he wished for gloves. And a heavier coat.

Martine wasn't wearing any coat at all. Just jeans that fitted snugly to every curve and a long-sleeved touristy shirt paying homage to New Orleans's chicory coffee that did the same. She hugged her arms across her middle as they watched the snow in companionable silence from the doorway. Comfortable silence. The only thing that would make it better was if they were watching from her window upstairs, where the air was warm and the bedroom was only a few yards away.

"You like snow?" she asked after a moment.

"Nope. But when it's like this, all fat and thick and nothing's turned to ice yet, it's damn pretty to watch." He knew he should leave: tell her good-night, wait to hear the locks click and the planter scrape as she dragged it back into place, then clear enough of the car windows to get himself home. He was tired. She was cold. Standing here would just make him more tired and her colder.

But it was hard to take that first step over the threshold.

He shoved his hands into his pockets, felt the keys there held together with a small wire loop and remembered one of his reasons for coming over tonight. "Here are the keys to your new lock." He pressed them into her hand, her fingers already cold. "I know it's a hassle, but for right now you need to open it from inside the courtyard. The chain is looped around that cast-iron planter, and the lock is against the planter, so no one can reach it to cut it."

"Can't they just cut the chain again?"

Thinking of the chain he'd damn near had to drag across the driveway, he grinned. "They could, but not without being noticed."

She gave him a skeptical look, then stepped outside. His first impulse was to catch her hand, pull her back inside out of sight of whoever happened to be looking. But considering how reasonably she'd cooperated with his requests to restrict her movements, he let her go, instead closing the door, following her down the steps, into the covered driveway and back to the gate.

Her laugh upon seeing the tow chain that made the old chain look like a length of twine was fresh and sweet and normal. He appreciated the sound of it, and the feel, and couldn't wait for the day it came naturally and often.

If she let him come around again once the case was closed.

The lines across her forehead eased, revealing more relief than he suspected she knew. "Thank you, Jimmy. I'll reimburse you for it tomorrow."

The old Jimmy could give her a list of various types of reimbursement he would prefer over money. The new Jimmy—the smarter Jimmy—kept his mouth shut, because after a long time of trying, Martine was starting to like him again, and he wasn't about to risk that for a sly, flirty, maybe sleazy remark.

"You'd better get back inside before you turn into an icicle." His voice was quiet, the sound hollow as the brick arch reflected the words back.

But she didn't move. "I'm not that cold." Also quiet, hollow. Her gaze locked on his.

He reminded himself to breathe, but his lungs wouldn't fill, not with the tightness around his chest that came from nowhere. Her own breaths were shallow, causing the slightest lift and fall of her chest, and her cheeks were red, her lips tinged blue, belying her comment.

Slowly he lifted his hand to feather back a strand of hair that had fallen across her forehead. "The first time I saw you…"

She'd been with Evie, who had come by the station to see Jack, and he'd thought a lot of things: she was gorgeous. She had killer long legs, and the curves of her breasts, waist and hips gave her exactly the lush type of body that he preferred. Her smile was incredibly easy and passionate. She wasn't his usual sort of woman, but they would be great in bed, and at the time all he'd been interested in was a great time in bed.

Instead of choosing one of those things to tell her, he changed the subject, sort of. "I haven't dated anyone since before Alia and Landry got married." Did Martine remember scowling at him through the ceremony or deliberately spilling champagne on him after the cake was cut? She had snubbed his every attempt to talk to her—talk, when he'd really wanted to take her in his arms, dance with her, touch her and persuade her that he was deserving of another chance. Her iceberg act had made him the butt of jokes for the other cops in attendance. Not the first time, not the last, and he'd deserved it.

Her deepening flush suggested she did remember.

It passed quickly, though, and her gaze narrowed on his. "Define *date*."

"Gone out with. Had a meal or drinks with. Spent time with a woman with the intention of starting or building a relationship."

The corners of her mouth twitched. "Wasn't there an exotic dancer you were serious about?"

He'd been working a series of murders with Alia at the time, murders that had brought Landry into her life. Nina had been a sweet girl but temporary. She'd been ten years younger by age, double that in life experience. For a stripper, she'd held on to her naïveté pretty fiercely. By the time the murders had been solved, the relationship had been over.

"We were a mutually agreed-upon short-term thing." His fingers were still in her hair. He slid them over icy black silk to her shoulder and gave the taut muscles there a squeeze. "Does it bother you that she was a stripper?" He knew what a lot of people thought of exotic dancers—and the people who got involved with them. Alia, wiser than most, had been amused. Would Martine, or would she fall back on her judgmental attitude?

"Does it bother you that I dated a stripper?"

His gaze widened, and so did her smile.

"His name was Nico, and we were together about six weeks before he moved on to Dallas. He was a nice guy—had a degree in engineering but found out he could make more money dancing—and he taught me some *mo-oves…*"

She swung her hips in a sensual shimmy that ended with her chilled body skimming across the front of his. Again Jimmy's breath caught in his chest, and for one long moment he couldn't remember how to let it go, how to replace it with fresh oxygen to feed his starving brain cells.

"Does not dating mean not having sex?" she asked, and what little bit of breath he'd caught rushed out again.

"You don't pull punches, do you?" he asked wryly.

"What's the point?"

"Yes, not dating means not having sex."

"Wow. In…" Silently she counted up the months since Alia and Landry's wedding. "I'm impressed."

"Wow," he echoed. "I've been trying to impress you for six years, and all it took was giving up sex for a year? You're not an easy woman, Martine." Something about his words surprised her—the trying-to-impress part? Her mouth formed a small *oh* of surprise, and because it was too tempting, and because his body was still tingling where she'd barely touched him, he cupped his hands to her face and bent over her. "Lucky for me, I like a challenge."

His mouth covered hers, cold lips, hot breath, eager tongues. When her arms wrapped around his neck and she rose onto her toes to press her body against his, his hands moved without thought, sliding from her face to her shoulders to her spine, gliding downward to cup her butt and pull her hips against his erection. The cold didn't matter anymore, or the snow or the case or the murders. Nothing mattered but getting closer to her, touching, seeing, tasting, needing every bit of her, satisfying the hunger she'd stirred six years ago that had never gone away.

Her moan echoed in the small space, given strength by the unusually quiet night and by the need that scraped across his nerves with a painful sting. He'd heard that sound from her before, had made that sound with her before, and welcomed it again. The first time—last time—had been ruined by the ring of his cell phone and his mention of his wife. At the time, he'd thought it was the stupidest thing he'd ever done, but now he knew better. Just being with her then, kissing her, wanting her, had been wrong in ways he hadn't comprehended then.

He did now.

Anything more that happened between them now would have to be a rational, clearheaded decision on both their parts, or he would lose another chance with her, and this one would likely be the last.

That would be the stupidest thing he'd ever done.

Reluctantly he ended the kiss—the hardest thing he'd ever done—and nuzzled her throat, her jaw, her ear, before murmuring, "I should go."

Part of him hoped she would say, *No, you should stay.* The weaker part hoped she wouldn't.

Her breath was slow, audible, forming a tiny cloud in the air. "You probably should."

"It's not that I don't want you."

Her lips quirking into a smirk very much like his own fallback expression, she shifted her body against his, making his breath catch, his nerves tingle, his muscles damn near spasm with pleasure. "I know that. But we should be sure."

I'm damn sure. "Rational," he agreed.

She nodded. "Reasonable."

"Certain we can set aside the past."

"Make a calm decision not based on emotions of the moment."

The need inside him that wasn't about to go away anytime soon snickered. If any decision should be based on emotion, it was this one. But he ignored it. "Certain you can trust me."

She stilled, then her gaze sought his in the dim light. For a long time, she looked at him, her expression all serious and complex and intense, making his breath catch once more. When it eased, so did the tension inside him, and when the corners of her mouth turned up in the smallest of smiles, the tightness in his body eased, too.

"I do trust you, Jimmy," she said, and the honesty in her voice humbled him. "I trust you with my life."

And he would protect her with his life. And maybe, when all of this was over, she would trust him with her heart, too.

Chapter 7

After a surprisingly peaceful night, Martine woke to find a mostly pure blanket of white coating everything. Cradling a cup of coffee between her palms, she looked down on the courtyard, undeniably a magical fairyland with all the snow, and grunted with a distinct lack of appreciation. Sunshine. She wanted sunshine and warm breezes and no more of this winter crap.

In the living room, the morning news anchors were talking about nothing but the snow and its complications. Lists of schools closed for the day scrolled across the bottom of the screen while lists of areas to avoid due to traffic accidents were updated every few minutes. *Stay home unless you really need to go out*, the cheery blonde said with exaggerated sincerity.

Between sips of coffee, Martine texted Niles and Ramona and told them not to come in today, then gave

Anise a choice. She usually needed the money more than the other two. If she could get to the shop safely, Martine would open and work beside her today. She could use some company.

Niles replied K. Ramona said, Thnx. Regretting the slow disappearance of the written language as Martine knew it, she was rewarded with Anise's message: I'll be there before ten and will bring lunch.

Mention of lunch made Martine's stomach rumble. She got a chicken drumstick and the last few scoops of potato salad from the refrigerator and took it with her coffee into the crafts room. With the lights on, the heater running and the curtains open, it was the least claustrophobic place in her apartment. If she ever needed to defend herself there, she had plenty of sharp or heavy objects, from scissors to paper cutters, in addition to the Taser and the pepper spray.

She was in the process of selecting a new project to start or an old one to finish when her cell phone rang. Spying Evie's name, she put it on speakerphone and forced the happiest greeting she'd managed in a while.

"Hey, the kids haven't seen you in nearly a week. You want to come and have an early lunch with us?"

"Hmm, when the kids invite me somewhere, there's usually a hook, like the waiters are six-foot-tall rats."

"They were mice. You've seen enough rats down by the river to recognize the difference. But you will need a coat. Maybe two of them. And a hat. A scarf, gloves, boots, maybe earmuffs if you have any."

Evie's amused voice was interrupted by Jackson's shout. "Aunt Martine, we're having a picnic in the snow. Please come!" A second later, Isabella added her pleas, and a garbled message from little Evangelina suggested she was doing the same.

Evie wrestled the phone back from her children. "Now it's my turn to talk."

"It's always your turn," Isabella said archly.

"When you have your own phone—"

Martine interrupted. "Which will probably be for their next birthdays so Jack can keep track of them."

Evie snorted. "He would have the vet plant tracking chips in them if he could."

"Is he back yet?"

"No. He's snowed in in Omaha."

Martine felt a niggle of guilt because she hadn't even given Jack more than a thought or two since he'd left. She hadn't spent much more attention on Evie, home alone with the three kids who were definitely Daddy's boy and girls. Ordinarily, she'd be helping Evie distract them in the evenings, but this wasn't an ordinary week.

"I appreciate the invite," she said, grateful she had a legitimate reason for turning it down. Sitting outside to eat and drink in the snow didn't make the happy girl inside her jump and cheer.

"But you've got more sense than I do."

"No. You know I'd do it, but... I'm not supposed to go anywhere where someone might see me, and I wouldn't want to risk anyone following me to your house, scaring the kids or—or hurting..." She couldn't think beyond that. Her brain just refused to.

"I'm sorry, Martine. I didn't forget. I just didn't realize. Without Jack here to keep me updated, I just thought things were the same as Tuesday. Are you in danger?"

Martine's gut clenched. She didn't want to tell her best friend that Paulina's killer knew her address, had been to her house and sent her messages, but she also didn't want Evie showing up at the apartment or the shop to keep her company, either. "Enough that you should forget you know me for a while."

Evie gasped. "I can't—I won't—"

"For the kids' sake, Evie." Martine could actually feel the moment Evie relented. Her friend was a strong woman, loyal to the friends who made up her family and fiercely protective. She also understood thoroughly that having kids changed the dynamics of that family. In matters of safety, the kids always, always came first.

"Tell the little monsters that I'm sorry I can't join them on their snow picnic, but send me pictures."

"I will. We will." A tremor shook Evie's voice. "You be careful, Martine. And tell Jimmy if he doesn't do his absolute best on this case and keep you safe, I will put a curse on him that will make his dangly bits shrivel up and ruin him for any other woman the rest of his life."

Martine winced at the threat. Evie's powers were of the foretelling-the-future variety, but if anyone knew someone who could do what she'd threatened, it was her. Martine decided to give her good news—or, at least, interesting news—to offset the bad. "Oh, no, don't do that," she said, a little bit of slyness working its way into her voice. "*I* intend to ruin him for any other woman for the rest of his life."

There was a moment of stunned silence, then Evie squealed. "Are you being bad with NOPD's baddest boy? Jack said if you didn't kill him in the first twelve hours, he'd probably be okay, but this sounds like way more than okay. Give me details, Martine. I need gossip."

"Oops, I think I hear Anise downstairs," Martine lied. "Gotta go. Love to the kids and love you, too. Don't freeze on your picnic."

Though she knew she'd frustrated Evie—exactly as she'd intended—her friend's laughter pealed before the call disconnected. Smiling, she wiped her fingers on a wet wipe from the box on the bookcase, shook out an inexpensive vinyl tablecloth to cover the table, then began taking items from the shelves. She had ninety minutes before Anise would arrive downstairs and no desire to spend it being idle, where her mind could wander wherever it wanted.

Painting fabric was one of her many hobbies, one that helped justify having an entire room just for crafts. She'd made gorgeous watercolor cushions for her patio furniture last year and had bought a plain white hammock on closeout last fall with the intent of doing it to match. She already loved her courtyard and was sure she would love it more with the hammock tucked near the niches built into the brick wall that held candles inside hurricane glasses. With plenty of soft pillows, it would be the perfect place to relax on a lazy evening, and with the double-sized hammock, there would be plenty of room to share it with Jimmy.

Or some other guy, she reminded herself. Just because they both wanted to give this thing a chance didn't mean it would work out. Yeah, it could be another guy. Maybe Nico would come back through town, or maybe someone she hadn't yet met.

Or Jimmy, the stubborn part of her repeated. Maybe it wouldn't work out for the long term, but for a few months, enough for the evenings to get warm enough to laze outside, yeah, it could last that long. Long enough to surprise everyone who knew him. Maybe long enough to surprise everyone who knew her, too.

Maybe even…

She rolled her eyes, not willing to go there, and focused on her task. After taking her breakfast dishes to the kitchen, she returned with two cups of water, one for the paint medium and the other to wet the watercolors. The pigments were strong, vibrant colors that spread across her canvas in swirls and swoops, seeping into the fabric as the water helped move it along and toned down the hues to a dozen shades of gorgeous pastels that made her happy just to look at them.

By the time the phone interrupted her again, she was applying the last swipes of paint medium. Pleased with her efforts, she traded the brush for the phone, arched her back in a stretch and answered without looking at the caller ID. "Hey, Anise, perfect timing. I'll be down in a few minutes."

There was no response. No, that wasn't true. She could hear something in the background—a rustle, a whisper, really just a sense of a sound—then the bell downstairs buzzed. Jumping, she almost dropped the phone before calming her heart and her nerves and jogging down the stairs.

Anise stood on the stoop, bundled up as if the worst blizzard in the history of the world was raging. Only her eyes and the bridge of her nose were visible, and ice crystals decorated her yellow ski mask where it covered her mouth. Martine undid the locks and pushed the planter to the side so she could open the door. "Too cold to even say, 'Hey, I'm here,' before you hang up?" she teased.

"If I didn't already suffer from seasonal depression, this weather would do it to me," Anise said flatly. "Hey, I'm here."

Martine's smile faltered. "Didn't you just call my cell to let me know…"

Anise shook her head.

A shiver seeped through the open collar of Martine's shirt and raced along her skin, trailing up her spine and down into her suddenly queasy stomach. "Oh. Okay. Um, why don't you come in? I just need to grab a few things. Coat. Bag."

"Shoes." Anise looked pointedly at her socked feet. "Go on. I'll wait here." Though she walked the ten blocks between home and the shop twice a day, Anise didn't do stairs unless they were unavoidable. That, she insisted, was why God invented elevators.

Turning, Martine dashed back up the stairs. As soon as she rounded the corner out of her assistant's sight, she yanked the phone from her pocket and checked caller ID. Her heart stopped, giving a stutter or two before it managed to find a rhythm again, and stone-cold ice spread through her. Unable to depend on her legs, she sagged against the wall, and her gaze went unfocused, scanning the room without making sense of anything until it reached the kitchen window, then the back door.

The apartment was filled with windows and doors, entries and exits, window glass easy to break, doors easy to kick. Even with locks, even with Jimmy's weapons, even with her sense of security—false sense?— she wasn't safe here. The killer had found Callie. He'd found Paulina in a strange city that no one knew she was even in besides Martine. He'd already proved he knew where to find her.

It was just a matter of time.

"Don't hurry on my account," Anise called up the stairs. "Just because it's twenty degrees colder down here than it is up there."

The girl's voice was enough to shake Martine from her shock. She hustled into the bedroom, pulled on a pair of comfortable boots, grabbed her purse from the kitchen table and a coat from the coat tree. Before she reached the stairs again, she drew a deep, deep breath to control the panic inside her. She forced herself to walk down the steps at a sane pace, to follow Anise outside, to lock the door securely, then tiptoe through the snow to the shop's stoop.

The weather-sensitive door creaked and groaned, but within seconds they were inside, where she made a beeline for the storeroom. "I'll start the coffee," she called, not entirely a lie since she intended to do that, too. First, though, she had a phone call to make.

"DiBiase." Jimmy's voice was warm and confident and would have done tingly girlie things to her inside if she wasn't too chilled to tingle.

"Hey, Jimmy, it's Martine."

His voice went softer, sweeter. "It's not even ten o'clock. Miss me?"

More than you know. "Um, listen, Jimmy, I just got a phone call."

"Yeah?" Interest and concern in one syllable.

"Yeah." Her fingers clenched tighter, and she had to force air into her lungs before she could get the words out.

"Caller ID said it was from Callie Winchester's phone."

When Jimmy was a kid, swearing was strictly pro-hibited in the DiBiase household. Convinced that his parents would somehow find out he was breaking the rule, he abided by it until he was about twelve, when he wrecked his bike and skidded twenty feet along the pavement, shredding the skin exposed on his arms and legs. *Damn*, he'd muttered, and it had lessened his pain a little, so he'd repeated it, like a mantra, until he'd vented all his frustration and hurt. Now the word kept running through his brain. *Damn damn damn damn.*

It wasn't lessening anything this time.

It took too long to get a warrant to Callie's cell service provider, then too long to get back the location of her phone when the call was made—though instantly would have been too long—and finding out made the hairs on the back of his neck prickle. He rose from his desk, too edgy to sit still, pulled on his coat and headed out to his car.

Whoever had called Martine had been in Jackson Square, specifically in the corner nearest Café du Monde. Far too close for comfort, but not as close as earlier. One of the towers the phone had pinged before the call placed it on Royal Street less than ten minutes before.

The killer had walked past Martine's apartment, had possibly stood outside and watched the building while she was oblivious inside, going about her pre-work routine. Then she—his gut was leaning heavily toward a woman, and although he remained open to all possibilities, he didn't argue with gut instinct—had gone to Jackson Square and placed the call, frightening Martine without saying a word. Then, according to the service provider, the phone's signal had disappeared, meaning either the phone was turned off or the battery went dead.

He was pretty sure this woman, this person respon-sible for two murders, hadn't been careless enough to let the battery die.

Which meant she could be back on Royal Street, watching Martine's place. Hell, she could be in the shop posing as a customer.

Dread shuddered through him. He was generally well acquainted with the feeling—that came from going to too many crime scenes, from investigating too many victims—but this dread was different. It was sharp edged and left him in some odd limbo before numbness and angry raw fear.

Head ducked against the cold, he got into his car and started the engine, shuddering as cold air blew out the defroster vents, fogging the windows.

When he pulled away from the curb, he automati-cally headed in the direction of Royal. Martine had to close the shop. Had to get out of her apartment. Had to go into hiding someplace where she couldn't be found.

Like Tallie Winchester. Robin Railey. Irena Young.

He knew exactly where he wanted Martine to go.

And it wasn't going to be easy to get her there.

Like most Southern cities, New Orleans's policy for dealing with snow was simple: wait it out. Eventually the sun would come out and the air would warm and the snow would go away on its own. It was a good time to hibernate. He just wished he could.

Parking next to Martine's car, he stepped out, and the snow crunched beneath his feet. Trails were worn in the white stuff, including a mess of prints going up and then down Martine's steps. The same prints marked the shop's steps, though his own bigger foot-prints obliterated them. He jiggled the knob and pushed at the door until it gave, stomped his feet to clean his shoes, then went inside. When he closed the door, a mild shock shot through his fingers. "Damn," he muttered, and a dozen feet away, Anise gave him a curious look.

"How was it?" She cocked her head to one side. "The same as before? Stronger? Weaker?"

Remembering her comment the first time it happened—*That wasn't the effect I was going for*—he scowled at her. "Where's Martine?"

"In there." She cocked her head toward the door marked Private.

Jimmy went that way, but before opening the door, he turned back. "A little stronger than before. Is that the effect you were going for?"

Smiling serenely, she shrugged and returned her attention to the shelves she was rearranging.

The door opened into a medium-sized room with display counters, shelves, cabinets and tall jars and bins holding who knew what. There were no windows, the only lighting artificial and not nearly substantial enough. Though no candles or incense burned, an exotic, acrid smell drifted on the air.

Goose bumps raised along his arms. This was the real stuff, the merchandise she sold to real practitioners.

"Are you looking for me or just looking?"

The voice came from the right and shifted Jimmy's heart into overdrive. His hand had already shoved past his overcoat and jacket to his pistol before it registered as Martine's. After sucking in a sharp breath through his teeth, he turned to find her standing a few feet from him, her dark clothes and black hair blending with the shadows in the corner. "Holy crap, Martine, don't you know better than to sneak up on an armed man?"

She raised both hands palm out. "I didn't sneak. I didn't move at all." Then she did move, coming into the light, resting her hands on the glass countertop. "You must have bad news."

"Why do you say that?"

"Fabulous news gets delivered in person. Good or so-so news can be passed over the phone. Bad news usually requires a face-to-face visit." Her gaze raked over him, and a thin smile turned up the corners of her mouth. "You don't look like you've got fabulous news."

Lines furrowed around her eyes, her forehead and tagged the smile as less than authentic. She looked soul weary, as if the call from her dead friend's phone had been the very last straw. It made him want to wrap his arms around her, to hold her until she remembered that she wasn't alone in this, to give her some bit of strength to help her through.

By God, she *would* get through.

"The cell towers show the call came from Jackson Square, but they put the phone on this street just before then," he said grimly.

Even in the dim light, he saw the color blanch from her face. "*My* street?"

"Yes."

"While I was making coffee, I went to the living room window and looked out to see how much snow we'd gotten. I saw a few people on the street and thought they were more suckers for punishment than me. They just seemed normal, people on their way to work. None of them stood out." Her gaze scanned the room as if danger might lurk in every shadow before coming back to him. Fear darkened her irises, but she was making an obvious effort to contain it. "But that's the problem, isn't it? Whoever killed Callie and Paulina, whoever left that envelope on my car and cut the chain to my gate, they just looked normal, too, didn't they? The kind of person you'd smile at and say hello to on the street. Not some crazed psychopath who might drag you around the corner and crack your skull open."

He moved his hand to her shoulder, rubbing away the shivers there. "You're a wise woman to be scared, Martine, but—"

"I think I should close the shop for a few days."

The comment surprised him. He'd figured she would give him an argument about closing, about hiding and letting someone else control her life. He'd thought he would have to persuade her, pointing out that it was just temporary, that it was safer for everyone if she avoided the shop, that being smart and alive was better than being independent and dead. It took him a moment to catch up with her and nod. "I agree."

Again her gaze skimmed the room, stopping on the door he'd left open behind him, focusing on the world outside. A dangerous world. "The thing is…" Once more the pretend smile touched her mouth. "I don't feel safe in my apartment. This morning, after that call, it just really hit that the murd—" She swallowed hard, corrected herself. "The person who killed Paulina and Callie is here, waiting for me. I lock myself in my apartment, but there are ways in. He or she could walk into the store at any time, and I wouldn't know, I wouldn't suspect, until it was too late. They could be watching outside when I leave with you, they could follow us, they could have a tracking device on your car, and the minute you turn your back—"

When he'd first walked into the room, he'd wanted to hold her—just as he'd wanted to keep holding her when he'd walked away last night—but he'd waited. Now he took a step to reach her and pulled her close to him. She was so slender and insubstantial, a shaky mass of emotions dominated by fear. "Hey, don't insult my cop intellect," he lightly teased. "I check my car every day. No one's gonna follow me unless I want them to. And I'm the best at ID'ing vehicles driving the same route I am, sticking too close or taking too many of the same turns."

Bless her, Martine made an effort, even with her face pressed to the soft wool of his coat. "Huh. Jack says he's the best at all that stuff."

"Well, Jack may say it, but with me, it's really true. You would be amazed, Tine, at all the things I'm best at. You come stay at my place, and I'll show you. Or tell you." He hesitated, then returned to his original word choice. "No, show you."

Tension ratcheted through her body as she lifted her head, staring at him. Was she thinking that in a tourist destination like New Orleans, there were a thousand better places to stay than with him? Wondering what people would think? Wondering what *he* would think?

Or wondering what *she* would think. Feel. Do.

Or not do.

"I've got room," he went on. "It's safe. There's a security system. A doorman. No one will know you're there. Seriously, of all the places you could hide out, who in this city would ever believe you'd choose mine?"

She stared a moment longer before a real smile came to her face. Among their friends and acquaintances, it was well known—and a source of amusement for most—that the mere sight of him pushed her irritation level to the max. The closest she ever came to a smile around him was the baring of her teeth, and anything she had to say, she said in a fearsome growl. He figured all that was going through her mind, too, because curiosity and possibility both seeped into her expression.

"They say you always go to your lady friends' homes so you don't have to meet the minimum standards of cleanliness in your own."

"Or so I can leave the next morning pretty much when I want to."

She was relaxing a little in his arms, warming to the subject of what he was sure had been many conversations about his failings and shortcomings. "And that you prefer crappy apartments in crappy areas so women don't feel safe going there alone. That way no one ever shows up without an invitation and an escort."

"Aw, that's not true. But sometimes," he said drily, "I do try to live within my salary, and cheap apartments are often crappy ones. It also has the advantage of putting me close to the calls I work."

"They also say—"

"Wow, they talk an awful lot about me when my back is turned, don't they? And you listen to an awful lot of it for someone who professes to hate me."

She smiled innocently. "Have I ever actually used the word *hate*?"

He was too lost in looking at her to answer right away. She was beautiful and sexy, and she had this way of gazing at a man that made him feel she was giving him everything—every bit of her attention, emotion, desire, need. She had another way of looking that could make a man go weak, pretty sure she might leave him a boneless, brainless puddle and grateful for it. But add innocence to the sexiness and sensuality, and he was a goner.

He lost track of the conversation, instead maneuvering her even closer against him, bending to kiss her ear, to make her shiver. "I'm more interested in words you might actually use in the future," he murmured even as a rattle sounded outside the room. Anise's voice filtered in the air, along with a stranger's, their words impossible to make out. Jimmy didn't know if he went taut first or if Martine did, but he put her away and pivoted toward the door.

It was an older woman talking to the clerk, wearing a coat too thin for the day, silvery hair peeking out under a knitted New Orleans Saints cap. Not Irena. Not Tallie or Robin. Neither predator nor prey.

Nope, not exactly right. Irena might be his favorite choice for the killer, but that didn't mean he could rule out anyone else. A sweet lined face and pure white hair weren't enough to take that stranger out of the running for anything. When he didn't have a clue who his suspect was, then it could be anyone. Good reason to get Martine out of sight and keep her there.

Martine, moving soundlessly, eased the door shut and sighed. "At least we won't lose much money. The whole week's been a bust. Please, God, may the sun shine again Monday."

"As soon as Anise's finished, we'll lock up and give her a ride home. Don't tell her or anyone else where you're going. Oh, and I'll need your phone." When he held out his hand, she gave it to him with just a little reluctance. He powered it down and slid it into his pocket, heard the doorbell ring and sneaked a peek to find Anise alone. "Come on, Tine. Let's go."

Martine had lived in her apartment nearly twenty years and she loved it more than the day she'd moved in, but a heavy sense of unease prickled through her as she climbed the stairs. Even with Jimmy two steps behind her, she was afraid to reach the top, to notice a window cracked open, the back door unsecured, signs of an intruder soiling her space and spoiling its aura.

There weren't any windows cracked open, and the back door was still locked, and not a single thing had changed from the last time she was there, but the unease didn't go away. She grabbed a backpack from the coat tree and a cardboard box from the workroom, along with a handful of the shop's logoed bags. She filled the backpack and the box with clothing and shoes, with toiletries and makeup going into the shopping bags. She didn't want anyone who saw her to think she was running away but maybe making a delivery for the store.

"I do have luggage," she said to Jimmy, leaning against the doorjamb, arms crossed, just in case he thought she was one of those people who really did pack in cardboard and plastic.

"Luggage says 'I'm going somewhere.' Boxes and bags say 'But I'll be back in a few hours.'" He grinned. "Didn't think I caught the subtle nuances of that, did you?"

"I didn't know you knew a thing about 'subtle' or 'nuances.'" But there was no sting to her words. She glanced around the room, thinking of nothing else she wanted besides the laptop in the living room and a heavier coat from the rack. "I guess I'm ready."

She swung one strap of the backpack over her shoulder while Jimmy picked up the box and the bags. When she scooped up her computer, he shook his head. "No."

"No?" she echoed.

"You can't send email, use social media or surf the net. Providers are too easy to follow. You can use mine, but you still can't do email or social media. Okay?"

Swallowing a sigh, she put the computer in a desk drawer as she passed, then started down the stairs. She hadn't brought any projects, any books, any music. She would probably go stark-raving mad within twenty-four hours.

Unless Jimmy found a way to entertain her.

Had he noticed the condoms she'd sneaked into the bag with her hand lotion and other stuff? Smart women were never caught unprepared, right? Neither were smart men—or easy men—but given that he'd been celibate for a year, she thought it best to provide recently purchased protection.

Even if she didn't get to use it.

She waited inside the door while he put her bags in the trunk of his car. Then they returned to the shop and helped Anise close up. If the girl thought something was wrong, she kept it to herself. All the way to her house, she spoke only in partial sentences to give Jimmy directions.

There she swung her legs out the rear door, then paused. "You want me to let Ramona and Niles know?"

"Yes, please. Tell them I'll still pay you guys."

Anise fixed a grim look on her. "It's not just the

money. We're responsible. We could keep the shop open."

"I know you could, sweetie, but..." Martine didn't want to even hint that the store could be a dangerous place right now. If the killer was frustrated by Martine's disappearance, what revenge might he take on her employees?

"I really think it's best if we just all take a break. If you need anything, call my cell, okay?" Martine assumed Jimmy would be keeping it at work, in case the killer called again, and he could keep her updated on any other calls.

"Okay." Anise stood up, then ducked down inside again. "You'd better not let anything happen to her," she said to Jimmy, "or those shocks are just the beginning."

He acknowledged her with a relatively serious nod. She straightened, slammed the door and picked her way carefully through the snow to the porch of the small house she shared with her father.

"Are you still getting shocked by the doorknob?"

He gave the fingers of his left hand a rueful look. "Yeah. I think they're getting stronger."

Martine frowned. "I adore Anise, but...that's a little scary."

"You doubted her powers?"

"Well...yes. Anise's a dabbler. So is Niles, only he's not much of a believer. Creating a ward that shocks only one person, and the same person every time... who knows what she might do if she finds a talented mentor willing to work with her?"

"Like you?"

She shook her head. "I'm not talented. I can put together protection bags and charms and make cleansing potions and healing potions, but the difference between, say, me and Auntie Katrine—you know her, right?"

An eye roll accompanied Jimmy's nod, as if to say *everyone* in the NOPD knew Auntie Katrine. She was a fixture in the French Quarter, her business set up in good weather or bad on the sidewalk in front of her small shotgun house, painted hot pink and lime green. She was short and fat—she'd *tsk* if you used any other word—and she came from Trinidad, or maybe it was Antigua or West Caicos. She'd been here forty years going on seventy, and she'd birthed fourteen children and buried five husbands…or was it ten children and seven husbands? With Auntie Katrine, details always varied, but one thing didn't. She was on better terms with the spirits than anyone Martine had ever known.

"Take the executive chef at the best five-star restaurant in the entire world, and that would be Auntie Katrine. I would be the perpetually stained, sweaty, steamy peon in the back washing dishes. We'd both be in the restaurant business, but that's where the similarities end."

He squeezed her fingers lightly. "I'd like to see you sweaty and steamy for the right reasons."

This time it was her eyes rolling, but she wasn't annoyed. Some of his lines, his practiced smiles, his flippant comments, could still set her hair on fire, but her ticked off–meter wasn't nearly as sensitive as it used to be with him.

You need to get to know him, Evie always said. *When you figure out what's real and what isn't, he's a good guy.*

Of course, Evie was already happily married to the love of her life at the time she met Jimmy, so she was never the target of his over-the-top charming smiles or his sweet-talking ways.

In an attempt to distract herself, Martine gazed out the window. "Where do you live?"

"You'll be surprised."

Acknowledging that she likely would, she changed the subject. "Did the killer take Paulina's cell phone?"

"She left it at home when she ran away. The one she used to call you was a burner phone. It didn't have anything personal on it."

"So he took Callie's because it did have stuff on it—names, pictures. So she had no clue what was about to happen. She was going about her life as usual, and one night she died." She considered that for a moment. "I think I might prefer it that way—the surprise, you know. Poor Paulina looked like she'd been living in hell. She was afraid to stay in one place, to look over her shoulder, terrified of what she might see. But it didn't help her. She knew death was coming. Her only surprise was when, and maybe who."

"Paulina didn't get help," Jimmy said quietly. "She could have gone to the police. Her family could have hired bodyguards. They could have spirited her away to some isolated place on another continent or put her on a yacht in the middle of the ocean."

"Maybe she thought she didn't deserve any of that. Maybe she thought death was what she deserved."

Or maybe not. Her last known act had been to warn Martine. Without that, the killer could have grabbed Martine the very next day or anytime since. She would have been vulnerable and helpless and most likely have ended up like Callie and Paulina.

She didn't focus back into the present until the clicking of the turn signal pulled her there. Jimmy was turning into the parking garage of a tall building just a short distance from the river, stopping, waiting for the security guard to step out of the shack, give him a wave, then activate the iron gate. There were expensive shops on the ground floor of the building, the kind outside her budget except for very special events—which were pretty much outside her lifestyle—and she vaguely remembered hearing about condos upstairs.

Jimmy DiBiase, who according to legend had never cared one bit about the places he called home, lived in a sky-high condo in the Central Business District of the city. He had been right. She was surprised.

He parked in one of two spaces marked 805. Silently, they gathered her belongings from the trunk and hustled to the elevator fifty feet away. It was marked Residents Only and required a swipe card to operate, and it took them quickly to the eighth floor.

The condo had great bones, easy to tell because it had very little in it: a sofa that had seen better days. A television mounted to the wall above the fireplace. Stools at the counter that separated the kitchen, which didn't hold a single one of the usual items that tended to clutter counters. No dishes, no soap, no can opener, no sugar or coffee, nothing but half a roll of paper towels. Through an open door down the hall, she saw the corner of a mattress set, resting directly on the floor.

He set her stuff on the counter, and she added the backpack to the pile. "Are you planning to finish moving in soon?" she asked pleasantly, drawing a growl from him as she walked to the tall windows that looked out over the city. "Somehow, I didn't picture you living in an actual apartment—with a living room, kitchen and everything. I figured all you needed was a bedroom and a bathroom. You know, like a motel."

He looked as if he didn't know whether to be annoyed or to agree with her. Finally, with a grin, he opened his arms to encompass the mostly empty space. "I'm finished moving in. What you see is all I've got."

"Are there dishes in the cabinets?"

"Nope. No food, either. I *have* dishes. They're in boxes down the hall. I haven't had time to unpack them. And I'll get groceries today. I've just been a little preoccupied."

With this case, Martine knew. With her. "I appreciate your preoccupation."

His grin appeared again before he gestured toward the hall. "Want the five-second tour?"

It actually took about ten seconds. There was the master bedroom: the mattress set, a lamp sitting on a box, a closet, a bathroom and a wall of windows. The hall circled around behind the kitchen, leading to another bedroom, smaller in all senses, including the windows, then went back into the living room, passing the guest bath on the way. Neatly labeled boxes were stacked in the hall, and there was no furniture—zip, zilch, nada—in the guest room.

"So I'm sleeping on the couch." The idea tickled her: after practically jumping his bones the second time they met, and regretting not doing it on more than one occasion, the first time they spent the night in the same space, she'd be passing it on an old, worn, comfy sofa.

He gave her a long, serious, tantalizing look. "You're always welcome in my bed, Martine. I made that clear a long time ago."

"Yes, but you were *married*, Jimmy."

After another moment, he slowly smiled. "I have to admit, I admire the fact that it mattered to you. I even admire your unwillingness to let it go. I like that kind of commitment to your beliefs."

She believed him, especially when he touched her so gently, his fingers stroking along her jaw. The contact made her all warm and melty inside, made her forget all the ugliness and let her just be a woman with desires and needs and uncertainties.

"What are you committed to, Jimmy?" Her voice was barely a whisper, and the sound was unsteady, shaky, like her legs that didn't want to support her, like her fingers that trembled when they cupped his hand where it rested on her cheek.

He moved closer, brushed his mouth across her forehead, kissed a trail to her ear, then glided down to the corner of her lips. He toyed with her, sliding his mouth back and forth, teasing her lips apart, briefly tasting her, giving her a taste of him, before he lifted his head and met her gaze. His was fiercely protective and possessive and hot.

"You, Tine," he answered gruffly. "I'm committed to you."

Chapter 8

In all his years with the department, Jimmy couldn't recall ever not wanting to work as much as he did when he had to leave the apartment and Martine. It was a strange feeling. From the time he'd graduated the academy and started his first day with his training officer, he'd counted himself lucky for loving the job. From doing traffic stops to refereeing domestic disputes to drug arrests, he'd never gotten up in the morning and thought *I don't want to do this today*.

Right now, though, he didn't want to return to work. Two thoughts kept running through his mind, one that knotted his gut and another that could make him a believer in spontaneous combustion: Martine was in danger, and damn, the things they could do if he didn't leave. God knew, he'd worked enough long hours over the years to justify taking an afternoon off, but that wasn't the way he did things.

Instead, he kissed her again and left the apartment, arranging with the building's concierge service to take care of the shopping, and returned to the station.

When he got to his desk, he called Paulina's husband, back home in Alabama with the unenviable job of planning his wife's funeral. Shawn Bradley didn't sound as if he had gotten past the shock of her death.

"Your wife left her cell phone behind when she left. Is that right?" Jimmy asked after apologizing for bothering the man.

"Yes, she did."

"Did any calls come in on the phone after her disappearance?"

"A lot of text messages. Most of the calls were from me. At first I didn't know she was gone, and then I just… I wanted to hear her voice on the outgoing message." Bradley's voice cracked, and he took a deep breath to steady it. "In the first few days, there were calls from friends and coworkers who didn't know she'd disappeared. Those dropped off for a while, then it was like something jogged their memory and they called to see if she was back. Now it's down to her parents and me."

"Did you know most of the callers?"

"By name if not personally. Paulina liked to share the details of her day—who made her laugh, who ticked her off, who she had lunch with. The rest seemed to be just acquaintances, not part of her regular life. People who heard that a Paulina Bradley was missing and wanted to make sure it wasn't her."

He fell silent, so still that Jimmy thought they might have lost their connection. He was about to speak when Bradley did.

"Then there were the hang-ups. Though if I recall, one of them…" His tone turned thoughtful, and the rustling of papers sounded in the background. "Paulina *hated* missing a call—we used to joke that the phone was glued to her hand—so in the beginning, I kept track of them all since the phone would only store so many numbers. Okay, here it is. Two weeks after she went missing, she got a call from one of the Christmas-card friends I told you about—the sisters. Callie Winchester, from the 206 area code. No message, just a hang-up."

So the killer hadn't been watching Paulina, hadn't known she'd run away. Why the change with Martine?

Because the killer had found Paulina in New Orleans, and it was convenient to take care of her and Martine at the same time. Because Paulina had warned Martine. Because with Tallie and Robin already in hiding, Martine had been the only one the killer could easily locate.

"Does that help, Detective?"

"Yes, Mr. Bradley, it does." He got the cell carrier's name and Paulina's number so he could confirm the call through the company, said goodbye, then tapped his pen in the air above the notebook.

He'd been blessed with some cases so easy to close that a monkey could have done it: an angry avenger still holding the weapon, a remorseful spouse covered with the victim's blood and gunshot residue, a rival proud to have put the competition out of business. But there was no challenge to those kinds of cases, and he did love a challenge.

"Uncle Jimmy!" The cry came from the doorway an instant before Isabella and Jackson Murphy charged around his desk, each determined to reach him first. He slid his chair back in time for Isabella, ducking nimbly around her brother, to leap into his lap and press her cold cheek to his. "I won," she said with a dazzling smile.

"She cheated," Jackson complained as he climbed up, too.

"I don't think she cheated, buddy. She was just a little bit faster."

"Because Mom says I can't shove her out of the way."

Evie, carrying Evangelina, slid into the chair that faced Jimmy's desk. "She doesn't get to shove you, either, Jackson." As soon as the admonishment was spoken, she turned her gaze on Jimmy. "What have you done with Martine?"

Grinning, he pressed his hands over Isabella's ears. "I can't answer that in front of the kids."

Evie's gaze narrowed. "We went by the store, and it's closed, and she's not answering her door or her phone. Even if you were *n-a-k-e-d* in *b-e-d*, she wouldn't leave me standing in the snow frantic about her."

Picking up a pen and finding a piece of paper, Jackson carefully started writing. *N-a-k*. "What comes after the *k*, Uncle Jimmy?"

He deliberately misunderstood. "What comes after *k*? *H-i-j-k-l-m-n-o*—"

"*P!*" the older two shouted before dissolving into giggles.

Jimmy took advantage of their distraction. "She's someplace safe."

Evie's scowl spoke to her dissatisfaction. "I know that. I want to know where. Your apartment?"

Holding on to both kids, he shifted position. "You think she'd consent to that?"

Tilting her head to one side, Evie studied him before smiling slyly. "I think she'd consent to that and a whole lot more."

Images of the things Martine might consent to, and with him, thickened his brain and notched up the temperature a few uncomfortable degrees. If he let them linger at all, he would embarrass himself with the kids and give the other detectives one more thing to joke about. Deliberately he changed the subject. "Any idea when Jack will be back?"

"Tomorrow, if God takes mercy on my sanity. You'd think Omaha would have been better prepared for snow. They live up north, for heaven's sake."

"I bet people up north say things like that about New Orleans and hurricanes."

"Yes, but when I say it, it makes sense." Evie nudged Evangelina, sitting quietly. "Sweetie, give Uncle Jimmy the goodies we brought."

For the first time he noticed the paper bag Jack's youngest was clutching, the same pink as her jacket. Eyes wide and two fingers stuck in her mouth, she shook her head and held it tighter.

"We made you cookies," Isabella said, and Jackson prodded, "Give it to him, Vangie."

Evangelina shook her head again. Evie whispered something in her ear. After considering it, the girl took her fingers from her mouth and thrust it at him. "Here, Uncle Jimmy."

He accepted the bag, still faintly warm and smelling

of chocolate chips and oatmeal and raisins, and thanked each of the kids. "What did you tell her? Maybe I can use it next time I'm questioning a suspect."

"She's a little girl, not a suspect." Lips thinned, Evie added in a murmur, "At least, not yet. Kids, are you ready to get back out in the snow?"

Jackson wiggled to the floor, then held up his hand to high-five Jimmy. Isabella pressed her cheek to his once again before sliding down, and in a blur of movement and noise, the Murphy clan disappeared down the hall.

It wasn't until quiet had settled again that Jimmy realized Evie had left his question about her tactics unanswered.

But with the comment about Martine, she'd given him more than enough to think about.

There were no food or dishes in the kitchen, Jimmy had said, but by three o'clock, Martine's hunger pangs had led her to snooping. He was almost totally correct: the cabinets and drawers were empty. But the big gleaming silver refrigerator... Everything else might be bare, but occupying the top shelf was a large pizza box, and inside the box were two pieces of pie. It was from one of her favorite places, and the order tag still clung to the box, indicating he'd bought the pizza on Wednesday. Good enough for her.

Using paper towels as both plate and napkin, she warmed the slices just enough to soften the cheese, then climbed onto a barstool and took a ravenous bite. The flavors of the sauce, the meats, the cheeses, and especially the onions and peppers, settled and soothed the grumbling in her stomach. Too soon the pizza was gone. She washed her hands, then carried her stuff into the guest room.

Unpacking was simple: her folded clothes went on the shelves in the closet, her shoes on the floor underneath and her toiletries in the guest bath cabinet. She wandered back into the hall and around to the other bedroom and stood in the doorway. The bed was queen-size—she'd seen so many massive beds that she'd doubted anyone but her owned a smaller size—and the sheets were light blue. A blue blanket covered them, and a shades-of-blue quilt was pushed to one side. It was handmade, with perfectly aligned corners and tiny stitches.

So this was where the infamous Jimmy DiBiase laid his head at night.

This was where she could lay her head at night. For a while. Maybe a long while.

I'm committed to you, Tine.

Maybe for the rest—the best—of her life.

When a loud buzz sounded, she shrieked and whirled around, then sagged against the door. Intercom. Alarm system. Doorman. Concierge service. Jimmy had told her about them before he'd left. He hadn't told her someone might be calling, but that was okay. As soon as she stopped shaking, she would answer like a normal adult.

"This is Stefan from the concierge desk." The voice was young, male, the accent distinctly not Southern. "We have Mr. DiBiase's grocery delivery. Shall we bring it up now?"

Martine told him yes, then smiled faintly on her way to the door. So that was how people with money did their grocery shopping. It was a perk she could get accustomed to.

Within minutes, Stefan was at the door, pushing a trolley loaded with canvas shopping bags. He made polite small talk while unloading everything onto the kitchen counters, and bless his heart, his smile never wavered when it became clear that no tip was forthcoming. With a pleasant reminder to reset the alarm, he left, and she returned to the kitchen, regretting her habit of never carrying cash.

"Yeah, like you woke up this morning thinking you'd be tipping the concierge for a delivery," she murmured as she began unpacking. She wasn't sure she'd ever even stayed at a place with a concierge before, much less used their services.

There were a lot of shopping bags—natural, she supposed, for someone who was starting from scratch. All the staples were there: flour, sugar, spices, oil, condiments. A selection of canned, frozen and fresh vegetables. Shrimp, beef, chicken and pork. Rice, pasta, bread, deli meats and cheeses. Lots of cheeses, and three boxes of crackers. So Jimmy was a cheese-and-cracker guy.

Smiling at the image of him hunkered on a barstool, making a dinner of that and one of the sodas or beers, she opened the last bags and found two large cartons of ice cream, an apple caramel pie fresh from the bakery, an assortment of chocolates and coffee. The final bag, one Stefan had placed carefully in a corner of the counter, held tall paper sleeves, each cushioning a bottle of liquor: Bailey's, Kahlúa, bourbon and rum. Four of the spirits she'd offered him at the apartment.

It touched her that he'd remembered.

It seemed odd, deciding where food would go in someone else's kitchen. Once she'd taken care of that, she folded the empty shopping bags, stored them in a drawer, then retrieved a box of dishes from the hall. Now that she had dish soap and had discovered a stash of kitchen towels, she might as well unpack some of his supplies so they could make use of the groceries. Besides, she doubted Jimmy was going to be letting her out of the apartment every time a meal rolled around. That seemed to defeat the point of hiding.

With the television turned on for company, she washed and dried insulated glasses, plastic giveaway cups, logoed coffee cups and cereal bowls. There was a set of dishes so artfully mismatched that they seemed beyond Jimmy's ability to choose. A leftover from Alia? No, Alia loved food, but she didn't give a damn what it was served on, and she wasn't into subtleties of tones and variations any more than Jimmy.

Maybe another former girlfriend had chosen the vintage floral-pattern dishes. Heaven knew, he'd had plenty of them. It was a fact of his life, part of how he'd become the man he was. He'd made mistakes, and he said he'd learned from them.

She believed him.

Never get involved with a man with the intention of changing him, her mother's lifelong best friend and serial divorcée, Rona, liked to say. *Accept him the way he is, or move on down the road, honey, because that ride you're on is gonna get real bumpy.*

Bette had said Rona's ride was never going to smooth out until she swore off either marriage or divorce. Going on ten years single, it seemed she'd made the right choice.

After unpacking, washing, drying and putting away six boxes of kitchenware, Martine walked into the hall for a seventh, stopped and stretched, feet apart, arms high in the air, then slowly bent at the waist to ease the kinks out of her spine. As her fingertips brushed the floor, a key turned in the front door lock, and an instant later, the door swung open to reveal an upside-down version of Jimmy in the hallway. Immediately her face flushed deeper than could be blamed on the position, and just as immediately a grin spread across his face.

She stood more quickly than she should have, hair tumbling back into her face, heat rushing through her but not from embarrassment. The way he'd looked at her, the hungry, needy glaze in his eyes, the memories of their kiss and of his quiet declaration—*I'm committed to you...* They all combined to make her feel warm and quivery and nervous and excited and very, very girlie.

Summoning a normal voice from somewhere, she said, "You should give a person warning."

He stepped inside, shrugged out of his overcoat and hung it in the closet. "I figured using the intercom or ringing the bell might startle you, and if you tried to use the Taser or the pepper spray, I could duck back out and close the door really fast." He removed his jacket, too, and loosened the tie around his neck as he approached her. A whiff of cold, fresh air came off him, and an aura of satisfaction surrounded him.

"You have a good day?"

He shrugged. "In between. I learned a little. Not enough." He glanced at the stack of empty boxes teetering on one side of the hallway. "Wow. You got a lot done."

"I know I should have asked, but I had no way to get hold of you, and what good is food without dishes?"

"You didn't need to ask." He shoved one hand in his pocket and pulled out a cell phone. "I got this for you. It's prepaid, and with the number blocked, no one you call can press Redial and get you. It doesn't have all the bells and whistles, but it'll do what you need. Don't give the number to anyone, not even Evie. Not even your mom. I'll let you know if you get calls to return, and you can do those from my phone, okay?"

She reached for the phone, and he caught her fingers, pulling her closer. She didn't even pretend to resist. "Keep this with you all the time," he said, pressing the cell into her hand. "I've got a few numbers programmed already—mine, Jack's—he should be back tomorrow—and Gus. He's head of security here. His office is on the second floor. If anything happens, call all three of us. You know how to use it?"

She pulled her hand free and studied the phone. It was simpler than her smartphone—a good thing since she'd discovered she wasn't as clearheaded in a panic as she'd always thought she would be. "Yeah, I can figure it out."

"Good. Let me change clothes, and I'll help you in here."

Martine made sure she did understand the workings of the phone before sliding it into her pocket and going back to work. She hung the damp dish towel over an empty box, took a new one from its drawer and filled the sink again with hot sudsy water. The next box she opened held mixing and storage bowls, along with lids. Surely in one of the remaining cartons, she would find some cookware. She could easily see Jimmy preferring standing over a smoky grill with a beer in hand, but the only thing the apartment lacked was a balcony to hold said grill.

He returned from the bedroom wearing jeans, a snug-fitting T-shirt and socks. Even though, in deference to the situation, his gun was still holstered on his belt, something about him without shoes struck her as so...homey. So ridiculously right and cozy. He smelled good enough to wake her girlie hormones if they hadn't gone on high alert just at the sight of him, spicy and woodsy and rich.

"You know, I washed the dishes before I packed them." He lifted a milky-green bowl from the second sink, rinsed and began to dry it.

"I suspected as much. But who knows how long they've been in these boxes, or where the packing paper came from?" She gave him a sidelong look. "I do like your dishes, though."

He opened cabinet doors, looking for a place to set the bowl, then frowned. "You haven't seen them yet."

"Those pretty floral plates?"

"Oh. My sister made those. Running the family business and homeschooling the kids don't keep her busy enough, so she also dabbles in stuff. She made 'em, painted 'em, glazed 'em, fired 'em...whatever all it takes. She said I should use those instead of my real dishes."

"What's wrong with your real dishes?" Martine could make a pretty good guess, considering the other surprises she'd gotten about him this week.

He dropped the towel, brought in another box, lifted out a dinner plate and handed it to her. It felt as delicate as a fine sheet of ice, as if she dropped it, God forbid, it would float rather than fall to the floor. The colors were delicate, pale flowers on a creamy background, and the whole glowed with a lovely translucency.

She very carefully handed it back. "You were eating off those?"

He set it back in its nest in the box. "They're dishes. That's what they're meant for."

"No, by the time they get that old, they're meant for display and *maybe* a once-in-a-lifetime celebration." She narrowed her gaze. "I bet your mother's holding on to any other family heirlooms you've inherited, isn't she?"

He grinned, not the least bit embarrassed. "I tell her I could use the dining table because I don't have a desk and that the cabinet that goes with the dishes would make a great place to store stuff like files, footballs, shoes, but she just turns pale and pretends she doesn't hear me."

Martine appreciated the affection in his voice when he talked about his mother. She knew so many adults who had little to no relationship with their parents—Evie, Jack, Landry, Reece and Jones. Even, when it came to her father, herself. Jimmy, though, seemed on good terms with all of his family, and she admired that.

Admired him.

More than admired him.

The sun had abandoned New Orleans, there was snow on the ground, and Martine Broussard was falling in love with Jimmy DiBiase. Had stranger things ever happened?

Jimmy hadn't spent enough time in the apartment to have gotten accustomed to being there alone—he'd moved in only on Sunday—but he did wonder, after a while, why it didn't seem odd that Martine was there. He'd never been the sort to entertain at home. From the time his social life had begun, dinner with a date had always meant going out; quiet evenings at home were at *her* home; his bed was best for sleeping in alone. Even Alia, in the months before they got married, hadn't been to his place more than a handful of times and had never spent the night there. Though, to be honest, that was her choice as much as his.

But it felt right to have Martine here. She made it feel really and truly like home, and that was a sensation he hadn't had in longer than he could remember.

They had fixed dinner and eaten it, washed the dishes and returned the kitchen to its neat state. In her unpacking, Martine had found the coffee maker, and now they each had a cup, dosed with enough Irish cream to warm from the inside out, and the gas logs in the fireplace crackled and popped without the hassle— or the charm—of the real thing.

"So." Martine shifted at the other end of the couch, kicking off her shoes and turning to face him with her feet tucked underneath the cushion separating them. "The places you've chosen to live in the past are legendary for their undesirability. Why make such a drastic change?"

"I don't know. Maybe subconsciously I knew I would meet a damsel in distress who would need a safe place to stay."

The look she gave him was skeptical. "You already knew me."

"Not really. We'd already *met*. There's a difference."

She acknowledged that with a nod, then her eyebrows drew together. "A damsel in distress?"

"Hey, if it weren't for the saying, I wouldn't even know what a damsel is. I would just say 'a white female, five feet eight inches, one hundred and thirty pounds with black hair and brown eyes.'" And nice breasts. A narrow waist. Sweet hips, an incredible butt and legs that stretched all the way up to her eyebrows.

He wondered if she would object to the weight he'd guessed—he'd learned a long time ago on the job that little was more dangerous than guessing a woman's weight and getting it wrong—but any dissatisfaction she might have felt didn't stop her from smiling.

She was so damn beautiful when she smiled.

"You ever forget you're a cop?"

He didn't need to follow her gaze to the pistol on his hip. After so many years, it was second nature. Its absence would be more unusual than its presence. "No. I'm always prepared."

That earned him another smile. "Sometimes I think you like to play the stereotypical jock. Big, dumb, likes to party, all about easy sex and lots of it, not the sharpest knife in the drawer."

"Play?" He drank from his mug, watching her over the rim.

"Yeah, *play*. As in 'pretend to be.' You're a lot smarter, a lot more mature and empathetic, than you want people to believe. You cultivate this image, and not very many people get past it."

What did it say for a forty-year-old man that being called mature and empathetic was one of the best compliments he'd ever been given? And considering its source… Sweet damnation, Martine considered him mature. Nothing she could have said—not even *Let's get out of these clothes and into bed*—could have made him feel better.

"It's not an image so much," he admitted, dragging his fingers through his hair, "as who I really was. It took me a while to grow up. I'm an only son in a family that loves its daughters but really loves its sons. I was top ranked in football in high school. I played college ball for four years. I've been a cop for eighteen years, and just like football, the job has its groupies. Things have always come pretty easy, and I've always been… shallow, except when it comes to my job."

That wasn't as easy to admit as he'd thought it would be. It wasn't as if she didn't already *know* he'd had about as much emotional depth as a puddle after a rainstorm. She'd spent six years hating him because of it. Still, the words were tougher to say out loud than he'd expected. If things didn't feel so damn right between them, he wasn't sure he could have gotten them out.

She leaned over to set her coffee on the floor, then rested one arm on the back of the sofa, her cheek pressed against her fist. Her hair fell forward over one shoulder, catching and reflecting the light from the fire. "What did you major in in college?"

"Football and sex." It was a flippant answer that came as naturally to him as breathing. Immediately, though, he relented. "General studies. Liberal arts. Not that I'm particularly liberal about anything."

"Except sex." There was a lightness to her voice, like none of that mattered anymore. It stirred something in his gut, hard and hot, and sent a flush through his body as if the temperature in the room had soared.

He set his own coffee down, too, not trusting his hands to remain steady. Not wanting them busy doing anything else. "I used to be. Not anymore." His voice was husky and thick and no steadier than his nerves that had gone tingly. Like the shock touching the door-knob of the shop gave him, only magnified a million times.

"I believe you."

"I'm honored." He was, too. He'd wanted her, been intrigued by her, for so long, but after that disastrous night, he'd thought he didn't stand a snowflake's chance in hell. He was sorry it had taken two mur-ders and death threats against her to undo the damage he'd done back then, but he believed something good always came out of the bad. Martine could be his good, and he could be hers.

"Did you ever want to play pro ball?"

"Nah. Football's too hard on the body after a time, and I didn't want to spend half my year living, playing or practicing someplace else. New Orleans is home. And I wanted to be a cop. I just had to get a degree to make my parents happy first."

"And making your parents happy was important?"

"They deserved a little payback for all the time, money and frustration I cost them."

Had she moved a little closer? It seemed so, but he couldn't say for sure because somehow, he was closer, too, and he couldn't remember leaning away from the sofa arm behind him. But there was definitely less than a full cushion between them now, and even that dis-tance disappeared as she shifted onto her knees, then leaned over him.

She wrapped her arms around his neck and touched

her mouth to his with no hesitation, no slow buildup, no uncertainty at all. Her tongue slid along between his lips, then dipped inside his mouth and stroked. Hell, yes, it had definitely gotten warmer in the room, like closing-in-on-the-sun at supersonic speed, and his clothes had turned heavy, trapping heat and constraining everything flowing through him all at the same time.

He wasn't dumb, she'd told him, but for an instant, he felt it. His muscles were taut, his synapses firing constantly, and his brain was so overwhelmed, its orders were muddled. Hold her? Touch her? Kiss her? Tear her clothes off? Carry her off into the bedroom or just trade places with her on the couch?

Or relax and enjoy?

Oh, yeah, that sounded good. Relax as much as he could with a raging hard-on and enjoy it even when the pleasure left him broken into a whole lot of pieces of happy nothingness.

His hands shifted to rest on her spine, one at the base of her neck, the other low on her back. Even through her clothing, the contact felt unreasonably intimate. When they got undressed, when he could touch her bare skin, nothing between them anymore, no anger, no smugness, no misunderstandings...

Finally she made the last small move he'd been waiting for, sinking down, taking her weight from her knees, her body stretching the length of his, her hips cradling his erection, her breasts pressed against his chest, the pleasure of her desire crashing hard against the pain of his.

Sliding his hands upward, he skimmed them beneath her shirt, over the soft skin of her back, higher to the barrier of her bra, then back down again. They resumed their upward movement on the outside of her shirt, not stopping until he'd reached her ponytail. Even with his eyes closed, he didn't fumble over the clasp that held it, tossing it aside and letting her hair fall, long and silken over his hands. He stroked it, caressed it, then laid his palms flat against her head, held her still and took control of the kiss, plunging in his tongue to fill her mouth.

She whimpered softly, not in complaint or protest, and when she glided her hands along his body to his groin, he groaned far less softly.

Wriggling together, they were working their way into a prone position on the sofa when his cell phone rang. Martine's breath caught—hard to miss when his tongue was in her mouth—and her body, for an instant, was as rigid as his own before she pushed herself up onto her arms. The intrusion, both of the phone and the unwelcome memories it brought, washed over him like an ice bath, stopping his heart midbeat, making his hands shake. No, damn it, not this time... He'd waited so long...

The phone rang again, and suddenly her body went all soft again, pressing against him in the most sensitive places. A smile that was part frustration and part sly touched her lips before she pressed a chaste kiss to his mouth, then pushed herself off the couch. "See if you need to answer that," she said, raising her hands to the buttons of her black shirt. She undid one, then two, then three, head ducked, hair falling across her face, before catching his stunned gaze and smiling. "I'll wait for you in the bedroom."

Skimming through the rest of the buttons, she

slid the shirt off her arms, let it fall to the floor and walked—sauntered—sashayed—away before he had a chance to notice much more than the bright orange of her bra and the smooth brown of all that skin.

He had to roll onto his side to work his cell from his pocket and to grind out a nongreeting. "This better be important."

"Some information came in on your missing heart case." It was Steve Lawson, one of the detectives on shift.

Jimmy rubbed the back of his neck, his frustration subsiding. Nothing else was, thankfully. "Text it or email it to me, will you? Just don't call me the rest of the night."

"Aw, DiBiase's committing assault with a friendly weapon," Lawson said in an aside, and in the background a couple of people snickered.

"You guys ever gonna grow up?"

"That's rich, coming from Detective Peter Pan. Check your email when you're done. What'll that be? Five minutes?"

"Screw you, Lawson." He hung up before any of the guys could respond and left the phone on the kitchen counter on his way to the bedroom.

The only light in the room came through the windows, dampened by the screen that kept peepers from seeing in while still allowing a view out, and it all seemed to gather on Martine, standing beside the bed.

All those years ago, she'd been sort of a challenge: something he'd wanted and expected to get. Like he'd told her, everything had come easily...until her. His untrustworthiness had turned her into an opportunity missed, one that he'd regretted ever since. But here she was. With him. Wearing jeans and socks and frilly bits of silly orange lace that would soon be gone.

Here she was, giving him another chance, not just for great sex but everything he'd wanted…and some things he hadn't even known he wanted.

God help him, he wouldn't screw it up this time.

Warm air drifted over Martine's bare skin—so much of it—as the central heat kicked on, chasing away the goose bumps on her arms but doing nothing to settle the butterflies in her stomach. She wasn't new to standing naked, or partly so, in front of a man— her sex life was a healthy one—but something about this felt new.

It wasn't the gorgeous apartment. She'd dated men with money before. It wasn't the fact that her body wasn't quite as toned and firm now as it had been ten or even five years ago. She was growing older as graciously as she could. It wasn't even all those years of hostility and yearning and anger she'd harbored for Jimmy.

It was this moment. The yearning now. The need. The intensity. The seriousness of it. The not-just-sex-ness of it. The he-was-getting-too-important-ness of it. It was wanting to please him and wanting to please herself and being oh, so grateful that doing one would naturally accomplish the other.

She let her gaze slide over him: his dark hair still mussed from running his hand through it; the familiar devilish and sly and boyish and charming gleam in his eyes; the stubble on his jaw that indicated a long day; the navy T-shirt, bearing a large gold star and crescent of the New Orleans Police Department's badge, that stretched broad across his chest but clung to his flat stomach; the faded jeans that clung everywhere, and quite impressively. "No phone?"

He shook his head. "I left it out there. I told them if they called back, I'd shoot 'em." As he spoke, he lifted his shirt on the right side and removed his pistol from the holster, skirting around her to lay it on the night table next to a Taser and a canister of pepper spray.

She reined in her smile but couldn't help the easy, light tone to her voice. "Is that it on the weapons?"

"Depends on your definition of 'weapon.'"

"You are ready for everything," she teased. "You happen to have any condoms?"

"Somewhere."

"Don't bother looking." She took off her own Taser and pepper spray, added them to his, then reached into her hip pocket to remove a sleeve of condoms. "I come prepared, too."

Finally he moved toward her, and all the warmth she'd felt a few moments ago disappeared, chased away by the shivers racing through her. These were good shivers, though, the kind that promised delight and satisfaction, the kind she would never grow tired of.

He reached her with four steps, but instead of pulling her close for a hard kiss, as she expected, he stood a bit away, raised his hand and touched her cheek with a gentleness that humbled her. "You're an amazing woman, Tine."

She forced back the lump rising in her throat, blinked back sudden moisture in her eyes and, when his fingertips skimmed close to her mouth, she caught his hand, guided it to her mouth and pressed a long, slow damp kiss to his palm.

His free hand cradled her nape and pulled her against him, while his right hand reached lower on her spine, to the thin closure of her bra. With her hips pressed to his, his arousal seemed even more impressive, and she couldn't deny that the silly woman who still peeked out from her brain from time to time was amused by his one-handed dexterity with bra closures. A moment of subtle movements, and the garment fluttered, shifted downward until the straps caught on her shoulders.

"Oh, you're good at that," she murmured before he took her mouth. She slid the straps off and let it fall, nibbled at his tongue, then began exploring his still fully clothed body. The shirt was soft, like an old favorite, but not as soft as the skin it covered. Living art, an expansive canvas that invited her to touch rigid muscles, sensitive nerves, the network of bone that drew her hands downward. *The collarbone connected to the rib bone, the rib bone connected to the hip bone, the hip bone connected to the pelvic bone* and… Hallelujah. She was a happy girl.

Groaning, he shifted his hips out of her reach, so she grabbed handfuls of his shirt and began peeling it upward, forcing them both to break the kiss or be strangled in the process. She stared at him, her thoughts too chaotic with emotion, at the small knot of scars on his right shoulder, at another scar that ran across his biceps, at the gorgeous even tint of his skin and the way it stretched across his rib cage and dipped low over his abs.

"You forgot to say that you're handsome as sin," she murmured, her hands touching here, gliding there, savoring over there. "That's the biggest reason women were so easy. The money helped, the football and the badge, too, but being so damn gorgeous with that naughty-boy grin was the icing on the cake."

He rested his forehead against hers, his gaze heavy and all-seeing at such proximity. "It truly surprised me to find out that not all women—namely you—found my naughty-boy grin charming."

"At this moment…" Her voice was fading as drawing air into her constricted lungs became harder. "…I'm sure I would find everything about you totally charming if we could just get out of these clothes."

It was if she'd unknowingly discovered the magic words to send him from languidly touching and kissing and looking to stripping off his own clothes with breathtaking speed. He took a moment longer with hers, undoing the button and the zipper on her jeans, pulling the flaps of denim away from her body to glimpse inside, then yanking everything off as efficiently as he'd done with his own.

"I've never been with a woman wearing orange panties," he said with a broad grin as said panties sailed across the room inside her jeans. "Come Mardi Gras, we'll have a private party—you in those panties and bra and me in nothing. I'll even give you beads if you show me your breasts."

Mardi Gras. That was the end of February, not even two months away. Would they be together then?

Not the time to think about it, her rational mind decided. Damn sure not the time to wonder if she would even be alive then. This was now, and she was going to make the absolute best of it.

Without a frame, the bed sat lower to the floor, and when Jimmy took hold of her shoulders to lower her back, her breath caught at the falling sensation. A foot above the mattress, he let go and let her fall, and she bounced on the shades-of-blue quilt with a laugh. The mattress bounced again as he joined her, but his mouth on hers stopped her laughter, and his body over hers sent shivers and need rushing through her. In bed, there was always time for play, but right now, with fire dancing in her stomach, with hunger long too unsatisfied burning through her and his dark eyes stark with that nothing-matters-but-you look, playtime was over.

When he knelt between her knees, plastic crinkled beneath her hip. She groped blindly for the string of condoms, tore off one packet before throwing the others aside, then smiled her sweetest, most innocent smile. She pushed up, and he obligingly rolled until he was on his back and she was kneeling just a few inches below where she needed to be. "Let me put this where it goes—" she drew her fingers over the length of his erection "—and then I've got a promise to keep."

She was going to ruin him for other women.

And herself for other men.

For the rest of their lives.

Nothing could wear a man out like a long week at work, days spent mostly with Martine and nights spent mostly worrying, thinking, wanting her, besides a couple of hours of impressively good sex. Jimmy lay on his stomach, the pillow he hugged underneath his head nothing compared with the silky skin he'd been touching and tasting and just looking his fill of. He was pretty sure, if he had a bit of artistic talent, he could draw a perfect replica of her perfect body, with every bump, birthmark and pore exactly in place. That was how intently he'd studied her.

She lay on her back, her hair spread over the other pillow, her cheeks flushed, her smile radiant. Sex was a great pastime—no one would ever get an argument on that from him—but sex with someone special was... well, special.

So much for Martine thinking he was smarter than he let on. Blame it on his oxygen- and blood-deprived brain. That part of him was still processing the fact that Martine had actually had sex with him, that she'd given him a second chance, that she was looking at him as if third and fourth and endless chances might be forthcoming.

Don't get too ambitious, buddy. You might act like a kid, but you're still forty. Those all-night workouts are a thing of the past. Though if anyone could bring them back into the present, it would be Martine.

She turned onto her side, bunching the pillow under her head, and gazed at him. "If I'd known you had a thing for orange lingerie, I would have worn it sooner."

"If *I'd* known I had a thing for it. For what it's worth, pink works, too. Red. Yellow. Green. Purple. Brown. Black. White. Beige."

"So, basically, every color known to man."

He wrapped a tendril of her hair around his finger, taking care to not pull. "Every color known to this man. And all the millions I have no clue about."

"So...was it worth the wait?"

Letting her hair uncurl, he moved his hand to her stomach, caressing with just the tips of his fingers across her concave belly, up to her breasts with their sensitive nipples, over her hip bones and lightly, just barely, between her legs. "Haven't I stroked your... ego enough tonight?"

With the pause, he penetrated the damp curls and made her breath catch, sending hundreds of little quivers along her nerves. She caught his hand, lifted it away and pressed a kiss to his wrist. "That wasn't the reward I had in mind."

"Reward?" He grinned. "I like rewards."

"Was it worth a piece of warm apple pie with vanilla ice cream in bed?"

His grin gave way to laughter. Martine had a weakness for apple pie. That was going to make life easy when he needed a quick apology, a little persuasion or just a little treat to give. A man could find good apple pie anywhere.

"It deserves the whole damn pie. Stay here, and I'll get it." He kissed her and swung his feet over the side of the bed just as his cell phone rang. He sighed.

"At least their timing is better." Martine slid up to lean against the headboard, the sheet tucked under her arms. She was the prettiest sight he'd ever seen.

He tugged on his boxers, then headed down the hall, snatching up the phone as the next ring started. "Didn't I say don't call me again tonight?"

Lawson responded, "Hey, we gave you a couple hours. Even you can get laid in that amount of time. Besides, we're working. Why shouldn't you?"

He glanced down the hall, where he'd pulled the bedroom door until it was almost closed. The sound of water came faintly from behind it. Martine was in the master bath. He turned on the speaker, set the phone on the counter next to the stove and got the ice cream from the freezer. "Oh, I don't know. Because

I put in all my hours for the week and already made a good start on next week's hours?" After peeling off the plastic lid from the pie, he plated two large pieces and popped them into the microwave. "What's up?"

"We got something new on your lonely heart case."

"Don't call it that."

"That NCIS agent—"

"The cute one," another voice chimed in. Detective Petitjohn.

"The cute one that you didn't used to be married to," Lawson clarified. "She called it the lonely heart case, and you know it fits. Poor heart out there, wondering where the hell its body got off to. Besides, all good serial killers need a name of some sort."

The microwave dinged, and Jimmy removed the hot bowls and started spooning up ice cream. "Forget the name. What about the case?"

"A woman took her dog out for a walk a little bit ago. He ran off into the woods and came back chewing on something."

Petitjohn took over. Jimmy had never met a detective, himself included, who didn't like having his say in a conversation. "This woman's a surgical nurse, and she recognized it right away as a human heart. Your victim's, we assume. We got no shortage of heartless killers around here, but yours is the only heartless victim at the moment."

A soft rustle came from behind him, a sound Jimmy couldn't identify. He spun around and saw Martine, wearing the white button-down shirt he'd tossed on the bathroom counter after work and leaning heavily against the doorjamb where her legs had apparently given way. Grief and revulsion etched deep lines into her face, and the blood that had drained left her so pale, he thought she might faint.

Damn it. Dropping the spoon, he took a step toward her, but she backed away.

"They cut out her heart? Her *heart*?" Horror echoed through the words and showed on her face and in the crumpling lines of her body. She sagged, and he lunged for her, catching her on the way to the floor, sinking with her the last few inches.

As he lifted her into his lap and wrapped his arms around her, Lawson's voice came distantly. "Uh, look, sounds like you have your hands full. We just, uh, thought you'd want to know. Later, man."

He assumed the phone went silent, but he couldn't tell because Martine's panicked attempts to draw a full breath were too painful to separate out any other sounds. He held her snugly and stroked her tousled hair back from her face. "Breathe, darlin'. Just focus on that, one slow breath… That's good, Tine, now take one more… Breathe a little deeper this time… That's it, sweetheart."

Unlike most men, he had a natural talent for dealing with distraught women. Being big brother to two drama princesses had given him a good start, and his job had taught him the rest. He'd never been the sort of cop who stood by stoically while a victim or family member broke down and wished for a female officer to deal with them. He knew the value of a touch, a hug, a hand to hold and a few quiet words.

The floor was hard and cold, and the air was still, carrying a hint of cooling apple pie. After a few minutes of rasping breaths, Martine grew quieter, but shudders racked through her. Somehow, the fact that he felt her sobs more than heard them made them that much worse, as if she couldn't find the strength inside to give them voice.

He couldn't guess how long she cried. Long enough for his butt to go numb, for the muscles in his arms and legs to get stiff from the awkward position. Long enough to drain whatever energy she had, but nowhere near long enough to find any real comfort.

When her body grew still and her tears subsided, he continued to stroke her hair. "I didn't intend to tell you. It's information the public doesn't need to know, and I knew it would…" *Break your heart*, he'd been about to say. "It would be too much to hear about someone you loved. I'm sorry you found out, and I'm sorry you found out this way."

She lifted her head an inch or two so she could see him. Exhaustion and revulsion etched lines into her face. "Is there any good way—" a hiccup interrupted her "—to find out your friend's heart was cut from her body after she died?"

By sheer will, Jimmy kept his muscles from contracting. *Don't ask, don't ask, please, God, don't let her ask*. He didn't think he could tell her that Paulina hadn't been dead when the killer started carving. She was too shaken. Learning that her friend didn't die a relatively easy death from blunt force trauma to the head but instead was butchered alive was too much for her to take in at one time.

Was there ever a good time?

Her head sagged against his shoulder again. She shifted, wiping away dampness from her cheeks, then switched her focus again to breathing. The tremors slowly faded, and her muscles very slowly relaxed.

For a long time, she was so quiet that he thought she might have fallen asleep. Her week had been as long and stressful as his, her evening as energetic and cathartic. Now all he had to figure out was how to get his feet under him and stand up without jarring her too much, then carry her to bed.

Ten years ago, he could have done it without much effort. Tonight, just thinking about it made him consider the possibility of sleeping on the tile floor, uncomfortable as it was.

Before he'd moved, she pressed her cheek harder against him. "When I asked you if Paulina's death was related to Callie's, you said yes. That the details of the cases matched. Does that mean Callie also…?"

Her voice was soft and weary, and it fueled the rage deep inside him. He hated people so bitter, so angry with the world, that they thought they had the right to destroy other people's lives. No parent or spouse or child should ever have to know that someone took their loved one's life for any reason. If Irena Young or whoever the hell had committed these murders couldn't bear to live as long as her victims did, then she should have damn well killed herself. Problem solved.

"Yes."

"So this person who wants me dead…he intends to remove my heart, too." She raised her hand protectively to her chest, as if she were saluting a flag. "Promise me you won't let that happen. I'm very attached to this heart, and I really don't think I could bear losing it. I know I'd be dead and wouldn't know it, but please, Jimmy…" Her tone edging closer to hysterical with each word she spoke, she clamped her jaws shut, keeping any other plea inside.

He laid his own hand over hers. "I won't, Tine. I swear on my life."

She breathed, then nodded, but it was clear she didn't entirely believe him. He couldn't even take offense. He could promise her anything, and he could mean it with his heart and soul and even his life.

But that didn't mean he could force it to come true.

He would do his damnedest, though. Or die trying.

Chapter 9

The rest of the night and Saturday morning passed in a blur for Martine. She woke to a dark gray sky, rolled over and went back to sleep, snuggling against Jimmy's body. The next time she woke, the sky was light but still dreary and Jimmy was gone from the bed. She slid into the depression where he had lain, faintly warm and smelling of his cologne, and fell asleep again with her head on his pillow.

The third time she woke, she felt thickheaded, as if she'd closed down a few Bourbon Street bars all on her own. Her body ached, and her stomach was so empty that it was distressing her brain. Her eyes were too puffy and sore to make out the numbers on the bedside clock, but she thought there were only three, so it was past noon, not yet night.

She needed a shower. A toothbrushing. A delete

button on her brain to clear out ugly memories she would never forget.

Paulina, Callie, I'm so sorry. I never should have let things end the way they did.

They *walked away from* you, her internal voice reminded her. They *forgot* you.

Sliding to the edge of the bed, she rubbed her empty stomach and decided the one thing she needed most of all: Jimmy. She didn't care that she looked like she'd tested her hair in hurricane-force winds or that yesterday's makeup was smeared and clumped or wiped off completely. She just wanted to feel his presence. Just wanted to feel safe.

Leaving his bedroom, she tiptoed around to the guest room for warm socks and fuzzy slippers. On impulse, she grabbed a pair of leggings and squirmed into them, then proceeded to the living room. The logs were ablaze again in the fireplace, and the central heat spread warmth to the spaces too far for its reach. But being this cold from the inside out, she wasn't likely to warm up very fast.

Jimmy had pulled three empty boxes over to form a table in front of the couch and was studying papers, notes, photographs and such from the files spread out. She was careful not to look at any of them. She didn't want to see anything her brain wasn't ready for.

He sat back and watched her circle the boxes to join him. She would have sat at the opposite end, but when he extended his hand, she grasped it tightly and let him pull her down next to him. For a long time he just looked at her, then he gently combed his fingers through her hair, undoing some tangles. "You okay?"

"I'll survive." It was the most hopeful answer she

could give and had the added benefit of being true. She *was* going to survive this thing. She might never be the same person again, but she would, at least, *be*.

Jimmy maneuvered them until he was leaning back against the sofa arm and she was tucked up close. She liked being so close.

"The temperature is in the forties today, so the rest of the snow should be gone soon. Jack's back in town and grumpy after spending so much time with his fugitive. I saved you a piece of apple pie, but first you've got to eat something. Breakfast, lunch, your choice."

Even though her first thought was to turn down food, her stomach growled so loudly, it would have been a refusal nobody believed. "How about toast?" She could keep dry white toast down, right?

"How do you want your egg? Scrambled or fried? Over-medium or -hard? I'll warn you, I don't do over-easy. The goop on top is just gross."

"Toast will be fine."

"I'll make it over-hard so the yolk doesn't drip. What kind of cheese do you want? We have Swiss, cheddar, gruyere, pepper jack, provolone..." His expression was innocent, as if he wasn't ignoring every word coming out of her mouth.

Since he was sweet enough to care, and she would like to see if he could actually fry an egg properly, and she really was hungry, she relented. "You choose, and I'll eat it."

He kissed her forehead, then brushed his mouth across hers before standing. "While you wait, you might want to..." One hand circled in the general area of her face, which she took to mean *Wash your face, brush your teeth, get your hair under control.*

Okay, so when she returned to the bathroom, she looked all ready for Halloween. She took a shower, scrubbed her face and brushed her teeth twice before dressing in the leggings again and a red sweater. Underneath she wore a matched set of violet lace lingerie.

Wonderful aromas filled the air when she went back to the living room: fried eggs, melted cheese, artisanal bread and coffee. Jimmy was on the couch again, and he'd cleared a space on the boxes for her meal. She sat on the hearth instead, savoring the heat of the fire, the buttery warmth of the toasted egg-and-cheese sandwich and the sight of him, in disreputable jeans and another NOPD T-shirt. Even though he hadn't shaved, even though his hair stood on end, he was the most beautiful man she'd ever known.

The first bite of sandwich made her moan softly. "The man can cook," she murmured to herself, but his grin showed he didn't need to hear the words to understand the compliment. She polished off the sandwich far too quickly for good manners and drained half her coffee before wiping her hands on a napkin and gazing at him. He was sorting through papers, making notes in that cramped little style of his.

After a moment, he looked up. "Are you ready for the apple pie?"

"Not yet." With her backside blazing warm, she shifted along the hearth, propping her feet on the stone so they could get warm, too. "Is there anything new you can tell me?"

He put his ratty notebook down and raised his arms high above his head in a tension-relieving stretch. Lacing his fingers together, he rested both hands on the back of his head, propped his feet on the corner of a box and sighed. "Everything I've got on Irena Young is a dead end. If she's worked since her mother's death, it's been under a different social security number or she's gotten paid off the books. She still has the same cell phone, according to the provider, but hasn't made a single call since the week after her mother's death, and it's rarely turned on. Those calls went to family back in Idaho, but they say they haven't talked to her since and don't know where she is or what she's doing. She hasn't updated the address on her Louisiana driver's license, but she doesn't have a license from any other state, either."

That was a sad way to live: having no contact with her family, no friends, apparently no one who mattered in her life beyond her mother. Martine loved her mom dearly, but even Bette, with her larger-than-life personality, wasn't enough to fill up all that space. Where would she be without friends, coworkers, acquaintances and lovers?

"Her father's out of the picture, too. He moved down south—way south, like Panama or Colombia—when he retired and hasn't been back to the States since. The Marquitta police can't find anyone there who maintained contact with Irena or Katie Jo after the murder. There were no identifiable fingerprints on the letters or the pictures, no saliva from licking the envelopes, no spores or microbes or anything." He loosed his hands and shrugged. "We've got a lot of nothing."

Warm enough at last, Martine left the hearth to curl up on the sofa. "What—" Nausea rose in her stomach, but she forced it down again and steadied her voice the best she could. "What will they do with—with Paulina's—her—"

Compassion and tenderness—two things she'd never thought the superficial Jimmy capable of—softened his gaze. "Her heart?"

She nodded.

"DNA will confirm that it's hers. Then her husband will have the option of having the coroner's office dispose of it, or it can be returned to her body for burial, or he can have it cremated. Her funeral is scheduled for the early part of next week, and the results probably won't be back by then. I don't know if he'll delay it or have the heart placed later or what."

Logically, Martine knew Paulina was beyond caring that her heart was gone. Emotionally, she couldn't imagine her friend's spirit feeling anything but distress. How could she rest in peace without her heart?

Wrapping her arms around her knees, she contained the tiny shivers passing through her before they could grow in intensity. Forcing her thoughts away from that one terrible point, she quietly said, "I can't go, can I?"

Jimmy shook his head. "A lot of killers attend their victims' services. The local police will be there. They'll photograph everyone at the church and the cemetery. You'll have to look at the pictures to see if you recognize anyone."

Her smile was sad. "I barely recognized Paulina herself. Tallie, of course, will look a lot like Callie. Robin... Irena... Only as long as they haven't changed very much."

Or they could be looking for someone else. Someone she would never expect to find in the photos. Someone she'd forgotten or hardly known, someone she might not have known at all. If she had known him, he couldn't possibly be the same. Surely whatever led him to such horrific actions against girls he'd known would have left some sort of mark on his spirit and his soul, if not his face. And if she didn't know him, she would be worse than useless to Jimmy.

It was a good thing he wanted more than just information from her.

She hoped he wanted everything she had to give.

It was shortly after three when the doorman called up to announce a visitor. Jimmy cleared him, and a few minutes later, Jack rang the bell. Proving the meteorologists right, his only jacket was a hoodie, and he carried a stack of files and a folding chair, kept handy in his vehicle for cookouts and the kids' soccer games.

"Look, he hasn't even seen the place and he brings along his own chair," Martine teased.

Jack snorted. "He hasn't had enough furniture since that time we were moving him when two patrol officers tried to stack the armchairs and make it down the steps in one trip, and they dropped them from the third-floor landing."

"Would it have killed them to climb the stairs twice?" Jimmy asked.

"In that neighborhood, quite possibly." Jack tossed the files on the table, unfolded the chair nearby, then bent to hug Martine. "You haven't hurt him yet. I'm proud of your restraint. How are you?"

"I'm okay."

It wasn't a ringing endorsement, with a sort of woefulness to it, but Jimmy knew Jack would accept it as the best they could expect. Being an intended victim wasn't easy. Jimmy was proud of her for managing that much.

"I'll get some coffee—"

Martine interrupted. "I'll do that. You guys do all your ugly-part discussion while I'm out of the room." She rose, squeezed his hand as she passed as casually as if Jack's presence didn't change anything. Being just one more of Jimmy's girlfriends, especially in front of his cop friends, wasn't always easy, either. Expectations for them were usually pretty low.

Jack made only one dry comment. "You know, if you hurt her, you're going to have my wife to answer to."

"I'm not afraid of your wife."

"You should be."

Reclaiming his seat on the couch, Jimmy glanced at Martine, her back to them in the kitchen, lowered his voice and caught Jack up on everything they'd learned—or not learned—during his absence.

Jack hadn't been idle, either. Snowed in in Nebraska, he'd had plenty of time for phone calls, internet searches and records requests, and he'd taken on Jimmy's least favorite task: investigating the subjects' financial backgrounds. He had a lot of printouts, but nothing that grabbed for attention. They might still miss information that would make sense of it all. They might have it and just not got the pieces together properly. Or they might never get it all.

That was an outcome Jimmy couldn't accept.

"I kept trying to get hold of Callie Winchester's parents, and their lawyer finally called last night," Jack started. "The Winchesters are grieving the loss of their daughter. They have nothing to tell us that could possibly help in our investigation, and the subject of their daughter Tallie is strictly off-limits, for her own protection. She's somewhere safe. On what continent, he wouldn't say. He has no clue whether her parents have been in contact with any of the other parents, and he has no intention of asking them."

That seemed about right for the people who'd lived in the pretentious house at the end of the Broussards' street. "I've never understood families who won't do everything they possibly can to find their child's murderer."

"If everyone did things the way a reasonable person expects, we'd be out of a job, James. Unlike you, most of us need it."

"I need it," Jimmy protested. "If I was phased out, I'd have to move back home, where they'd probably make me handyman and security guard for the house. The kids would make me a badge from cardboard covered with aluminum foil, and my parents would drive me stark-raving mad urging me to get married, have kids and carry on the family name."

"There's a lot to be said for marriage and kids."

Jimmy resisted the urge to look in Martine's direction or give any hint that he was even vaguely interested in how their future looked. It was a long-standing joke at work that certain words had never been in his vocabulary, like *forever. Commitment. Monogamy. Fidelity.* When he and Alia had gotten married, his fellow officers had started a pool on how long it would last, and not one of them had given it more than a year.

He regretted that he'd been so immature and easy to read.

"Is it safe to come back?" Martine asked from the kitchen.

"Sure." Jimmy murmured, "She's a little squeamish about the heart."

"Who the hell isn't?"

Martine carried a sterling tray, ornately decorated and heavy enough to give a fifteen-year-old boy a concussion, as Dani and Becca had found out in a practical joke gone wrong. Jimmy had been the one injured, and also the one punished since the joke had been his. He'd never again sneaked up on the girls late at night when there was metalware within reach.

After they'd fixed their coffees, she asked, "Are you done with the ugly stuff, or do I need to leave the room?"

Jimmy didn't want her to go. Though she couldn't possibly be safer than she was at the moment, he felt more comfortable being able to see her. "You already know pretty much everything." Except that both hearts had been removed while the victims were still alive, and he'd already warned Jack of that.

Jack gave her a moment to get settled on the couch before he started. "I did a lot of checking into finances while I was in Omaha. What do you remember about the different families' money status when you were kids?"

Martine blinked blankly. "I don't know I ever thought about it. We all lived in the same neighborhood, though the Winchesters' house was definitely the biggest and nicest and Robin's house was kind of small. We couldn't have sleepovers there because it was too crowded, and she didn't really ever invite us. Her parents were nice enough, but they didn't socialize much with our parents except holidays or parties. Mom and Paulina's and the twins' moms had lunch every other Tuesday, and our dads played golf every weekend, but not the Raileys."

"Was she ever left out of your activities because of money issues?"

Jimmy looked up from his notebook—he was the dedicated note taker in this partnership—and watched Martine's gaze go thoughtful. Were Jack's instincts pointing to Robin? Jimmy was open to any suspect, preferably one they could stop, and Robin was as good a candidate as any, though she needed a motive. Maybe she'd never felt as much a member of the group as the others had. Maybe she still harbored some jealousy or anger toward them.

It was scary to think how little things that happened as kids could have such profound effects on people twenty or thirty years later, but he'd seen enough examples of it himself. Jealousy turned to envy turned to resentment turned to bitterness turned to rage, and rage trumped everything, even love.

"There were times she couldn't spend the afternoons with us because she had to work—she had a part-time job to pay for her cheerleading costs—but we did the same things all the time. It wasn't really missing out." Martine hesitated, as if she wanted to say something, even took a breath and opened her mouth, but closed it again right away.

Do you think Robin is the killer? Jimmy would bet that was what she wanted—and didn't want—to know. It was hard to accept that two of her friends had been brutally murdered. Harder still to know the killer wanted to do the same to her. It just might be impossible to believe it was another of her friends who hated them so.

"The Winchesters had a lot of money, didn't they?" Jack asked.

She smiled drily. "When the twins turned sixteen, their parents gave them each a brand-shiny-new convertible. Paulina and Robin and me—we were blown away, but their dad just grinned. He couldn't expect them to share a car, now, could he? What was another forty thousand dollars when his girls' happiness was at stake?"

"Damn," Jack muttered. "Jackson and my girls will be lucky if I allow them to leave the house by themselves when they're sixteen."

One of the downsides of police work: a cop knew better than anyone the danger lurking in the outside world. A cop who was a parent couldn't help but make some of it personal: *What if that was my kid?* And it extended beyond that. Too often the last couple of days, when Jimmy remembered the sight of Paulina lying dead in the cemetery, he wondered, *What if that becomes Martine?*

It wouldn't. Couldn't. Jimmy DiBiase didn't fail, and Jack Murphy didn't fail, and between the two of them, they *would* keep her safe.

Jack had more questions about Tallie and Callie—their relationship, their spending, their habits, their attitudes. Martine found the conversation surreal. He actually suspected Robin or Tallie of killing Paulina and Callie. She had great admiration for him as a detective, but this time he was wrong. She was certain of it.

Closing her eyes, she called up images of her old friends. Except for the end, their years together had been good times with so much laughter. They were peas in a pod, her father had teased, one personality split between five girls. They had shared meals, clothes, classes, activities, friends, families, experiences. They'd had a sort of conversational shorthand that allowed them to communicate with no more than a look, a word or two, and had led them into adventures and disasters. They had lived such *fun* lives.

Could either of them have become a killer?

It was unfathomable. Even trying to consider it made her stomach clench with revulsion. It had to be Irena Young. Irena didn't know Martine and the others, didn't love them. Or someone else, someone who'd thought he had reason to kill Callie, then had gone after Paulina to misdirect the investigation. Someone who'd never met Paulina or Martine or Robin or even Tallie.

It would still break her heart that Callie and Paulina were dead, but it would be easier to deal with if the real reason had nothing to do with the teenage bond they'd shared.

Was that selfish of her?

Before she could find the answer to that question inside her, she was startled back to the present when Jimmy and Jack both stood. Her knees were drawn up, her hands clasped around her now cold coffee. Jimmy's notebook lay open on the boxes, the one page visible filled with his tiny printing, and Jack's chair was folded, tucked under his arm.

"Give Evie and the kids a hug for me," she said wanly.

He said he would before walking to the door with Jimmy. They talked a moment longer while she gazed into the fire. Uneasiness crept through her like the past week's fog, filling all the empty spaces inside, worse than it had been before Jack's arrival. Sure, Jimmy had considered everyone a suspect but her, but actually being questioned about Robin and Tallie gave the situation a reality she wasn't prepared to accept.

She didn't know if she ever would be.

Jimmy returned, tugging her coffee cup from her hands. He took the empty mugs into the kitchen, then came back a moment later with a bottle of water for each of them. He circled behind the couch, pressing a kiss to the top of her head, then took his seat again at the other end of the couch. "Let's talk."

In her experience, when men said, *Let's talk*, it didn't bode well for the relationship. Either they wanted more than she was willing to give, or they wanted out. Intuitively, she knew Jimmy wanted her to talk, and he would listen, and then he would offer what comfort he could. Gratitude warmed her to her core, but it didn't shake the edginess.

She drank from the bottle, then fiddled with the cap before finally meeting his gaze. "Tallie wouldn't kill Callie." She infused the words with all the certainty in her heart, but a few beats later, more words escaped. "Would she?"

"Tallie's lived in London for twelve years. According to the State Department, Callie hasn't been there for more than fifteen years, and Tallie's trips to the US have been few and far between. There wasn't much in the way of phone calls, emails or texts between them, either."

"They're *identical twins*. Two halves of a whole. My mom used to say they lived in each other's back pocket."

"Or each other's shadow."

Martine was an only child who had longed for a sibling until she'd met Paulina, then the others. It was hard for her to think that sisters could be *too* close. And despite the two-halves-of-a-whole bit, they were still people with their own personalities, quirks, weaknesses and passions. Individuals who had been treated as one for the first eighteen years of their lives.

All four of them had cut Martine off without a word. Was it so unlikely that the sisters had had a falling-out, as well?

And what about Robin? Had she felt like she was in the shadows, too? That somehow she didn't measure up to the rest of them because her parents didn't have as much money? Had she resented them without their even knowing it?

Her head ached from the rounds of no-she-couldn't and maybe-she-could-have. Switching the water to her other hand, she pressed her palm to her forehead, letting the cool dampness left from the bottle ease her heated skin.

Her sigh was soft and tired. "You know what? I'd like to have one hour where I don't have to think about anything from the past."

Jimmy's grin was smug and sweet. "Take those clothes off, and I'll give you two."

"You're so charming."

"Hey, I think that's a pretty good offer. You get naked, and I give you two hours of fun and forget-fulness."

"Sadly, I think the forgetfulness is the more appealing of the two right now."

He set his water aside and made room for her—a

very small bit of room—beside him. She shifted around and settled between his hard warm body and the back cushions of the couch, and he wrapped his arms around her. For a long time, he just held her and she just savored it, letting her eyes close, her memories shut down, her brain concentrate on nothing but how good he felt and how good she felt with him.

"It'll be okay, Tine." The softness of his voice slid over her, easing muscles and soothing fluttering nerves.

"How do you do it?" Peering through her lashes, she watched him cock his head in question. "How do you spend every single workday with people at the worst time of their lives without letting hopelessness and despair take over your own life?"

He didn't have a pat answer, as she'd expected. Instead, he gave it a few moments' thought. "I have an occasional drink. I have good friends. I have great sex. From time to time, I go a little bit crazy for a few days. Then I get back to it." His shrug flowed through his body and into hers. "Someone's got to do it, Tine. It might as well be me. I'm good at it."

"You see so much ugliness."

"And a lot of good. And I do some good."

She rested her cheek against his chest, absorbing the quiet *thud-thud* of his heart. *Someone* had to do every tough job: care for babies whose lives were destined to be short; hold the hands of elderly patients as they passed from this world; fight fires and wars; advocate for abused children; counsel victims who lived; autopsy those who died, and find the persons responsible.

She couldn't be that *someone*. Put her in the shop, with its tourist- and voodoo-related items, and she was great. Ask her to do something so vital as heal, touch, love, grieve, protect, defend and find justice for those who couldn't do it for themselves, she would get lost in the darkness and never find her way out again.

"I'm impressed."

"By what?"

She lifted her head to see if he was serious. He was. "You. Your commitment. Your passion."

Surprise flitted through his eyes, then his expression softened. He raised her hand to his mouth and kissed it in such a gentlemanly fashion that she almost didn't notice the swelling of his erection as he turned onto his side to face her. "Contrary to popular belief, I do know how to commit to something." He settled her hand on his hip, then tilted her face so he could nuzzle her jaw. "And to someone. I may be a jerk, Tine, but I'm trainable, if you'll just give me the chance."

She cradled his cheeks in her hands and kissed him thoroughly before making a show of checking her watch. "It's four forty-five. My two hours start…" The old-fashioned second hand swept, *tick-tick-tick*, around the watch face before finally reaching the twelve.

She gave him a greedy, hungry, needy look and slid her hand down his flat stomach to his groin, making his breath catch, before she said the magic word.

"Now."

She jumped up and dashed away from the couch. "Hey," Jimmy called, scrambling to follow her, catching hold of her narrow waist just as she dived onto the bed. They landed in a tangle of limbs and covers, laughing, pulling at their clothes, struggling to get naked and to get him suited up before the need burned through them like a wildfire. It was fast and hard and funny and touching, and it led to a slower, lazier, easier, harder, damn more intimate second time. It left him feeling…

The Jimmy he'd been most of his life couldn't find words to describe what he felt. The Jimmy he'd been slowly evolving into wasn't sure, either, but was willing to give it a try.

Connected. Lucky. Tender. Protective.

Blessed.

In a culture where *Bless your heart* was an insult as often than not, *blessed* was in his vocabulary, just not used much. His family said the blessing before meals. His sisters' kids sang a song about counting their blessings, and he was on the receiving end of plenty of *bless-yous* when he sneezed.

Looking at Martine, though, lying quiet in his arms, the sweat drying from her body, her hair covering the pillow, her hand lightly resting on his chest, he was definitely feeling blessed.

Her eyes closed, her face sleepy, she murmured, "I heard you tell Jack you aren't afraid of Evie. He was right. You should be. She threatened to put a curse on you that would make your dangly bits shrivel away and ruin you for any other woman."

"Ouch. I hope you asked her not to."

Her eyes opened to bare slits, and a womanly smile curved her mouth. "I told her *I* intend to ruin you for other women."

He kissed her forehead. "You've accomplished that, sweetheart."

She closed her eyes again, but the smile widened as she resettled in silence.

He liked Evie, he thought as he stroked Martine's

silken skin. Even loved her in a sister-who-could-kick-his-ass way. She was fiercely protective of the people in her world. She gave Jack unfailing support, gave the kids unconditional love, gave Jimmy unasked-for but always appropriate advice, and she was the best friend that Martine deserved. The other four had let her down, but not Evie. Jimmy loved her more for that.

Dusk had settled, followed by dark, though it was never really dark in downtown New Orleans. A small snore from his side indicated that Martine had drifted off, and if he closed his eyes for a few minutes, he was pretty sure he could, too. Why not? Security was at their posts downstairs, the door was locked, the alarm was set, and the nightstand was crowded with their weapons. Nothing was going to happen tonight, besides snuggling with Martine and maybe a few more rounds of forgetting, or at least dreaming about it...

The ringing of the cell phone was harsh, out of place. He was dreaming, in the mountains where he vacationed, with tall trees, crisp air, the sun shining brightly, the water of a snow-fed creek tumbling across rocks, and Martine. Why would he take his phone there and leave it turned on? Most days he didn't even have reception there.

Dream-Martine turned to look at him, brows raised questioningly, and real-Martine thumped him with her elbow as she rolled away. "Answer the phone."

Slowly he came out of the dream, saw the lit screen of his cell phone on the table and picked it up. Groggy, much preferring the sunny Colorado mountains over reality, he grunted a greeting.

"Detective DiBiase?"

The voice was familiar. Clearheaded, he would have

no problem putting a face and a name to it, but clear-headed, he was not. "Yeah."

"Sorry for waking you, sir. This is Chaz Jordan."

A patrol officer in the Quarter. Tall, broad shouldered, weight lifter. He would come in handy on Jimmy's next move, and he wouldn't be dropping anything from a third-floor landing. "It's okay, Jordan. What's up?"

"We got a call about a disturbance on Royal Street." He gave the number, and Jimmy's heart missed two or three beats before starting again. "It's nothing big, but someone started a fire on the stoop. The person who called it in poured bottled water on it before it got really going. There are a few scorch marks on the door but nothing a coat of paint can't cover."

"Can you tell what was burned?"

"Pictures. Old ones. I know you've got a case involving the woman who lives here, and she's not answering the door, so I figured I'd let you know."

"Listen, Jordan, can you stay until I get there? It won't be ten minutes."

"Sure. I'll see you."

Jimmy spotted his jeans as he stood, yanked them on, then grabbed his shirt, socks, shoes. The mattress shifted behind him while he pulled on his socks, and Martine bent close. "What happened?"

Damn, he hated that fear in her voice. She couldn't have figured out from his side of the conversation that the call involved her, but she worried anyway.

"It's not a big deal. Someone set a fire on your doorstep. Guy put it out and called the police, and the cop's waiting for me to pick up what's left over." He shoved his feet into running shoes without untying them, tugged his shirt over his head, then started threading his belt through the loops on his jeans.

"I want to go with you."

"Martine—"

"I won't get out of the car. I won't talk to anyone. No one will even notice me. I just… I need to see that everything's okay. Please, Jimmy."

He tried to stand his ground, but it was a losing battle. "It's not fair to ask favors when you're sitting there naked," he grumbled. "You'll stay in the back seat, and I'm locking you in. Give me any trouble, and I'll take you to jail. We've got cells for people like you."

She dressed more quickly than he did, grabbed the Taser and the pepper spray as if she'd been doing it for years, and was in the hallway heading for the door before he finished securing his own weapons. Shaking his head, wishing he could just handcuff her to the bedframe—not that he had a bedframe—he caught up with her at the door where she was putting on her jacket.

He pulled on his own jacket, then grabbed a hoodie from its hanger. It was black, big enough that she could wear it over her coat, bulky enough to add a little camouflage to her slender body. She didn't argue, just slid her arms into the sleeves and stood impatiently while he zipped it, then pulled the hood over her hair, casting her face into shadow.

"If you tie it, I'm going to look like that cartoon kid on TV."

"Kenny. You watch *South Park*? You don't seem the smart-ass bratty-kid type."

Her smile was sarcastic. "My best friends have kids. I pick up popular culture by osmosis."

Holding on to the edges of the hood on both sides, he ducked his head to give her an intense look. "We're taking my department car, and you're seriously riding in the back seat, out of sight, and I really am locking you in when we get there. You good with that?"

She nodded firmly. "I'm good."

The elevator was empty, and no one lingered in the garage, either. The air was cold and muffled sounds from the nearby streets, but it was warmer than it had been that morning. Maybe a normal winter was on its way back to New Orleans. Maybe everything would be back to normal soon.

Except him and Martine. He intended to make these last few days their new normal.

And keep it forever.

His gaze constantly scanning, he opened the rear door of the vehicle so she could slide into the seat, closed it and got behind the wheel. Glancing into the rearview mirror, he cautioned, "Stay out of sight. I don't want the security guards to see you."

Silently she disappeared from view.

Only one guard was at the entrance, the other one probably making rounds. Jimmy acknowledged him with a wave, then turned toward Royal Street.

Jordan's patrol unit was parked in front of Martine's apartment. Jimmy stopped on the opposite side of the street in front of the shop, where shadows would help hide her. This late at night on this particular block, he wasn't concerned about impeding traffic, not that he cared much. "I'll be back."

She didn't reply, move or even, as far as he could tell, take a breath. She was, for all intents and purposes, a ghost.

No. Not a ghost. Just invisible.

Jordan climbed out of his car and met Jimmy at the stoop, carrying a large evidence bag and a pair of gloves. The smell of charred paper lingered in the air, thin and acrid, made sour by the water poured on it.

"Thanks for waiting."

"No problem, Detective."

"Aw, you can call me Jimmy." Rank didn't mean a lot to him. He preferred to be on good terms with everyone, best terms with the officers on the street. They saw things, knew things, that came in damn useful to him. He wasn't about to stand on formalities with someone who would eventually make him look good.

Jimmy pulled on the gloves and felt the top of the pile. The uppermost layers had burned, but beneath were intact photographs, some areas turned to ash, others scorched, edges curling. They were cool to the touch, no dormant flames smoldering underneath.

"Thanks, Detec—Jimmy." Jordan held the bag open. "Is the woman who lives here okay?"

"Yeah. She's staying elsewhere." Jimmy flipped through the top few layers carefully, making note that the pictures appeared older, faded, the subjects young and unaware of what was to come. His brain registered a couple of shots of a teenaged Martine before he carefully scooped up the pile and slid them into the bag. He didn't bother to seal or initial it. Ordinarily, he would take them to the office and study them before logging them in as evidence, but it was the middle of the night. He would take them home, examine them and spread them out so the damp pages could dry thoroughly before he rebagged them. First thing in the morning, he would deliver them to Evidence.

With his hands free, Jordan shined his flashlight on the door. "You can see where a few flames got it, and it looks the paint bubbled a bit, but it's not much. I checked the lock, and it's secure. I also checked the gate to the courtyard and the door to the shop, and they're okay, too." Jordan looked up and down the street, then lowered his voice. "Isn't this part of that murder case—the woman found in the graveyard?"

"Yeah, it is."

"Cool." Immediately an abashed look came over his face. "I mean, damn. Too bad."

Jimmy grinned, remembering a time when he would have traded his next fifty routine calls for just one with a little depth and excitement to it. He followed Jordan's lead and looked from one corner to the other, from one side of the street to the other. When the killer had called Martine Friday morning, she'd stood out here first. Not the first time she'd come there, not the last. But he and Jordan were the only people out. A hundred people could be watching from the windows and doors of the buildings across the way, but the premises concealed them.

The back of his neck prickled as he turned toward the cars. "Thanks a lot, Jordan. I really appreciate it." He crossed the damp pavement in long strides, got in his car and started the engine. When he took a calming breath, he smelled Martine in the light flowery perfume that clung to her skin, in the honey scent of her shampoo and in the faint, barely there essence of fear.

As he drove, his gaze shifted from the street ahead to the rearview mirror, back to the street. He made a series of random turns, circling the block, making absolutely certain no one was following them.

"I assume you don't see any crazies."

Martine's voice came from lower in the back—not the seat itself but the floorboards. He grinned. She'd taken his don't-be-seen admonition to heart.

"Just the one driving this car. We're coming up on the garage entrance." Not only were they not being followed, he had seen very few cars. It seemed everyone was giving the city one more night to get over the snow and cold before they flooded the streets again.

At the gate, he stopped. "Hey, Travers, if you see anything odd—car keeps driving by, someone paying too much attention—let me know, will you?"

The guard, standing in the open doorway of the guard shack, blew on a cup of steaming coffee. "Always, Detective. They got you working late, huh?"

"At least it was a short trip this time." Smiling, listening to the even tenor of Martine's breathing, he drove through the gate and to his space.

Martine stood near the counter, watching as Jimmy, wearing gloves again, meticulously separated the top pictures on the stack, reduced to ash, from half-burned photos in the middle and, at the bottom of the pile, mostly undamaged shots.

When he finished, she counted thirty-five pictures, filled with familiar faces and memories. There were only four of the girls in most of the photos, except for the ones where the camera was handed off to a bystander—usually a boyfriend, a friend or someone eager to be a friend.

Jimmy pulled out his cell phone and took his own pictures of the pictures, no doubt to add to his growing pile of folders. Unlike Jack, who was pretty much all digital, Jimmy liked his evidence the old-fashioned way, in hard-copy form that he could look at, touch, highlight, process in his own way.

He slid onto a stool, then gestured her nearer. "Have you seen them before?"

"I've probably got copies in my storage bin."

"Who's the photographer?"

It was mostly a rhetorical question. It was easy enough to see from the array who was missing from most of the shots. "The camera…" Her hands started to tremble. She clasped them tightly. "It was before cell phone cameras. We all had little dinky versions, of course, but this was a thirty-five-millimeter SLR film camera. Pricey, fun to use, took great pictures. It was… It was Tallie's."

The name hung there in the air as invisible bands tightened around her chest. She forced out the next words with too little air to give them substance. "It doesn't mean it was her. She always got multiple copies and gave them out. Those could be anybody's— Callie's or Robin's or even mine."

"If the killer had stolen them."

But her place was secure; nothing was missing from Paulina's house; and there had been no report of a theft before or after Callie's death. Which left Tallie or Robin.

Martine's knees buckled, and Jimmy grabbed her, lifting her onto the stool next to his. She bent forward, pressing her forehead against her knees, taking rapid breaths that left her feeling light-headed and confused. She needed another hour of forgetfulness—an entire day of it. She was tired of knowing the worst about people she'd loved, suspecting the worst about other people she'd loved. Tired and sick and disillusioned.

Jimmy patted her back until her breathing was under control again, but she could tell when his attention wandered back to the evidence. His shadow shifted over her as he picked up one photo, turned it over and examined it. "This one's thicker than the others. Maybe it's two stuck together or…"

Martine straightened and watched as he pulled the knife from his pocket and gently worked the blade point into one corner, separating one piece of paper from the other. With that start, they came apart easily, each bearing the same wrinkles where they'd connected, but the second piece wasn't a photo.

Thick black letters, like the first message she'd received, were centered on a file card: *It's too late to hide, Tine.*

Jimmy slid to his feet, crossed the living room and rooted through the piles on the makeshift coffee table. He came back with the yearbook, open to the twins' senior pictures, set the notecard on the opposite page and looked at Martine.

The yearbook adviser had insisted on labeling their pictures Callista and Taliesin, and the girls had insisted on inking those names out and writing in Callie and Tallie. The *t*, the *a*, the *l*, *i* and *e* from the card bore an eerie resemblance to Tallie's handwriting in the yearbook.

"How could this happen?" Her voice was small and weak, the same way she felt. "How could so much love turn to that much hate?"

Jimmy didn't answer. What could he say? *I don't know. It just happens. Life gets screwed up.* She could come up with those answers on her own. The only one who might know the truth was Tallie, and it was too late for her to share. The other half of her whole was dead.

Don't meet any other old friends who happen to call, Jimmy had warned Martine a few days earlier. At the time, she'd taken it to mean that the killer might be watching. She much preferred that to the knowledge that the old friend was likely the killer.

Jimmy left the counter again, going to the fireplace. A moment later, blues music drifted into the air from speakers hidden around the apartment. There were no lyrics, just sexy, sweet instrumentals that made her muscles relax and stretch and long to move.

He came back, pulled her to her feet and shut off the light over the pictures, leaving the room illuminated only by the city's lights spilling through the glass wall. She half expected him to lead her toward the bedroom, but instead he wrapped his arms around her, drew her near and slowly, sensuously danced her toward the center of the living room.

"Not too sad for you?" he murmured in her ear.

The raspy sexy sound of his voice drew a smile she couldn't have summoned on her own. "My mother says if dancing to the blues makes you sad, then you're not doing it right."

"I'd like to meet your mother."

Martine rested her head on his shoulder, let him lead her in languorous steps around the gleaming tile floor. Comfort was slowly seeping into her body from his body, from the rustle of the air, from the lament of the saxophones. "You would like her, and she would like you. But I have to warn you, Jack is her favorite man in the entire world."

"Only because she hasn't met me yet. Does she come to town often?"

"When she's stopping off between trips. I'm going to ask her to come soon. While this is incredible—" she nodded to him, then herself "—sometimes…"

"A girl needs her mother."

"Yes." Just the thought of Bette in her bigger-than-life mama-lion mode was enough to bring a tear or two to Martine's eyes. "She'll charm you. She charms the whole world."

"And I'll charm her right back."

Another smile worked its way out. "That'll be a nice change. She hated my ex-husband."

"Parents are supposed to hate their kids' exes. Every time I see Alia's grandparents, they say rude things to me in Vietnamese."

"Do you speak Vietnamese?"

"No. But some things don't need translation."

And there it was—a laugh, when she'd begun to think she might never laugh again. She slid her arms around his neck and left a trail of kisses along his throat before brushing her mouth to his, sighing softly. "I've known you for six years—"

"Five days," he corrected her, and in a very real sense, he was right.

"And I never imagined I'd say this, but… You're good for me, Jimmy DiBiase."

And with that, she kissed him.

Chapter 10

In cases of emergency or convenience, cell phones were a wondrous thing. There ought to be times, though, Martine was convinced, when people should be unreachable, and this early on a Sunday morning was one of those times. She burrowed deeper under the covers, trying to block the ringing of Jimmy's phone, but once it had penetrated her sleep, she couldn't shut it out.

Thankfully, it went quiet after a moment…until the message alert sounded. A few seconds after that, the ringing began again.

Shoving back the covers, she looked at him, sprawled on his back, dead to the world, then slid out of bed. The tile floor was cold on her bare feet, making her do a little dance around the bed to the phone. All she intended to do was mute the ringer, then wake him up in case it was police business he needed to deal with. The number displayed on the screen stopped her.

The call was coming from her shop. The only people in the world with a key to her shop were her and Anise. Had her employee gone by there and seen something wrong? Encountered some problem? Found another message from Tallie?

She answered with a quiet "Hello" as she shrugged into Jimmy's shirt from last night, then left the room. The music still played in the living room, the same sort of sexy, sad songs she and Jimmy had danced to, made love to, fallen asleep to. She found the remote on the mantel and shut it off, then checked out the window to see that the fog had returned. From this vantage point, it looked as if the buildings were floating atop a drab colorless cloud.

"Hello," she repeated.

Anise's response, somewhere between relief and a whimper, came suddenly. "Oh, thank God, Martine, it's you! I've called and called, and I was so afraid, I didn't know what to do!"

The hairs on Martine's nape stood on end, and goose bumps covered her entire body. It was just that the room was cold, she told herself, and the tile floor even colder, but she couldn't even pretend to believe it. Something was horribly wrong. She felt it in the nausea sweeping over her, the trembling that made her clutch the phone, the roiling in her stomach. Even so, she managed an even, reasonable tone when she spoke. "Take a deep breath, Anise, then tell me why you're at the shop this early when you know we're closed today."

Anise obeyed, her first breath ragged and painful, the next a little less so. "Niles left some stuff here, and I'm meeting him this morning for breakfast so I said I'd pick it up for him, but when I got here— Oh, God,

Martine, I'm so sorry I did this! I just didn't think—I didn't really believe—"

Martine padded to the couch, curled into a small ball and gripped the phone tighter. "What happened when you got there, Anise?" *Please let it be nothing, just some silly thing that she's overreacting to, God, please.*

There was a rustle of noise in the background—nothing she could identify, just a sense of sound, activity— then Anise spoke again. This time, the panic was mostly gone, her tone dull and heavy with regret. "I've got a message for you, Martine."

Another hesitation, another rustling, then… "Actions have consequences."

The call disconnected.

Dear God, Tallie was at the shop, and she had Anise. If Martine wasn't already sitting, her legs would have given way beneath her. "Anise?" she whispered, even though she knew her friend couldn't hear. "Anise, please…oh, please…"

She had to wake Jimmy, had to tell him, to take him with her when she went to the shop so he could arrest Tallie, so he could free Anise and bring an end to this entire awful mess. He would need time to call Jack and maybe some other officers, to make a plan, to get people in place and to keep Martine safe—

Halfway to her feet, she sank down again. Tallie wanted to deal with *her*, not the police. She had killed Paulina. God help her, she had killed her own twin sister. She wouldn't hesitate to kill Anise, too, if Martine sent the police in her stead.

Jimmy won't let you walk through that door. It's too dangerous.

But what about the danger to Anise if she didn't? She trusted Jimmy with her life. She had faith in his abilities to do his job better than anyone could, but she couldn't bear it if her young employee suffered because of her.

Grimly, she stood, hardly noticing the chill from the floor. She went to the guest room, dressed in jeans, a sweater and running shoes, got her slicker, then slipped into Jimmy's room to leave his phone where she'd found it. After sliding the weapons into her jacket pockets, adding his knife just in case, she couldn't resist stopping a moment, touching her hand to his arm and whispering without sound, "I love you, Jimmy."

Then, before her courage fled, she left the room, the apartment, the building. Shivering inside her slicker, she greeted the security guard as if she were just any resident out for a stroll. Once she turned the corner out of his sight, she began running.

She hadn't been anywhere alone in days, and she should have been relishing the freedom: the people she passed who paid her no mind; the eeriness of the fog, cool and damp where it touched her skin; the unusual quiet for a Sunday morning. She wasn't, though. All she could think about was the shop. If Anise was okay. What she would do when she got there. Whether she was a fool for sneaking out on Jimmy. If she would pay for it with her life.

Her fingers clenched around the pepper spray in one pocket, the Taser in the other. Maybe she would die, but Tallie wouldn't get away unscathed.

By the time she reached her block, deep breaths were impossible to come by and pain throbbed in her side. She slowed to a walk, gaze locked on her destination, mind racing to come up with a plan.

She had nothing. She sold T-shirts and postcards, anointing oil and John the Conqueror root, for God's sake. She didn't know the first thing about confronting psychotic killers who were holding someone she loved hostage. She was totally unprepared.

But she had no choice.

As she reached the edge of the plate-glass windows, she slowed her steps and peered inside. Only the lights over the checkout counter were on, not enough to dispel the gloom on a dreary day. She saw no sign of Anise or Tallie.

The sign on the door was still turned to Closed. It was impossible to make a stealthy entrance, given the door's habit of sticking, so she wrapped her fingers around the knob, took a deep breath and turned and jiggled and forced her way in with all the accompanying noise. It made more noise as she closed it, then all went silent.

Martine believed in evil, but her experience with it had been extremely limited. She read about it, saw it on the news, heard stories about it. But this morning she felt it in the air, smelled it in the overpowering scents of the incense display, heard it with every thud of her heart. She wanted to yank the door open and run screaming down the street. She wanted to race up the stairs next door to her apartment and hide under her bed. She wanted to be anywhere but here, doing anything but this.

Instead, she walked farther into the room. "Anise?"

Another silence, another rustle, then… "In here."

The door marked Private was open, a faint light coming out, too little to dispel the heavy darkness of the main room. Martine slowly walked that way, circling shelves that blocked her path, coming to a stop in the doorway.

Anise huddled on the stool behind the counter, her face a stark contrast to her black hair and clothing. She was trying to make herself look as small as possible, but no matter how small she got, it was hard to ignore the tremors rocketing through her. Her gaze was moving constantly in silent warning, from Martine's face to the shadows against the wall on her left.

Martine eased into the room to the other side, intending to stay as far from Tallie as the U-shaped counter would allow, but hardly five steps into the room, she tripped and fell against the glass. Thankfully, the counter was sturdy, the wood frame absorbing the force of her stumble. She regained her balance quickly, looked to see what had tripped her and gasped.

There, her dark clothes blending into the shadows, motionless—*dear God, please not lifeless, too*—lay Tallie.

Relief washed over Martine. They'd been wrong. Tallie hadn't killed their friends. She hadn't grown into some kind of homicidal maniac. Just like her sister, Paulina and Martine, she was an innocent victim. So who…

A whisper of movement interrupted the question as a slender figure stepped out of the shadows into the light. "It's nice to see you again, Martine."

Unable to draw a deep breath, Martine stared across the room into the face of her tormentor, her one-time friend and now her would-be killer. "I'd rather see you burning in hell, Robin."

* * *

Between the steady beeps of his cell phone, Jimmy surrendered, rolled onto his side and picked up the phone. He rarely turned it off, though he could, of course. Even in a job filled with emergencies, no one could legitimately expect him to be available twenty-four hours a day. It had just always been a thing with him. He'd rarely had any real reason to *not* be available.

According to the cell, he'd missed two calls and two messages. He squinted at the information on the screen, hoping it was just the sudden awakening that made it hard to bring the caller ID into focus and not his age. He also hoped the calls didn't have anything to do with this case, weren't anything that might call him away from home. It was Sunday, dreary and gray outside, a perfect day for a decadent meal, a game or two on TV and lazing in bed with—

He glanced behind him. Martine was already up—had been long enough for the sheets to cool. He didn't hear any noises from the bathroom, living room or kitchen, but she was the sort to stay quiet and let him sleep. She'd probably slipped out of the room for coffee and breakfast…though he swore he could smell fresh coffee from a hundred yards and no aroma lingered in the air.

"Martine?" He sat up, still grasping the phone. His call got no reply, and deep inside, he knew why: she was gone. There was a feel to the silence, an emptiness, that meant he was alone.

Swearing, he jumped from the bed and did a quick walk-through of the apartment, confirming his gut instinct. When he wound up back in the bedroom, he checked caller ID, better able to see now that he was wide-awake. His muscles went taut at the name of the shop. "Damn it, Martine—"

Hands shaking, he listened to the message. He needed a moment to identify the panicky voice talking double her usual speed and half an octave higher. *Detective, I need to talk to Martine. I know you know where she is, I know you can get in touch with her, and I know you won't want to, but it's an emergency. I have to talk to her right away. Call her right now and tell her to call me. This isn't one of those times you get to decide what everybody else does. Call her! Right now! It's important.*

The second call came as soon Anise finished the message. The anxiety in her voice was palpable, crawling along his skin as she left a message more of the same. Then, according to the call log, a third call was received—and answered. The conversation lasted just under ninety seconds. Long enough for Anise to report a problem, one significant enough to make Martine sneak out to meet her.

It wasn't hard to guess the nature of the problem. Martine had been so compliant with his requests and restrictions up to this point. The only thing that could lure her out in the open now would be a threat to someone close to her. They knew Tallie had been watching the shop and her apartment. It was a fair guess that she'd realized Martine wasn't coming back until the danger had passed—also a fair guess that if Anise had gone to the shop this morning, Tallie could have seen her arrive. It was far too easy to guess that she knew Martine would put her own life at risk to protect Anise's.

Fear spread through him, leaving fine crystals of

ice in its wake, freezing his blood, his heart, even his brain. This couldn't happen. He'd just gotten this second chance with her. He'd just fallen in love with her. He couldn't lose her now. He wouldn't.

His gaze shifted to the night table, its weapons looking lonely with the others gone. She'd taken his knife, too—a weapon of last resort. Pepper spraying or Tasing someone—that could be done from a distance, maybe ten feet for the spray, up to fifteen for the Taser. But a knife…that was up close and personal. That could give a person nightmares.

Most mornings, he needed a hot shower and steaming coffee to reach his mental best. This morning, panic was a pretty good substitute. He put the phone on speaker, then called Jack while he dressed. His partner wasn't very happy about being awake at such an unholy hour on a Sunday morning—it wasn't even eight yet—but at least he was used to it; his kids woke him early every Sunday.

Jimmy related the conversation, and Jack's grumpiness disappeared. "What do we do now?"

"We stop Tallie."

Jack snorted at the obvious answer. "We're assuming she's already got one hostage. Martine'll make two. We're going in? Just you and me?"

"Call Lawson and Petitjohn."

"Aw, man, they're idiots."

"Not when they're on the job." Then they were fearless. "Have them meet us on Dumaine at the intersection with Royal."

"We'll be there."

Jimmy was well aware as he left the apartment that they were violating department policy. He should report a suspected hostage situation higher up the chain of command, let them call the Special Operations Division, let the negotiator take the lead. Fine as they were, though, the tactical platoon didn't know Martine. Being emotionally involved with a subject definitely could have its downside, but there were advantages, too, one of them being that he would do *anything* to get her back safe. Besides, going through official channels took time, and he wasn't sure how much of that Martine and Anise had.

Stopping at the gate, he asked the security guard if he'd seen Martine. She'd left five or ten minutes earlier, on foot, friendly but not chatty, a woman with a purpose. Probably, the guard joked, of enjoying this wonderful sunny morning.

Jimmy parked his car nearer Jack's house than Martine's, grabbed binoculars from the trunk and jogged to the intersection nearest the shop. It wasn't the finest view he could have asked for, but it was enough to see no one was in the main room. Next he checked the car parked in Martine's driveway, calling in the tag number to dispatch. When footsteps sounded behind him, he didn't look around. Jack always walked like a man with a purpose. He had an aura of authority Jimmy would like to have when he was finished growing up.

A moment later, Petitjohn and Lawson arrived. They worked together, hung out together, vacationed together and showed up together any time they were summoned, so much that people wondered whether they were partners just on the job or in life, too. Jimmy didn't give a damn. Like he'd said, they were fearless, and that was what he needed.

Sliding back around the corner, out of sight of the

shop, Jimmy looked at his backup: alert, clearheaded, bulletproof vests under dark hoodies or windbreakers. He didn't need to see to know each of them was more heavily armed than he was. Good. Because Tallie Winchester wasn't walking out of here free.

"The car parked out front comes back to Phillip Malloy in Chicago," he said. "I don't know whether Malloy's somehow involved or just another victim."

Jack pulled a couple of papers from inside his jacket. "This is a sketch Evie did of the shop. Here's the front door. The back goes into the courtyard. The apartment has a courtyard door, too, on the second floor, and there's a gate here, but it's secure. There's no indoor access from the shop to the apartment."

Petitjohn pointed at the three smaller rooms inside the shop. "What are these?"

"Bathroom, break and storeroom," Jack answered, "and this is where she sells supplies to serious voodoo practitioners. Only one door into each of these spaces and no windows."

"So we need to find out which floor they're on." Lawson grinned. "I don't suppose your pretty wife sent a spare key to the apartment to help out with that?"

Jack let a ring with a lone key dangle from his finger. "I also brought pictures. They're not current, but they're all within the last five years. Martine—she's ours. Anise works for Martine. Tallie Winchester—we think she's the killer. Robin Railey—we think she's another intended victim. Railey may be halfway around the world, but just in case…"

Something clicked in Jimmy's mind. "She lived in Chicago. Robin Railey. She disappeared there after the first murder. Went into hiding, according to the second victim. Either she or Tallie could have stolen the car to get away."

Petitjohn took the key from Jack. "So we're gonna check the apartment and make sure they're not there," he said as Lawson took the sketch, which also included the layout of the apartment. All the time Jimmy had spent there, and there were three rooms he hadn't seen.

"I'm going with you," Jack added. "I'll take the courtyard stairs to the rear door of the shop."

"I don't suppose you have the spare key for that."

Jack shook his head.

"So you and I go in loud." If they all survived this, Jimmy hoped Anise would be grateful enough to remove her curse from the doorknob so he could come and go without absorbing ever-increasing voltage.

"One last thing…" This time it was Petitjohn handing something around: earbuds so they could stay in touch. One of the perks of working with a tech geek.

Jimmy tucked the earbud in, then the other three took off back the way they'd come. They would circle the block and come in from the opposite end. No one inside the shop would be able to see them without pressing right up to the window, which would allow Jimmy to see *them*.

Martine was in the shop. He knew it in his bones. He was hoping she'd left the front door unlocked, unless Tallie had ordered otherwise. A simple thing like that probably wouldn't cross her mind when Anise was in danger. And Tallie would want a quick escape, no dealing with locks and creaky sticking doors.

When Jack, Lawson and Petitjohn reached the apartment stoop, Petitjohn unlocked the door while the others ducked behind the car—letting the air out of the tires, Jimmy realized. A moment later, the three of them disappeared inside. He listened to the quiet, heavy and ominous, that came over the buds, his gut roiling, holding his breath so he didn't miss the faintest sound.

Sticking the binoculars in his pocket, he strode across the street and down the sidewalk. Halfway to the shop, a heavy exhale sounded over the link. "Nothing here but us cops," Lawson murmured. "Petitjohn's going out the back. I'm coming to you."

All right. Martine was just a few yards away and presumably safe for the moment. Big emphasis on *presumably*. Tallie could have met Martine at the door with a gun and walked her and Anise out of the area. Could have taken Martine and left Anise behind. Could be on her way right now to the place where she'd cut Paulina's heart from her chest. Could…could…could…

"You wait here," he murmured to Lawson. "Anyone who comes out, put 'em in cuffs."

When the detective nodded, Jimmy climbed the steps to the door and prepared to wrestle it open, announcing his arrival to everyone inside. His Taser drawn, he wrapped his fingers around the knob and got a hell of a shock, enough to make him spit out a silent curse and make his fingers twitch. "You'll hear me come in," he said to Jack, then pushed the door.

It opened as smoothly and silently as a well-oiled high-tech marvel. Stunned at his good luck, Jimmy headed toward the room marked Private. The door was open, a light was on inside, and the faint sound of voices drifted on the air. Though he neither recognized the voices nor understood the words, a jolt through his chest told him which one was Martine's. His knees damn near went weak with the proof that she was still alive.

Now, God help them, they had to make sure she stayed that way.

"Burning in hell?" Robin echoed the words with a serious helping of disbelief. "Really, Martine, twenty-four years since you've seen me, and the first words out of your mouth consign me to hell? So much for old friendships being the best."

"I didn't end the friendship. You guys did when you scattered like frightened little mice. You abandoned me, and you think you have the right to come back now and turn my life inside out?"

Martine listened to herself and wondered where the words were coming from. Certainly not from her own little frightened mouse, quaking in the corner of her brain. She'd assumed she would come in here, calm and in control, and reason with Tal—Robin until an opportunity to use her weapons arose. Apparently, calm, control and reason were hiding in the corner with mouse. Instead, Martine was angry—about Callie's and Paulina's deaths, about whatever Robin had done to Tallie, about the threat she'd made against Anise. She was furious about the past week, the fear, the grief, the sorrow, the guilt, the sadness and the regret, and she for damn sure wasn't going to make it any easier for Robin to kill her.

"Hey, I'm the one holding the gun here." Robin waved it in the air for a moment. "I have a right to do whatever I damn well please."

Martine's fingers flexed around her weapons. She would use the Taser, effective and with the least chance of hurting herself. Pepper spray could drift on the air and burn innocent eyes as well as evil ones, and the knife... Only if it was a choice between it and death. She did not want Robin's blood on her.

Martine moved a few steps deeper into the room. "Anise, leave."

Surprise emphasized the paleness of Anise's face. She slid from the stool to her feet, but her knees sagged before catching her weight. "I—I can go?"

"No!" Robin slammed her free hand onto the glass, and Anise hopped like a frog back onto the stool. "You can't give orders here, Martine. *I'm* in charge."

Calm, control and reason knew that, but anger and frustration had the direct line to Martine's mouth. She wasn't about to let Robin terrorize or kill an innocent young woman who hadn't even been born when their problems started. She continued to move toward the opening of the counter. "Go, Anise. This is between Robin and me."

This time Anise was prepared. She didn't ask permission, didn't walk to the pass-through but boosted herself onto the counter, spun around, hopped off on the other side and darted through the shadows to the door. Just as Martine had done, she tripped over Tallie, shrieked and said, "Sorry, sorry, I forgot. Sorry."

Shock held Robin rigid. "You—you—I can't believe you—" A laugh escaped her, as chilling as the fog. Then, requiring a great deal of control, she forced herself to relax. "It's okay. She was just bait. All I really need, I've got. Tallie's not dead, by the way. Not yet."

Her gaze locked on Robin, Martine strained to hear the sounds of Anise's passing through the shop. She tried so hard she wasn't sure whether the sounds she picked up were real or imagined: a shuffle of feet, a gasp, a whimper, a creak of wood and the reassuring rumble of what might have been a male voice. Hope surged inside her. Jimmy was here, or Jack, or...*oh, please don't let it be Niles*. Panic was his usual state of affairs.

Martine eased back in the direction of the door. "So all you need to be a happy woman is to kill Tallie and me." A bit of fresh air wafted through the doorway—because the front door had opened?—and barely detectable on the cold air was a dear scent. Jimmy's cologne, fresh and near and full of hope. He was out there, somewhere within screaming distance. She was going to be okay.

Robin followed on the opposite side of the room. She may have let Anise go, but Martine was sure if she tried to walk out, her old friend would use that gun.

She stopped a distance from the door to lessen the chances that Robin might look into the main room. Sadly, she couldn't see, either. "Why?"

Robin gestured with both hands, still holding that damn gun. "It's Callie's fault. I never would have come up with the idea on my own."

"Callie wanted you to kill us, starting with her?"

"Of course not." Robin backed into the shadows again. When this was over, Martine swore she would have new bright lights installed all through the shop. She didn't care how much her customers liked atmosphere. No one would ever be able to hide in here again.

"Did I tell you I got engaged? Of course not, because we haven't spoken for twenty-four years." Robin drifted into the light again to reveal a massive diamond on her left hand. Under normal circumstances, it would have taken Martine's breath away, but now, knowing that those hands cut their friends' hearts out of their chests, all she could see was the stone bathed in blood.

"First," Robin began conversationally, "let me catch you up on the years since we last spoke. I went to college—had to work my way through that, just like high school. Had a couple of decent jobs—too little pay for too much work. Got married—twice. Got cheated on and divorced—twice. Moved to Chicago for a new job. Pay wasn't great, but I met a lot of important people. Including Philip Malloy."

She paused, obviously expecting a response. "You don't know who he is, do you? Damn, Martine, you always thought the sun rose and set on this stupid city. Small-town Louisiana girl never could imagine anything bigger or better than New Orleans. Philip owns half of Chicago and a good chunk of the Midwest. He's got more money than Mr. Winchester ever dreamed of, and he wants to spend it all on me."

Robin gazed at the ring a moment, her smile sweet, the affection in it sincere. For her fiancé? Or for the millions he could give her?

"I told Callie. She and Tallie sent me Christmas and birthday cards sometimes. And you know what she did? She asked me for money. Can you believe it? *Money.* When I had to work for everything I ever got. Seems Daddy's generosity ended when she turned forty and still had her hand out all the time."

Martine wished she could be surprised by Callie's request, but the twins had been raised that way. They'd only had to ask, no matter how outrageous the desire, and they got it. Had anyone truly expected them to become self-sufficient adults?

"I knew better than to think it would be a one-time deal. If I paid her, she'd be back in a year or six months or a few weeks, wanting more. So I told her no, and she said she would tell Philip about the curse we put on Fletcher."

The slightest blur of movement flickered outside the door. Martine glanced that way, as if checking on Tallie, and saw Jimmy on his hands and knees. Her heart squeezing painfully, she wished she'd awakened him to tell him she loved him. What if she didn't get another chance?

He gestured toward Tallie, making a pulling motion, and Martine walked back along the aisle. Robin followed her on the opposite side.

"You have to understand that Philip is a very private, almost reclusive man. He avoids the media and shuns the spotlight. His good name is sacred to him. When Callie threatened to tell him… If I hadn't silenced her, I would have lost everything."

Martine's stomach clenched at her casual, reasonable tone, as if reputation and money were perfectly logical reasons for murder. "So you killed her and made it look like a ritual murder to throw suspicion on…who? Fletcher's family? One of us?" When Robin shrugged, Martine pointed out, "Ritual murder isn't a voodoo thing."

"Oh, for God's sake, Martine, how many people know that? I needed a distraction, and it worked. Then I realized that Callie couldn't talk, but you, Paulina and

Tallie could. If I was going to keep my secret safe…
Benjamin Franklin said, 'Three can keep a secret, if
two of them are dead.' Who am I to argue with one of
our founding fathers? Though, of course, four shared
my secret."

Two of them were dead, and one lay injured and
possibly dying. Finally, it became too much for Martine to resist a look toward Tallie. With the cabinets
and merchandise in the way, she couldn't see her, and
though she'd listened hard, she hadn't heard a sound.

"So…" Robin gestured with the gun. "Time to go.
I had planned on you and Goth Girl carrying Tallie to
the car, but now I suppose I'll have to help you. Then
we'll go to the same place I took Paulina, and…" She
let her shrug finish the sentence.

Martine didn't move. "You expect me to just go
along quietly?"

"Yes, because I'll shoot Tallie if you don't." With
another sweet smile, this time tinged with regret, Robin
sighed. "That's where we're different, Martine. You
still care about us. All I care about is Philip and me
and how incredibly happy we're going to be. So *move*.
Before Goth Girl comes back with the police."

Still Martine didn't move. Had Jimmy had enough
time to get Tallie out and reposition himself? What
if he could hear but not understand them? What if he
was vulnerable when Robin walked through the door?
What if she shot him instead?

That image forced her into motion, long strides
leading to the end of the counter. When Robin rounded
the corner and saw nothing but bare floor where Tallie
had lain, a keening sound escaped her, full of anger and

making the hairs on Martine's neck stand on end. Furiously, she charged through the doorway, screaming, the pistol up and ready to fire, and Martine charged after her.

Jimmy and Jack were near the shop's entry, Tallie cradled in Jimmy's arms, his back to them as he handed the woman over to Jack. Jack shouted a warning and Jimmy spun, but he'd holstered his weapon to pick up Tallie. Even as he grabbed for it, Martine knew it would be too late.

Her actions were pure instinct: she'd yanked the Taser from her pocket as she ran, had activated it and flipped off the safety. Now she centered the laser on Robin's back and pulled the trigger. It crackled and popped and, an instant later, Robin's body went rigid as she fell to the floor, her body convulsing from the electrical shock, her screams turning to curses.

Then reaction hit. Like Robin, Martine's muscles locked in place. She couldn't lower the Taser, couldn't control the shudders racking her body, couldn't breathe or speak or stop the tears filling her eyes. She stared at Robin as she twitched, the longest thirty seconds of her life, both horrified and perversely satisfied by the knowledge that *she* had dealt that punishment. Even more perversely, when the charge ended, she wanted to trigger it again: thirty seconds for each life she'd destroyed or tried to.

"Tine? It's okay, Tine."

Jimmy's soft, anxious voice came from nearby, and he tugged until her cramped fingers let go of the Taser. It clattered when he set it on a shelf beside them, then he wrapped his arms around her and held her so tight she could scarcely breathe. She wanted him to never let go.

His breathing was rapid and shallow, and he was shaking, too, but slowly he calmed, and so did she, breathing deeply of all his scents. Voices sounded behind them, and sirens wailed outside, but right there in his embrace, everything *was* okay. He'd kept his promise.

After a moment, he tilted her face back to stare into her eyes. "You saved my life."

It took a moment for the words to process, then she slowly smiled. "Yes, I did."

"There's an old saying that if you save a man's life, you're responsible for him ever after. Want to spend the rest of your life looking out for me, Tine?"

It was a serious moment, serious words, serious intent, and she couldn't stop the laughter bubbling inside her. "Really, DiBiase? You ask that now, surrounded by cops and paramedics and gawkers and a crazy psychotic killer who tried to shoot you?"

And there it was—the grin she loved with all her heart, smug and brash and overconfident and sexy and sweet, aw, damn, so sweet it made her ache. "If I wait until everything's back to normal, you might come to your senses and turn me down. I love you, Tine. I always will."

After years of nurturing her hostility toward him, she *had* come to her senses. She knew him. Wanted him. Loved him. Trusted him. Forever.

In reply, she cupped her hands to his face and kissed him, sliding her mouth from one end of his to the other before parting his lips with her tongue, dipping inside, tasting him, teasing him. "I love you, Jimmy," she murmured, "and I always will. Just one question."

When his brow quirked, she smiled innocently. "Will you let me keep the Taser?"

* * * * *

And don't miss out on any other suspenseful stories from Marilyn Pappano:

NIGHTS WITH A THIEF
BAYOU HERO
UNDERCOVER IN COPPER LAKE
COPPER LAKE ENCOUNTER

*Love pulse-spiking romance and
spine-tingling suspense?
Don't miss this exclusive excerpt from
FATAL THREAT
The latest FATAL book from New York Times
bestselling author Marie Force!*

A JOGGER SPOTTED the body floating in the Anacostia River just south of the John Philip Sousa Bridge.

"I hate these kinds of calls," Lieutenant Sam Holland said to her partner, Detective Freddie Cruz, as she battled District traffic on their way to the city's southeastern quadrant. "No one knows if this is a homicide, but they call us in anyway. We get to stand around and sweat our balls off while the ME does her thing."

"I hesitate to point out, Lieutenant, that you don't actually *have* balls to sweat off."

"You know what I mean!"

"Yeah, I do," he said with a sigh. "It's going to be a long, hot, smelly Friday down at the river waiting to find out if we're needed."

"I gotta have a talk with Dispatch about when we're to be called and when we are *not* to be called."

"Let me know how that goes."

"To make this day even better, after work I have to go to a fitting for my freaking bridesmaid dress. I'm too damned old to be a damned bridesmaid."

His snort of laughter only served to further irritate her, which of course made him laugh harder.

"It's not funny!"

"Yeah, it really is." With dark brown hair, an always-tan complexion and the perfect amount of stubble on his jaw, he really was too cute for words, not that she'd *ever* tell him that. Everywhere they went together, women took notice of him. For all he cared. He was madly in love with Elin Svendsen and looking forward to their autumn wedding. Wiping laughter tears from his brown eyes, he said, "I won't make you wear a dress when you're my best-man woman."

"Thank God for that. I need to stop making friends. That was my first mistake."

"Poor Jeannie," he said of their colleague, Detective Jeannie McBride, who was getting married next weekend. "Does she have any idea that she has a hostile bridesmaid in her wedding party?"

"Of course she does. Her sisters left me completely out of the planning of the shower, no doubt at her request. I'll be forever grateful for that small favor." Sam shuddered recalling an afternoon of horrifyingly stupid "shower games," paper plates full of ribbons and bows, and dirty jokes about the wedding night for two people who'd been living together for more than a year. The whole thing had given her hives.

But Jeannie… She'd loved every second of it, and seeing her face lit up with joy had gone a long way toward alleviating Sam's hives. After everything Jeannie had been through to get to her big day, no one was happier for her—or happier to stand up for her—than Sam. Not that she'd ever tell anyone that either. She had a reputation to maintain, after all.

She'd been in an unusually cranky mood since her husband, Nick, left for Iran two weeks ago for what should've been a five-day trip but had twice been extended. If he didn't get home soon, she wouldn't be responsible for her actions. In addition to worrying about his safety in a country known for being less than friendly toward Americans, she'd also discovered how entirely reliant upon him she'd become over the last year and a half. It was ridiculous, really. She was a strong, independent woman who'd taken care of herself for years before he'd come back into her life. So how had he turned her into a simpering, whimpering, cranky mess simply by leaving her for two damned weeks?

Naturally, the people around her had noticed that she was out of sorts. Their adopted thirteen-year-old son, Scotty, asked every morning before he left for baseball camp when Dad would be home, probably because he was tired of dealing with her by himself. Freddie and the others at work had been giving her a wide berth, and even the reporters who hounded her mercilessly had backed off after she'd bitten their heads off a few too many times.

During infrequent calls from Nick, he'd been rushed and annoyed and equally out of sorts, which didn't do much to help her bad mood. Two more days. Two more long, boring, joyless days and then he'd be home and things could get back to normal.

What did it say about her that she was actually *glad*

to have a floater to deal with to keep her brain occupied during the last two days of Nick's trip? *It means
you have it bad for your husband, and you've become
far too dependent on him if two weeks without him
turns you into a cranky cow.* Sam despised her voice
of reason almost as much as she despised Nick being
so far away from her for so long.

Twenty minutes after receiving the call from Dispatch, Sam and Freddie made it to M Street Southeast,
which was lined with emergency vehicles of all sorts—
police, fire, EMS, medical examiner.

"Major overkill for a floater," Sam said as they got
out of the car she'd parked illegally to join the party
on the riverbank. "What the hell is EMS doing here?"

"Probably for the guy who found the body. Word
is he was shook up."

Dense humidity hit her at the same time as the funk
of the rank-smelling river. "God, it's hotter than the
devil's dick today."

"Honestly, Sam. That's disgusting."

"Well, you gotta figure the devil's dick is pretty hot
due to the neighborhood he hangs in, right?"

He rolled his eyes and held up the yellow crime-
scene tape for her. Patrol had taped off the Anacostia
Riverwalk Trail to keep the gawkers away.

The closer they got to the river's edge, the more
Sam began to regret the open-toe sandals she'd worn
in deference to the oppressive July heat. The squish
of Anacostia River mud between her toes was almost
as gross as the smell of the river itself. She had her
shoulder-length hair up in a clip that left her neck exposed to the merciless sun.

Tactical Response teams had boats on the scene, and

from her vantage point on the riverbank, Sam could see the red ponytail belonging to the Chief Medical Examiner, Dr. Lindsey McNamara. She was too far out for Sam to yell to her for an update.

"Let's talk to the guy who called it in," she said to Freddie.

They traipsed back the way they'd come, with Sam trying to ignore the disgusting mud between her toes. Officer Beckett worked the tapeline at the northern end of the area they'd cordoned off. He nodded at them. "Afternoon, Lieutenant. Lovely day to spend by the river."

"Indeed. I would've packed a picnic had I known we were coming. Where's the guy who called it in?"

"Over there with EMS." Beckett pointed to a cluster of people taking advantage of the shade under a huge oak tree. "He was hysterical when he realized the blob was a body."

"Did you get a name?"

Beckett consulted his notebook. "Mike Lonergan. He works at the Navy Yard and runs out here every day at noon." He tore out the page that had Lonergan's full name, address and cell phone number written on it and gave it to Sam.

"Good work, Beckett. Thanks. Keep everyone out of here until we know whether or not this is a crime scene."

"Yes, ma'am. Will do."

"Why would anyone run out here during the hottest part of the day?" Sam asked Freddie as they made their way to where Lonergan was being seen to by the paramedics.

"For something called exercise, I'd imagine."

"When did you become such a smart-ass? You used to be such a nice Christian boy."

"Things began to go south for me when I got assigned to a smart-ass lieutenant who's been a terrible influence on my sweet, young mind."

"Right." Amused by him as always, Sam drew out the single word for effect. "You were easily led." She approached the paramedics who were hovering over Lonergan. "We'd like a word with Mr. Lonergan," she said to the one who seemed to be in charge.

He used a hand motion to tell his team to allow her and Freddie in. The witness wore a tank top, running shorts and high-tech running shoes. Sam put him at midthirties.

"Mr. Lonergan, I'm Lieutenant Holland—"

"I know who you are." His shoulders were wrapped in one of those foil thingies that runners used to keep from dehydrating or overheating or something like that. What did she know about such things? She got most of her exercise having wild sex with her husband. Except for recently, thus her foul mood.

Lonergan's dark blond hair was wet with perspiration. His brown eyes were big and haunted as he looked up at them.

"Can you tell us what you saw?" Ever since she'd taken down a killer at the inaugural parade, she was recognized everywhere she went. She hated that and yearned for the days when no one recognized her. But that ship had sailed the minute her sexy young husband became the nation's vice president late last year. Her blown cover was entirely his fault, and she liked to remind him of that every chance she got.

"I was running on the trail like I do every day, and

when I came around that bend there, I saw something in the water." He took a drink from a bottle of water, and Sam took note of the slight tremble in his hand. "At first I thought it was a garbage bag, but when I looked closer, I saw a hand." He shuddered. "That's when I called 911."

"How far out was it?" Sam asked.

"About twenty feet from the bank of the river."

"Was there anything else you could tell us about the body?"

"I think it's a woman."

"Why do you say that?" Freddie asked.

"There was hair." Lonergan took another drink of water. "Once I realized what I was looking at, I could see long hair fanned out around the head." He looked up at them. "Do you think it's that student who went missing?"

Sam made sure her expression gave nothing away. "We'd have no way to know that at this point." The entire Metro PD had been searching for nineteen-year-old Ruby Denton for more than two weeks. She'd come to the District to take summer classes at Capitol University and hadn't been seen since her first night on campus. The story had garnered national attention thanks in large part to the efforts of her family in Kentucky.

"I bet it's her," Lonergan said.

"Do me a favor and keep that thought to yourself for now. No sense upsetting the family before we know anything for certain."

"That's true."

Sam handed him her card. "If you think of anything else, let me know."

"I will." After a pause, he said, "I was out here

yesterday, and she wasn't there. I would've noticed if she'd been there."

"That's good to know. Thanks for your help."

"It's sad, you know? For someone to end up like that."

"Yes, it is." She stepped away from him to confer with the paramedic in charge. "Is he okay?"

"Yeah, he's in shock. He'll be fine. You think it's Ruby Denton?"

"I'll tell you the same thing I just told him—we have no way to know until Dr. McNamara gets the body back to the lab. Until then, we'd be speculating, and that sort of thing only makes a hellish situation worse for a family looking for their daughter. Ask your people to keep their mouths shut."

"Yes, ma'am. No one will hear anything from my team."

"Thank you."

"What's going on over there?" Freddie asked, drawing Sam's attention to the tapeline, where Beckett was arguing with a bunch of suits.

"Let's go find out."

They walked back the way they'd come, along the trail to where Beckett held his own against four men in suits with reflective glasses and attitudes that immediately identified them as federal agents.

"What's the problem, gentlemen?" Sam asked.

"There she is," one of them said in a low growl that immediately raised Sam's hackles.

"Let us in," another one said. "Right now."

"I'm not letting you in until you tell me what you want," Beckett said. "This is a potential crime scene—"

"We need to speak to Mrs. Cappuano." The one who

seemed to be in charge of the Fed squad took another step forward. "It's urgent."

Sam's heart dropped to her belly and for a brief, horrifying second she feared her legs would give out under her. *Nick...* Why would federal agents have tracked her down at a crime scene in the middle of her workday unless something had happened to him?

Please no.

Sam immediately began bargaining with a higher power she didn't believe in. She'd give up anything, anything in this world except Scotty, if it would keep the man in front of her from saying words that could never be unsaid or unheard.

Only Freddie's arm around her shoulders kept her from buckling in the few seconds it took for Sam to recover herself enough to speak. "What do you want with me?"

"We need you to come with us, ma'am."

"That's not happening until you tell us who you are and what you want," Freddie said.

In unison they flashed four federal badges.

"United States Secret Service," the one in charge said. "We need you to come with us, ma'am."

Sam didn't recognize any of them. Why would she? Nick's detail was in Iran, and Scotty's was with him. "I... I'm working here. I can't..." Bile burned her throat as her lunch threatened to reappear. With her heart beating so hard she could hear the echo of it strumming in her ears, she somehow managed to choke back the nausea. Later she'd be thankful she hadn't puked on the agents' shoes. Right now, however, she couldn't think about anything other than Nick. "Has something happened to my husband?"

Freddie tightened his grip on her shoulder, letting her know his thoughts mirrored hers. That didn't do much to comfort her.

Looking down at her with a stone-faced glare, the agent said, "We're under orders to bring you in. We're not at liberty to discuss the particulars with you at this time."

"What the hell does that mean?" Freddie asked. "You can't just take her. She's not under Secret Service protection, and she's working."

"I'm afraid we *can* take her, and we will, by force if necessary."

"What the fuck?" Beckett spoke for all of them. At some point he'd moved to the other side of her.

Like someone flipped a switch, they moved with military precision, busting through the tapeline, grabbing hold of her arms and quickly extracting her before her stunned colleagues could react. Sam fought them, but she was no match for four huge, muscled, well-dressed men who whisked her away with frightening efficiency.

In the background, she could hear Freddie and Beckett screaming, swearing—at least Beckett was—and giving chase, but they, too, were no match for this group. Before she knew what hit her, she was inside the cool darkness of one in the Secret Service's endless fleet of black SUVs, the doors locking with a sound that echoed like a shotgun blast.

"Move," the agent in charge ordered.

The car lurched forward just as Freddie and Beckett reached it. Freddie pounded once against the side window with a closed fist before the car pulled out of his reach.

Sam watched the scene unfold around her with a detached feeling of shock and fear. Something awful must've happened. That was the only possible reason for this dramatic scene. She was far too afraid for Nick to work up the fury she'd normally feel at being kidnapped by federal agents. Her hands were shaking, and her entire body was covered in cold chills.

If Nick had been harmed in some way or if he was… *No, no, no, not going there.* If he was hurt, what did it matter if Secret Service agents had grabbed her? What would anything matter?

She bit back the overwhelming fear and forced herself to focus. "Would someone please tell me what's going on here?"

Don't miss the explosive new book in New York Times *bestselling author Marie Force's* FATAL *series*

FATAL THREAT

Available August 2017 wherever Harlequin HQN titles are sold.

Most people gave him a wide berth, but not Mandy. He
shoved those thoughts away. She was nothing more to
him than a woman in trouble, and he just happened to be
in a position to help her. It was nothing more than that
and nothing less.

He left the bathroom and blinked in surprise. All the
lights were off except a nightstand lamp next to Mandy's
bed and the glow of two lit candles on the same stand.
The room now smelled of apples and cinnamon.

"I hope you don't mind the candles. I always light a
couple before I go to sleep."

"I don't mind," he replied. Hell yes, he minded the
candles that painted her face in beautiful shadows and
light. Hell yes, he minded the candles that made the room
feel so much smaller and much more intimate.

He walked over to the sofa and found a bed pillow and
a soft, hot pink blanket. He placed his gun on the coffee
table, unfolded the blanket and then stretched out.

HRSEXP0817

"All settled?" she asked.

"I'm good," he replied.

She turned off the lamp, leaving only the candlelight radiance to create a small illumination. Too much illumination. From his vantage point he could see her snuggled beneath the covers. He closed his eyes.

"Brody?"

"Yeah?" he answered without opening his eyes.

"Somehow, some way I'll make all this up to you."

Visions instantly exploded in his head, erotic visions of the two of them making love. He jerked his head to halt them. "You don't have to make anything up to me," he said gruffly. "Now let's get some sleep."

"Okay. Good night, Brody."

"Good night," he replied.

Seconds ticked by and then minutes. When he finally opened his eyes again she appeared to be sleeping. Candlelight danced across her features, highlighting her brows, her cheekbones and her lips.

He couldn't be her friend. She was too much of a temptation and he couldn't be friends with a woman he wanted. He didn't want to be friends with anyone.

He'd see her through this threat, and then he had to walk away from her and never look back.

Don't miss
SHELTERED BY THE COWBOY by Carla Cassidy,
available September 2017 wherever
Harlequin® Romantic Suspense books
and ebooks are sold.

www.Harlequin.com

THE WORLD IS BETTER WITH

Romance

Harlequin has everything from contemporary, passionate and heartwarming to suspenseful and inspirational stories.

Whatever your mood, we have a romance just for you!